why
she
left

BOOKS BY LEAH MERCER

A Mother's Lie

Who We Were Before
The Man I Thought You Were
The Puzzle of You
Ten Little Words

why
she
left

LEAH MERCER

bookouture

Published by Bookouture in 2021

An imprint of Storyfire Ltd.
Carmelite House
50 Victoria Embankment
London EC4Y 0DZ

www.bookouture.com

Paperback ISBN: 978-1-80314-008-7
eBook ISBN: 978-1-80314-007-0

To A, for continuing to inspire and support me every day.

ONE

ISOBEL

'Isaac, we're here!' Isobel yanked on the handbrake, wincing at the squeal of protest from her rusty old car. Thank God they'd made it – at one point in the two-hour journey from Brighton to London, she'd been afraid they'd break down on the busy motorway. Parked up among the gleaming black Mercedes, BMWs and hulking Land Rovers, her ancient Ford Fiesta looked like it was crashing a very posh party. She swallowed, thinking that was exactly how she felt right now, returning to the home she'd last seen as a teen. She may have grown up here, but she didn't belong.

She couldn't, not after what had happened.

'Isaac?' She turned, her heart squeezing as she took in her sleeping teenaged son stretched out on the back seat. His long legs were jammed against the door in what looked like a supremely uncomfortable position, but his face had the same peaceful, knowing expression he'd worn from the very first day she'd held him in her arms, all alone in the silent hospital room. But she wasn't alone, she'd reminded herself as she'd stared down at her baby. They had each other, and she'd do anything to encircle him in love; to keep him safe and protected.

Isaac yawned, then shoved his fingers into his eyes and rubbed furiously. Isobel cringed. Despite telling him off for years, he still did that when he was nervous or excited. And— She squinted at his fingers. Was he wearing black nail varnish? Her mother would love that. She'd probably hand Isaac the nail-varnish remover at the door and ask him to remove it before entering the premises.

Isobel shook her head, unable to stop a smile when she remembered how one day, she'd tried out a scarlet lip gloss all the girls at school were wearing. She'd thought she'd scrubbed it off, but her mother had recoiled, saying she looked like she belonged on the street, not the daughter of the headmistress of England's most prestigious school. Far from being offended, Isobel had spent the next ten minutes furiously trying to erase any trace of it. She'd snuck into her mum's room to sample her pale pink lipstick, then dashed up to Boots to buy the same shade. Her heart twisted as she realised that she still wore that shade, and pain shot through her of all she'd had to leave behind... and of how the past had clung to her, tormenting her with both longing and horror, despite her attempts to shake it off.

Now, fifteen years later, she was back in the heart of that longing and horror. And whatever her mum's reaction to Isaac's nail varnish, it would be nothing compared to a long-lost daughter and an unknown grandson turning up at the door.

'Sorry, Mum.' Isaac lowered his hands, then peered out the window. His eyebrows rose, disappearing beneath his heavy dark fringe. 'This is where you grew up?'

Isobel took a deep breath and forced herself to follow his gaze, staring out at the pristine white facades of the houses lining Burlington Square. The square looked exactly the same as when she'd left. In the late-October sun, the large plane trees glowed russet and gold. The black cast-iron fence lined the square's private garden like a soldier defending its turf. Front gardens were pruned to within an inch of their lives, with stubborn roses defying the change of seasons – just like the women inside, who seemed perfectly ageless. It was the very image Isobel had dreamed of for years after leaving, but in her dreams, the glossy beauty had been blackened with fear and panic, as if someone had doused even her happy memories in darkness.

She jerked as her eyes caught Burlington Square School, swallowing up one whole side of the street. It *was* the square, so much that locals and students called it just that: the Square. Her great-grandfather had founded it, and it had risen in prominence to become one of the best private schools in the country. It was everything to her mother, and it had been everything to her too. Isobel had planned to take over as the head when her mum retired. But then... The dark windows yawned towards her, and Isobel yanked her gaze back inside the car, breathing hard.

'Christ, Mum. Look at this place. Why did you ever leave? It's miles better than our dump back in Brighton.' Isaac blew his fringe away from his eyes, and she turned towards him, trying to calm her racing pulse.

'I just...' She paused, unable to conjure up any thought in the shadow of the Square. 'I had to get out.' That was true anyway. She couldn't be the same girl any longer. She couldn't be a part of this world, unless she wanted it to be destroyed – unless she wanted everything her mother held dear to be destroyed.

She had to be dead to everyone and everything in it.

And so, she'd become a different person: not a promising student from an affluent family with a brilliant future, but a young runaway with nothing. She'd built a new life, closing off everything to do with who she'd been before. Because if she let herself think for one minute of the mother she'd loved with all her heart – if she let herself remember the terror and shame that had propelled her from here – she would have drowned. And while there had been many times over the years that memories tried to pull her under, Isaac had been her light when the darkness threatened.

Could she stay afloat now? Could she keep the pain and fear at bay, now that she'd returned to the place she'd tried for so long to forget? The questions seeped into her mind, and she forced back the rising unease.

'I still don't understand why you never let me visit. Honestly, I thought all our relatives were dead or something, and that's why it was just us.' Isaac grabbed the camera that was constantly by his side. 'I'm going to take some photos.' He got out of the car before she could respond, his long slender form dressed all in black silhouetted against the white houses.

She watched as he snapped away, his words ringing in her ears as surprise and disappointment needled inside. What did he mean, 'just us?' She'd never thought of the two of them that way, and she hadn't realised that he did. He'd never asked about family... which she supposed was a little odd, but she was more than happy to accept.

She climbed from the car, trying to ignore the trembling in her legs. 'Come on,' she said to Isaac. 'Let's introduce you to your grandmother.' *Grandmother.* The word sounded strange in her mouth, and though she had tried to say it normally, her voice was tight and tense. Because in a way, Isaac was right. They didn't have any relatives. The woman she was today wasn't a daughter; a sister. The woman she was now had no family – no one besides her son.

But her past and present were about to collide. She was about to come face to face with the mother she'd adored... the mother she'd had to walk away from. What *would* her mum think when she opened the door? Would she let them in, or would she turn them away? Would she see the stranger Isobel was now, or would she embrace the daughter she'd thought was gone forever? Even if that daughter *was* gone forever, Isobel prayed it was the latter because they really did have nowhere else to go. She'd never have come here if they had.

She grabbed the carrier bags with their things from the boot and took Isaac's arm, unsure whether she was steadying herself or him. They climbed the steps together to the glossy blue door with the polished brass handle, and a memory flashed through her mind of the final click of the lock when she'd left all those years ago.

Isobel breathed in and pressed the bell.

TWO

RUTH

The buzzer sounds through the empty house, and I shake my head in annoyance. I've lived here so long that everyone – delivery people included – knows not to disturb my Sunday evenings. They are sacred: my time to get in gear and make sure everything is right for the coming week. After half-term break last week, I can't wait to walk the corridors tomorrow and see the faces of parents and children, happy and excited to be back at Burlington Square School, like I have for so many years. Like my father and his father did too.

The school has been a Kensington landmark for almost 75 years now, growing with every generation. My grandfather started it right here in this house as a boys' school for families who weren't keen to send their young sons to boarding school, and it soon became a place to rival any institution, with parents clamouring to have their children accepted. When it started bursting at the seams, my father relocated the school to a stretch of houses across the square, expanding to include more year groups. Following the zeitgeist of the times and the skyrocketing costs of maintaining the old buildings, I opened up the Square to girls just a few years before Isobel joined the senior school. And my eldest daughter

Cecily, now deputy head, began a sixth form a few years ago to cater for sixteen- to eighteen-year-olds – she's really sunk her teeth into getting that started. It's been so good for her to have a project of her own.

I glance out the window and into the falling light, thinking how strange life is. I always thought Isobel would be by my side – my quiet, shy girl so much more like me than her bolshie sister, who was a carbon copy of my ex-husband. But Isobel, well... I push back from the desk, breathing in. It's been years since she left, and I've managed to put to bed all the hurt, pain and confusion she caused. But sometimes, when the house is silent, I hear an echo of her laugh and an image of the two of us drinking tea by the telly rips through me, plunging me straight back into those awful days after she ran away... the days when I'd drift around the place for hours, looking for any hint of why she left.

For any hint of how I could get her back again.

I never found an answer – and I never found Isobel, despite my attempts – but the school kept me going. It kept me sane, just like it did when my father died and my husband left. The Square is the one constant; the one thing I *can* control in this shifting world. I've always felt a part of it. As a young girl, my father would sit me in the back of the class and tell me that one day, it would be mine.

But it's more than just a possession. It's my grandfather and my father, and everything they've achieved. It's the students and all their potential. It's the families and the community, and the way the Square's alumni have touched every corner of culture and science around the world. It lends me a power that makes me bigger than myself; bigger than any past hurt and pain. It lifts me up, away from a life where I'm alone.

I owe it everything.

And actually, I do have someone in my life: Cecily. She is the one who was here to support me after my stroke, and the one who kept things going at the superior level the school demanded when I needed her most. And when I finally retire, she's the one who will take over the family legacy.

I bite my lip, the constant worry circling inside that I *can* keep the school at its superior level. Even with all my efforts, it's becoming increasingly difficult. I've managed to keep up with the times (computer labs, 3D printers, and the like), but our buildings are old and in need of a massive – and costly – overhaul. And despite the school's reputation, our waiting list is nowhere near as long as it used to be. For quite a few years, we had a waiting list for the waiting list. Now, though, some parents have started sending their children to the local *state* school. I never dreamed we'd be competing on the same playing field, but I guess we're not the only ones struggling right now.

When I lie in bed late at night in the quiet, creaking house, sometimes I have the uneasy sensation that I am losing control of the school, no matter how tightly I grasp it. In the past few weeks, the building has staged a series of rebellions, from a crumbling front step and a clogged toilet flooding the girls' toilets to a leaky roof. And just last week, the police rang in the middle of the night to report that the front door was wide open. I tugged on a coat over my pyjamas and hurried across the square, beyond relieved when they told me they'd checked out the building and found nothing amiss except a cracked display case the door could have slammed into. The latch must be faulty, they said, then bid me good night.

I stood in the dark corridor, and for a second, it felt like the place in which I'd found such comfort and security was mocking me; sniggering at the very notion that I ever thought I had control. I laughed at myself and went home, but the strange feeling lingered.

The doorbell sounds again, more insistent this time, and irritation shoots through me. I slide off my glasses and get to my feet, feeling the familiar tugging at my chest. Anxiety pains, the doctor said, before telling me to slow down – which, of course, immediately made me more anxious, especially in the aftermath of my stroke... especially knowing my father died of a stroke, too, when he was still young. But I won't slow down. I'm not ready to. Not yet.

Who on earth is there? I peer out the window to the step below, brow furrowing as I spot a woman and gawky teen clutching carrier bags with items spilling out. I can't see their faces, but their clothes are baggy, hanging off them untidily. I know straight away they're not from the square. In fact, they may not be from anywhere – they may not have a home. Are they begging?

I march down the stairs. They've already disturbed me, so I might as well give them a piece of my mind. As a head teacher, telling people off comes naturally. I smooth down my jumper and arrange my face into a stern expression, then swing open the door.

'I've a good mind to—' The words vanish when I come face to face with the woman. She's not a stranger to the square. It's her birthright, actually.

A birthright she rejected.

Isobel.

Shock filters through me as I stare at my daughter, taking in her face – a face that used to be as familiar to me as my own. Faint lines score her forehead and her eyes look tired, but apart from that not much has changed: wide mouth, dark eyes with long lashes Cecily always coveted, curly dark hair set against pale skin. I blink, wondering if I'm imagining her presence, like when I had my stroke and I reached out to hug her, only to embrace empty air. Can my daughter really be here right now, in front of me? Every inch of me strains to gather her in my arms, but I'm afraid she'll disappear once more if I do.

'Hi, Mum,' she says, in a voice so much like the girl I remember, but tainted with age and life. Her mouth twists around the words, as if they're unfamiliar. My heart pangs as I realise they're unfamiliar to me too. Cecily rarely calls me 'Mum', Mother or any other permutation, having opted for 'Ruth' when we first started working together. If I'm honest, we're more like colleagues than anything else. 'This is Isaac,' Isobel continues, gripping onto the boy's arm. 'Your grandson.'

Her voice is barely a whisper, and I'm not sure I've heard the words properly. They hang in the air, floating towards me, before I can finally breathe them in and understand what she's saying. I have a grandson. I'm a *grandmother*. I turn towards the boy, taking in his dark hair, pale skin and long lashes like his mother's. Before I can stop them, images flood through my head: Sunday lunches together, tea in front of the telly, a house full of laughter and love... a world of family, of people around me, of a life I could have had.

'Can we come inside?' she asks, when I don't say anything.

I lower my eyes, trying hard to keep the emotion from my face as my mind spins. I can't let them in... into *me*; into the part of my heart that finally scarred over. I can't bear to expose that old wound again, not after all that happened. Then I meet Isobel's stiff gaze, and pain rips through me as I remember that this is the daughter who coldly cut me from her life, saying she never wanted to talk to me again. And by the tense way she's holding herself and the distance she's keeping between us, it's obvious that whatever the reason she's here, it's not to play happy families.

It's not for me to be a grandmother... or her mother once more.

I straighten my spine. I don't need anyone else in my life anyway. My thoughts may have run away with me for a second, but my world is full enough now.

'Come through,' I manage to say in a calm voice. The sooner the better, actually, because although the square may seem quiet and private, everything that happens here gets out. I can almost feel the prying eyes peeping from windows right now.

'I'm Ruth,' I say, extending my hand to the boy. I see Isobel tense even more at my formality, but what does she expect? Isaac may be my grandson, but I didn't know he existed until now. He takes my hand, and I cringe when I notice he's wearing black nail varnish. What kind of fashion is that? Certainly not one any Burlington Square School student would sport. But then, Isaac's not a student there. Isobel's rejection extends far beyond her. Despite myself, I feel the old hurt gripping me.

I manage to smile as I shake his hand, but inside my mind is churning. Why are they here? What do they want?

And why did my daughter leave in the first place?

Am I finally, after all these years, going to find out? Do I *want* to?

I take a deep breath and usher them in.

THREE

ISOBEL

Isobel kept her hand on Isaac's arm as they went inside, hoping he wouldn't feel her shaking. The collision between the world she'd left and the one she inhabited now sent shock waves through her, leaving her weak and unsteady. Every bit of her longed to turn and run, but she couldn't. All she could do was keep moving forward, further into the house, as memories bombarded her, each one like a dart straight to the heart.

Here was the vase she'd broken when she'd tripped on the doormat and crashed into it – she could still see where the bits had been glued together. Here was a nick on the wall where her older sister Cecily had thrown a glass when their mum had said she couldn't go out one night. And here was her mother... Isobel swallowed, trying to hold back the emotion swirling inside. Here was her mother, with grey threading her dark bob and a face lined with wrinkles, staring at her and Isaac as emotionless as if they were simply driftwood that had washed up on the beach.

After all this time, she hadn't hugged Isobel – or Isaac, for that matter – barely inviting them in. For God's sake, she'd introduced herself as *Ruth*! Isobel had seen Isaac's face drop when 'Ruth' held out her hand, but her mother hadn't noticed. Isobel breathed in against the stinging pain, telling herself it was for the best. She wasn't the girl who had lived here, and the further apart her past and present stayed, the better. Clearly, her mother felt the same.

Isobel slipped off her shoes and nodded to Isaac to follow her example, cringing when she saw the holes in his filthy socks. Despite the years that had passed, she knew exactly what her mum would think, and it wouldn't be good. As they followed her mother's regal walk to the lounge, Isobel remembered how Cecily had jokingly dubbed their mum 'the Queen of the Square'. It was true too: everyone within a square-mile radius practically genuflected whenever Ruth glided by. She held the keys to their children's future, so much so that husbands ran from their wife's side as soon as their baby was born, just to put their child on the school's lengthy waiting list. Once a famous footballer had offered a sizeable 'donation' for his son to attend, requesting a guarantee he'd make it to Cambridge in return. Her mum had turned it down, saying he'd have to join the waiting list like everyone else. They'd never be desperate enough to take bribes, she'd proclaimed proudly.

'Please, have a seat. Would you like some tea?' Her mother tilted her head. 'Isaac, would you care for a drink?'

'Do you have any Coke?'

Isobel cringed, anticipating the answer.

'I'm afraid I don't buy fizzy drinks,' her mother responded on cue. 'All that *sugar*. I can offer you some cold filtered water.'

Isaac muttered thanks and ducked his head.

'Just tea for me, please,' Isobel said. 'Milk, no sugar,' she added hastily, in case her mum had forgotten. Before she'd left, a cup of tea by the TV before bedtime had been one of the few things she'd shared with her mother. She was so busy during the day, but at night they'd watch whatever silly show was on, curled up on the sofa, until the news started and Mum went to bed. Her mother was softer then, as if the proximity to sleep had made her more vulnerable, gentler. More maternal and less like the figurehead Isobel had so admired. Pain shot through her once more, and she pushed away the memory.

Her mum disappeared into the kitchen, and Isobel let out a breath, glancing over at Isaac. She touched his hand at his tentative, nervous expression. Her son had always been an open book to her, ever since the day he was born. She may not have known how to put on a nappy, but she'd known in a heartbeat when he was cold, hungry or just needed some cuddles. As a young child he would tell her everything, from when he cried at school because he spilled his squash to when he missed the loo and splattered wee everywhere. Despite everyone warning her she'd be lucky to get a grunt out of a teenager, they were still as close as ever. Their relationship was a blanket of warmth and comfort, and she'd buried herself in being a mother.

'Okay?' she asked softly. He might have been excited at the prospect of family, but this strange place and meeting his grandmother was a lot for a sensitive young man to take in.

'I'm fine.' He nodded, but she could see by how he was grasping his camera that he was anything but relaxed. She patted his arm and glanced around the room, holding herself tightly as her eyes traced its familiar confines. The large metal-framed clock on the wall; the Victorian desk in the corner, lovingly polished and restored... this might be a family home now, but it had once been the original building for the school. As a little girl, Isobel had wandered in here, imagining eager boys listening to her powerful great-grandfather, and playing teacher, impatient for the day she'd take over, since Cecily had zero interest.

Sometimes, Isobel would gaze across the square to see the school returning her stare, its row of windows keeping solemn watch... as if making sure the family at the helm were doing everything possible to uphold its reputation. It had seemed like a living thing, more powerful than her mother herself. The thought had made Isobel shiver with admiration and awe, and she'd realised once again how lucky she was to be a part of it all.

'Here you are.' Isobel jerked at her mother's voice and reached for the saucer her mum was holding out.

'Thank you,' she said, taking a sip from the patterned china she recognised from her childhood.

'So.' Her mother settled into the armchair across from them and crossed her legs at the ankles, staring from Isobel to Isaac and back again.

'So.' Isobel cleared her throat. 'I'm sorry to turn up like this, especially on a Sunday night.' She remembered her mother always kept Sunday nights free to get ready for the week ahead. 'It's just... well, we didn't have anywhere else to go.'

Her mother was silent, fixing her with that unnerving gaze Isobel recalled only too well.

'You see, um, my partner – ex-partner – drained my savings account without me knowing, then threatened me not to say anything to the police. I have no money.' She shifted on the sofa, fear stirring inside her when she thought of Silas. They'd been together just over a year, and she'd thought he'd be the one to finally make her feel safe. Instead, he'd fooled her into thinking he wanted to be with her, all the while stealing behind her back.

She shuddered, remembering his fury when she'd confronted him, saying she'd go to the police. He'd grabbed her arms and shaken her, shouting in her face that if she ever told anyone, he'd make her pay. She'd twisted from his grasp and tried to run for the door.

'Where are you going?' he'd asked again, catching her elbow and squeezing so hard she cried out in pain. 'You're not leaving. I need you.'

'As a meal ticket?' she'd spat out, shaking with anger despite her fear. She'd shoved him away and he'd fallen onto the sofa – he'd been drinking, as usual – and before he could get up again, she'd raced into the bedroom and locked the door, jamming what she could into a carrier bag while he shouted through the flimsy wood that he'd find her, that she couldn't leave him, that she had to stay.

She'd waited, trembling, until he'd finally stopped shouting and started snoring – he must have passed out. Then she'd crept into Isaac's room, packed a few things, got into the car, and picked him up from school. She'd told him what happened and that they had to leave, shame and failure washing over her... emotions she hadn't felt in years.

They'd driven aimlessly, her mind spinning. Where could she go with only £27 in her pocket? Somewhere Silas would never be able to track her down? Between work and Isaac, she'd never really made any close friends. She hadn't been keen anyway – better to keep yourself to yourself and just get on with things. Credit cards and overdraft would only take her so far, and she'd never be able to pay them off. She'd swallowed as a sign for the motorway came into sight. There was only one thing for it; one place she'd never spoken of, not to anyone. One place no one who knew her now would find her: London.

Back to the square she'd grown up in, and the square she'd fled.

Back to the home where she'd once had everything.

'We just need to... we just need to stay for a bit, a few weeks, maybe,' she continued. 'Long enough for me to get a job and make enough to rent a flat somewhere. Shouldn't take long: I reckon there are hundreds of openings for nannies and cleaners in this area.' God, she hated this. She hated asking. She was proud of the life she'd built for her and her son, all on her own and with no help from anyone. She was proud of how she'd survived. But when she pictured Silas's face and the venom in his eyes when he'd shaken her, she knew she had no choice.

'That's fine. Of course it is.' Her mother made the words sound the exact opposite of their meaning. 'But there's no reason to become a cleaner or a nanny, for goodness' sake. Why don't you work in the school? I can set you up as an admin in the office – we had someone leave last week, so it's perfect timing.' She ran her eyes over Isobel, her lip curling. 'You'll need to tidy up, of course. Cecily can lend you some clothes, and—'

'Cecily?' Isobel interrupted, surprised. She'd never thought of her older sister as being here in London. Cecily had always said that as soon as she finished university, she was going to travel and pick the place she wanted to start a career. Isobel had both admired that view and found it terrifying at the same time. How ironic that it was her who had ended up leaving, and not her sister.

'Yes, Cecily is deputy head now,' her mother said, sipping her tea, oblivious to Isobel's astonishment. *Deputy head*? Cecily had vehemently opposed anything to do with the school, happily leaving Isobel to carry the mantle. How the hell had that come about? She tried to picture her mother and sister working together, but the image was almost unfathomable. A strange emotion jolted through her – something like jealousy, closely followed by sadness. That was supposed to be *her* role, her life.

She drew in a breath and looked over at Isaac, trying to anchor herself in reality. It wasn't her life now. It never would be again. And the less she had to do with it, the better – hadn't she just been thinking she needed to stay distant? Anyway, the thought of going back inside the school...

'Thank you, but no,' Isobel said firmly. 'I'll find something else.'

'All right.' Her mother took another sip of her tea, sitting back in the chair. 'Do you want to show Isaac his room? He can stay in Cecily's old bedroom.'

'Sure.' Anything to escape the tension in the lounge. 'Isaac?' She rolled her eyes as she noticed he'd slipped his headphones on. 'Isaac!' He glanced up. 'Come on. Let's get you settled.'

He slid off his headphones. 'Can I have something to eat first?' he asked. 'I'm starving.'

Isobel realised that in their rush to leave, he hadn't eaten anything since lunch at school – if then. Her son had always been slender, but as he shot upwards, he was becoming downright skinny. It didn't help that he spent most of his lunches avoiding the cafeteria and hanging out in the art room. He'd had a tough time settling into his school, coming home the first few weeks silent and withdrawn, so unlike her normally talkative boy who shared everything. She'd managed to uncover that some kids in his class had been bullying him... calling him the usual names reserved for quiet boys who preferred art and music to girls and roughhousing. She'd spoken with his teacher, then told Isaac there was nothing wrong with whatever – or whoever – he liked; nothing wrong with who he was. He was her son and she loved him. He could tell her anything he wanted, and she would always accept him.

Things had improved after that, the past few years passing without incident. He'd seemed to settle into his own skin, daring to express who he was a little more each year – the nail varnish was the latest. He knew that he didn't have to hide who he was from her or anyone else. She'd be forever proud and grateful that she'd done something right.

'I'll fix you a bite,' her mother said. 'Have a seat at the table, and I'll make you an omelette.'

Isobel was about to say that Isaac didn't really like eggs, but Isaac nodded shyly. 'That would be great. Thanks.'

Isobel raised her eyebrows, trying to quell the emotions stirring inside at the thought of her mother's omelette. Her mum had never been much of a cook, spending most of her time up at the school and leaving the girls with the nanny or, later, to fend for themselves. But she made a mean omelette, mixing the eggs with whatever was on hand and sliding the perfect steaming concoction onto the plate. Gulping it down had always warmed Isobel from the inside out, although she'd never been sure if it was because the food was piping hot or because her mum had made it. 'Isobel, do you want one?'

Isobel met her mother's eyes. She'd love one. She was starving too. But the thought of sitting at the table with her son, biting into her mother's signature special... it was too much. 'No, you two go ahead. I'll get settled.' But as she padded up the stairs, listening to her mum teaching Isaac how to crack the eggs, then laughingly scolding him for dropping shell in the mixture, she was feeling anything *but* settled.

We're only here for a short time, she reminded herself. *Just a few weeks, and then we'll be gone. We'll leave all this behind again and get back to our life – our real life.*

This place was the past and that was where it needed to stay.

That was where it *would* stay, no matter how hard it tried to invade.

FOUR

RUTH

I lie in bed, watching the red numbers on my ancient digital clock tick closer to midnight. I haven't been awake this late for ages: usually, I'm asleep by ten and up by five. The life of a headmistress necessitates an early start, and I like to be the first one at school. The hallways are empty of students, but full of potential for the day ahead. I love to stand there, breathing in the charged air. It invigorates me. It inflates me.

Tonight, though, I can't sleep, and tomorrow I'll need more than deep breaths in the hallway to inflate me. I've done all the things I usually do each night: lock the doors, turn off the lights, drink my camomile tea, and put a lavender sachet under the pillow – in that order. But as I listen to Isobel moving around in her room next door, even my usual rituals can't soothe me. Now that my daughter's back – with my grandson, no less – all the pain and confusion I thought I'd laid to rest have reared up again, blaring out the still unanswered questions.

Why did she leave?

Why did she never want to talk to me again?

What did I *do*?

Before I can stop it, my mind flips back to the moment I discovered the note on her pillow saying she was leaving... that she was fine; that she didn't want this life we'd planned out together. That I shouldn't try to contact her and that she wasn't coming back. If I close my eyes now, I can still see the loop of her writing, the careful cursive she'd practised for hours making fake report cards for my students before she was one herself.

I sank down on the bed, staring at the lined paper in my hand as confusion clogged my mind. Where would she go? And why? Girls like her didn't *run away* – that kind of thing didn't happen here. It must be a joke, I told myself, trying to stay calm. Hands shaking, I rang her over and over, but she never answered. I called Cecily, by then at university, but of course she didn't know where her sister was – not surprising; they'd never been close. I rang a few of the girls Isobel was friendly with at school, carefully probing to see if they knew anything without giving away that I'd no clue where my daughter might be, but they had no idea. I called my ex-husband, Alan, to ask if Isobel had been in touch, but she hadn't. All he could say was not to worry; that it was good for her to get a taste of life in the 'real world'. She'd be back before I knew it.

I only just refrained from pointing out that he'd never come back.

I stayed in Isobel's room for hours, trying to breathe through the anxiety, the fear and disbelief. She'd only just turned sixteen – and a young sixteen at that; nothing like Cecily, who was smart as a whip and could handle anything. Isobel knew little of the world outside this square. What on earth was she thinking? What had *happened*? Because something must have. She wouldn't change her mind; throw away her future. If I could just talk to her, then I could get through. Isobel and I, well... we were two peas in a pod. The future she wanted was exactly what I wanted for her: to work with me at the Square and to take over when I retired. She loved everything to do with the school, just as much as I did.

But it was more than that. She loved *me* – with an intensity that took me by surprise, catching me off guard after my elder daughter's independence. Cecily always pushed away from me, even as a baby. When I was with Isobel, I felt more than just someone to carry on the family legacy; the guardian of the premises. I was loved and I loved her fiercely in return. I would have done anything for her. I would have done anything to have her back.

I kept calling her mobile, but it was only when I threatened to involve the police that she finally rang, in a voice so cold and distant it didn't sound like her. She was fine. She was sixteen now, she said, and she could do what she wanted. She didn't want to talk to me again. I told her I loved her and begged her to come home, but she hung up.

I went to the police anyway, but they couldn't help. Like my daughter had said, she was sixteen, and legally, she could live on her own. Every part of me throbbed with worry and pain, but I forced myself to carry on... sure she would come home eventually. She had to: this was her family, her world. But weeks passed, and then months, and she never returned. Everyone asked where Isobel was, of course. I told them she went to Australia to visit her father and loved it so much she stayed, and though I could see some raised eyebrows, no one questioned me. No one ever questioned me. That was the status being headmistress afforded.

I tried to track her down many times those first few years, but I never found anything. She was simply gone, and eventually I learned to live with it. To live with the fact that the daughter I loved so much had turned her back so brutally – had thrown away her family and future at such a young age, without talking to me once. It was the worst kind of rejection.

Not just of this world, but of me. Of her *mother*.

I sit up and flick on a light, then open the drawer of my bedside table and take out a photo of Isobel, snapped a few months before she left. I put it in there after our last phone conversation. I couldn't bear to look at her smiling face each night, and yet I couldn't move her picture too far away. I know it's idiotic, but having it there made her feel close, despite knowing nothing about where she was.

I stare down at her image, her dark curly hair resting on the navy and red blazer, red tie knotted neatly. I can see so much of her in Isaac: same dark hair, same pale skin, same shy smile. I tilt my head, Isaac's face taking her place in the photo. He must be around the same age she was here – fourteen or fifteen, maybe? My eyes fly open as a thought hits: could *he* be the reason Isobel left? Perhaps she was pregnant and didn't want to tell me?

No. She would have told me, I'm sure. She knew I'd do anything for her; help her succeed any way I could. Besides, even if she wasn't comfortable, there are other ways to deal with an unwanted pregnancy without telling your mother... without leaving your life completely. If she'd really wanted to, she'd have found a way to stay. No, she clearly didn't want this life. For goodness' sake, she'd prefer to clean toilets than work at the Square! I saw the look on her face when I mentioned taking a job there. She rejected the school when she left and she's rejecting it now.

Isaac can't be why she ran away. She must have got pregnant soon after, though... so perhaps it was a boy who convinced her to go? Someone she was seeing outside the school, maybe – if it was a student, I'd have known. But why would she keep it secret? And when would she have had the chance to meet anyone? She may have been sixteen, but her school days were long and she'd never been one for big nights out. She was always so conscientious, so diligent. The perfect person to ensure our legacy continued.

So... *why?*

Frustration roils through me, and I put her picture back in the drawer, turn off the light, and lie down in bed. I'm not doing this again. I'm not going back to wondering, mulling over different scenarios, trying to answer questions that can't be answered. Whatever happened to Isobel is behind us, and unless she wants to talk about it, that's where it will remain.

I turn from the glowing digits of the clock, reviewing tomorrow in my mind like a lullaby. Five a.m. alarm, shower, my navy-blue suit, breakfast. Then cross the square to the school, where once the bell rings, I barely blink before it's four. I love that: love how the world engulfs me so much that I don't have time to think about anything in my own life. It's been my saviour ever since my father died, actually, when the grief and loss hit me like a bomb. He'd always been there, my only parent after my mother passed away when I was fourteen. By throwing myself into something he cared so much about, I felt a connection... like somehow, he was still by my side.

Isaac's face flashes into my mind, and it strikes me that as much as he looks like Isobel, there's something of my father in him too. The tilt of his head as he leans in, listening intently. The spark in his eyes when he learns something new – even if it's as mundane as making an omelette, like I showed him earlier. He isn't just my grandson, he's also my father's great-grandson. My dad lives on through Isaac, and he belongs *here*. With his family and at the school.

I know Isobel didn't want to come back. That much is obvious. And I know she won't be keen for her son to attend the Square. But I'm the headmistress, and my grandson is hardly going to sit at home while school is in session. Isobel may think that they'll only be here for a short time, but if I can make a connection with Isaac and get him into this world, then maybe... I suck in my breath. Maybe he'll stay.

Maybe he'll carry on the legacy Isobel rejected, just like my father would have wanted.

He can start tomorrow, I think excitedly. Good to get him settled as quickly as possible. I can't wait to see him in his uniform – I'll nip up to work early and find what he needs from the school store. My grandson: a Burlington Square student. I picture my father's proud gaze as he places a welcoming hand on Isaac's shoulder, and a warm feeling grows inside me, as if my dad is here right now.

I put my head down and close my eyes, sleep finally creeping over me.

FIVE

ISOBEL

Isobel stared at the cream-coloured ceiling the next morning, trying to figure out where she was. The silence felt strange – a long way from the squeal of braking buses, the chatter of people on their way to work, and the constant hum of traffic that seeped through the flimsy walls of her basement flat in Brighton. She sat up, dread creeping in when she remembered she was in her old bedroom. It was a far cry from the messy, lime-green den she'd left behind, but it was still unnerving to lie in a room from her former life... where the spirit of who she used to be hovered in the air around her, whispering memories in her ear at every turn, awaiting the moment she let down her guard. Last night, even in her sleep, she could feel the darkness lingering at the edge of her subconscious.

Thankfully, she'd held off any nightmares this time, but they'd invaded her for years after she'd left, creeping into her head while she slept each night, leaving her gasping for breath when she managed to drag herself awake – usually to find herself cowering in the corner of the room. Once she'd awoken in Isaac's nursery, cradling him close to her chest, as if protecting him from an invisible intruder. Only his wails had jerked her to consciousness, and she'd stayed awake the rest of the night, afraid she could have suffocated him. Finally, the vivid visions had faded, but they'd never completely disappeared, always threatening to burst into poisonous bloom from deep within her.

She grabbed her phone, groaning when she saw it was almost eight. She'd wanted to get up as early as possible this morning to start looking for jobs. The sooner she and Isaac could get out of here, the better. She yanked the duvet off and threw on the same clothes from yesterday, then headed downstairs towards the kitchen, where she could hear her mother and Isaac laughingly debating the merits of their favourite cereals: Isaac had gone for Frosties, while her mother preferred Shredded Wheat.

Her son's voice was louder and more animated than she'd heard it in the morning for years, and that same unsettled feeling from last night returned. Usually, Isaac went quiet around strangers. He hadn't spoken to Silas for a good month or so, relying on one-word answers and grunts. It was a different story with her mother, though: he was relaxed; he was at ease. Isobel sighed, thinking that he must really have wanted family around, after all. But they wouldn't be around long, and the less he connected, the better. When it came time to leave, she wanted nothing from this life to drag them down.

'Oh, you're up!' Her mother spotted Isobel lingering on the stairs. 'Come, have some breakfast. I'm afraid we don't have Frosties, since they'll rot your teeth' – she shot a playful smile over her shoulder – 'but we do have other options.'

Isobel nodded and followed her mother towards the kitchen, thinking how happy and excited she looked. It was a Monday morning, of course. That always made her mother happy. But why was she still here? Normally, she'd be at the school by now.

'You're up early,' Isobel said to her son as she rounded the corner. 'You—' Her mouth dropped open as she took in the boy before her, dark hair slicked neatly back and resplendent in the navy and red blazer of Burlington Square School. For a second, it was like her lanky son had disappeared, replaced by this neat, handsome young man who was every inch a student at London's most prestigious institution. It was a sight most mothers would embrace, but for her...

She blinked, wondering if she'd actually hallucinated; if she was so unnerved by coming back here that she'd conjured this up. But no: when she opened her eyes, there he was, still wearing the uniform. She breathed in, the shock waves from yesterday when she'd first seen her mother reverberating inside... widening their scope now to include Isaac. Her stomach churned, bile rising in her throat.

'What do you think, Mum?' Isaac asked, reaching up to adjust his tie. Isobel stared, a sensation flashing into her mind of how that tie had tightened around her throat, pressing in on her skin. She balled her hands into fists to stop from ripping it off him.

'Stand up and let your mother see you,' Ruth said, moving Isobel back so they could fully appreciate Isaac's uniform. She gazed at it in horror, every inch of her rejecting the image before her. She didn't want to hurt her son's feelings, but there was no way he was going to wear this. Actually, she couldn't imagine he'd *want* to wear it. The last time she'd been able to force a tie on him, he must have been five years old. What on earth had her mother promised to get him into this get-up?

Isobel waited for her son to slump off the chair and stand with his shoulders rounded, but the uniform seemed to have transformed him. He stood in front of her proudly, gazing at her with confidence. Isobel forced herself to take in his grey trousers, white shirt and red tie, and natty blazer. He had new shoes too: the shiniest black brogues Isobel had ever seen. Memories tugged at her mind, and she held her breath as if creating a shield.

'Doesn't he look smart?' her mum said. 'What a change!'

Isobel met her mother's eyes, feeling as if that red tie was choking her right now. 'What is this?' she managed to get out. 'Why is he wearing that?'

'Isaac, you carry on with your breakfast,' her mother said in a firm voice. 'We're just going to have a word.'

Isaac nodded, eyes wide, and Isobel's mother took her arm and propelled her away from the kitchen and into the lounge.

'Isaac's going to start at the school today,' her mum said smoothly. 'I thought it best to get him in at the beginning of this half-term.'

Isobel stared at her mother, realising that she was now taller than her. Why did it still feel like Ruth towered over her, then? 'No,' she said, her voice shaking. 'No, he's not. I told you, we'll only be here for a couple of weeks.' She cursed herself for not seeing this coming. Of course her mother would want Isaac to attend the school. She was the headmistress and he was her grandson. He was *family*, and family and the school were practically one and the same.

Besides, how would it look if he didn't go? Her mum had drilled into her the importance of 'community perception' and 'reputation'. One wrong step, her mother always said, and everyone would lose respect. And once that was gone... Isobel swallowed, attempting to stay calm. She didn't want to anger her mother, but she had no idea what she was asking.

'Isaac's already ahead with all his coursework,' Isobel said. 'Trying to get him settled into a new place for such a short time is more trouble than it's worth.' And although what she was saying was true, it was more than that. The school wasn't just part of the world she'd run from. What had happened there... that was what caused her to run.

That was what had ended her life here, forever.

Isobel shuddered. No. No way. Her son wasn't going anywhere *near* that building. She couldn't imagine he'd really want to anyway. What teenager wouldn't jump at the chance to have a few weeks off? Maybe he was playing along with his grandmother because he didn't want to offend her. Isobel could understand that. Once Isaac saw that Isobel didn't agree, she was sure he'd be only too happy to stay home.

'I'm sorry I didn't ask you first,' her mother said. 'But I knew what you'd say. You've made it clear that you don't want any part of this and that you only came back because you've nowhere else to go. But leaving is a choice you made, not Isaac.'

The words hit Isobel and she lowered her head against the force of them. A *choice*. If only that were true.

'Whether you want to be or not, you *are* here. And the school is such a great opportunity for him, you can't deny that. He's a bright boy and he deserves a place where he can shine.' Her mother's eyes burned into her. 'Just give him a chance. Surely you owe him that much.'

'Please, Mum.' They both turned to see Isaac in the doorway, and Isobel's heart sank. 'I really want to give the school a try. You never told me your family owned it!' His face shone with excitement, and her heart dropped further. 'Gran told me all about the art department they have – they've even got a photography darkroom. You have to at least let me check it out.'

The art department. Isobel gritted her teeth. So that was how her mother had convinced him. Isaac loved anything to do with photography, and he'd jump at the chance to learn some new skills. Isobel had to hand it to her mum: it had been less than a day since she'd met her grandson, and already she knew what to say.

'Anyway, you said you don't know how long we're going to be here,' Isaac continued. 'Wouldn't it be better for me to start now in case we end up staying longer? *Please.*'

'Isaac, I...' Isobel shook her head. 'I just don't think it's a good idea. We won't be stopping long enough to make it worthwhile, I know that much, and—'

'I'm going.'

Isobel's eyebrows flew up. She'd never heard Isaac sound so strong, so forceful.

'There's no reason not to let me,' he continued. 'Gran has already said yes. I'm ready to go. Mum, I'm going.'

Isobel held his gaze, her thoughts swirling. What could she say? She could hardly tell him the truth. He would never know what had happened there... he *couldn't*. For him, the school was simply a cool new opportunity, nothing more and nothing less. He was separate from the past that tormented her, and he always would be.

She sighed, thinking that perhaps it was easier to let him go – for now. While her mother might believe that Isaac belonged here, Isobel knew he didn't. This world of privilege, wealth and entitlement would be as foreign to him as the outside world had been to her. He'd probably come to reject it without her needing to do anything. Then she'd find a place where they could both belong, away from all of this.

'All right.' Her voice emerged as if she was being strangled. 'You can go. As long as you understand' – she turned to look at her mother – 'that we *will* be leaving as soon as I have enough for a rental deposit.' Guilt needled her as her mother's words echoed in her ears: how Isaac deserved to be here. Was she denying him a better future because she couldn't deal with her past?

She pushed the thought from her mind, telling herself that he'd been fine until now, and he'd be fine after this. Better to make your own way in the world than have everything handed to you on a golden plate, especially when the plate came heavy with expectation and responsibility. Sadness twisted inside when she thought of how she hadn't minded that at all. She'd welcomed it; wanted to rise to it.

'And I will take you up on that job in the school office,' Isobel said, turning to her mother. Her mum nodded, and Isobel could see the surprise in her eyes. She was surprised herself, but the decision was instinctive. She couldn't let her son face the place that had haunted her alone, even if she had managed to shield him from the truth of what happened there.

Isaac was an extension of her – the dearest, most tender part, where she was most vulnerable – and she'd continue to protect him with everything she had.

SIX

RUTH

Pride swells inside me as I cross the square with Isaac towards the school. With his hair neatly combed (we'll cut that dreadful fringe soon) and wearing his uniform, he's like a different boy. I can tell by the way he carries himself that he feels more confident too. Smart clothes have a way of doing that to a child.

Parents and students shoot him curious glances as we pass by, and he looks towards me as if for reassurance. I pat his arm, thinking what a big change this must be. I dread to picture his previous school, but *this* is where he should be. I'm glad he insisted on coming here too – glad he agreed with me and stood up to his mother. That certainly bodes well for the future... for his future. Isobel wanted to walk him up to the school, but as soon as she went to shower, Isaac took my arm and asked if we could go. Before I could answer, he'd propelled me out the door. Who am I to dampen such enthusiasm?

'Good morning, Mrs Cosslett,' James Richardson, a boy in Year 9, calls out. I nod, noticing that he finally got a new blazer that actually fits. With a father who designed the country's new fibre-optic network, it really shouldn't have taken so long to order one.

'Morning.' Celia Martin, a BBC news presenter with twins in

reception, shoots me a bright smile. 'Happy to be back after the break?'

'Always.' I gave up ages ago telling parents that I work through the holidays. They love to see teachers as having the life of leisure, constantly making comments about all the extra time off we get. If only they knew.

'Does everyone in this square know you?' Isaac asks, when at least five more people stop to have conversations with me. 'It's like you're a celebrity or something.'

I laugh and shake my head at the image of me strutting down the red carpet. 'I've lived here for years,' I answer, 'and when you're the headmistress, everyone wants to say hello.' As leader of the school, I quickly learned that people don't want to connect with *me*; they want to connect with the head teacher. I've played the role so long now that I can't imagine not doing it – can't imagine life without the respect and admiration tinged with fear in people's eyes. And truthfully, I'm not sure it's a role any more. The school and I are so intertwined, I don't know where it ends and I begin.

With all the parents and students eager to chat, it takes about three times longer than usual to reach our destination. It's a beautiful day, crisp and cool with sunlight streaming from a deep blue sky, and despite the late night and early start, energy courses through me. Here I am, about to enrol my grandson in my school... *his* school. I can scarcely believe it.

'Come on inside,' I say to Isaac, when I notice he's hesitating on the steps. My mind flashes back to Isobel's first day as a student here. The Square had only started admitting girls a few years earlier, and despite her begging to transfer from her old school, I'd asked her to finish there first: she needed to get the best marks possible on her exams, to prove the girls we admitted were the highest calibre. She'd paused the way Isaac is now, following behind me as I led her through the corridors and into her classroom. She'd reached out to hug me when I said goodbye – she was always affectionate, even as a teen – but I moved away. I was headmistress here, I'd thought, not her mother. But as I'd turned back and met her eyes, guilt had swept through me. I still wish I'd pulled her into my arms. I might have been her headmistress at school, but I was always her mother.

Before I can stop myself, I walk down the steps and take Isaac's arm. I know it's not exactly cool for teenage boys to allow affection, but he doesn't shrug me off. Instead, he turns to smile at me, and an unfamiliar warmth swirls inside. As we climb the steps, I can't hold back the hope that no matter what went wrong with Isobel, Isaac's return might make that scar inside me fade just a little.

'T.S. Eliot used to live here?' he asks, his voice full of awe as he spots the small blue plaque to the left of the door, proclaiming the poet resided inside for part of his life.

'You've heard of T.S. Eliot?' I raise my eyebrows, impressed. I wouldn't have thought his school was big on poets.

He nods. 'I used to read him at home sometimes. I love how he writes.'

'Well, you'll feel right at home,' I respond. 'He was a resident in this part of the school for a few years. The Square is made up of four houses, all Grade-2 listed properties built in the eighteen-hundreds.'

Isaac lets me lead him up the stairs and into the foyer, his eyes widening as he gazes at the high ceilings and the chandelier hanging above us, then down at the polished black and white chequered tiles.

'This is a *school*?' he asks, and my heart pinches as I think again of the dim, dark place he must be used to. I may have angered Isobel, but I've definitely done the right thing enrolling him here. In time, hopefully she'll see that too.

I smile at his astonishment. 'It is. And better yet, it's *your* school. Like I said last night, the family founded it.'

'I can't believe Mum never told me anything.' Isaac reaches out to touch a polished brass banister. 'But then Mum never told me anything about where she grew up, or my relatives... All I know is that my dad died when I was young.' He makes a face. 'She never said, but I kind of knew that I shouldn't ask about her past. I didn't want her to get upset.'

I nod, not surprised but fending off the questions still echoing in my brain. 'Come on. Let's get you registered. You're in Year...?'

'Year 10,' he answers, following me down the corridor. 'I just turned fifteen this month.'

I nod again, but inside my mind I'm doing quick calculations. Isobel has been gone for over fifteen years now. She left in the spring and Isaac was born in October, so... I draw in a breath. She *was* pregnant when she ran away. Who on earth was her boyfriend? How didn't I know anything? My heart aches as I think of her alone in a strange place with a newborn – or maybe her boyfriend went with her? *Why* couldn't she have just told me? I didn't imagine our closeness... did I?

I turn back towards Isaac, hardening myself against the past. I won't find any answers there. There's only the future. There's only my grandson.

'The office is just around this corner,' I say, pushing through another door. 'Hopefully your aunt will be there, so I can introduce you.'

'My aunt?' For the second time this morning, Isaac looks shocked. 'I have an aunt?'

'You do,' I say, pity for Isaac and anger at Isobel swirling through me. How could she have kept all this from him? He could have grown up with a family around him, a life without struggle. Instead, he was all alone... they were all alone. Except for a partner who stole everything they had. 'Cecily is your mother's older sister. She works here as the deputy head.'

I quicken my pace, eager to introduce Isaac. I wonder what Cecily will think of Isobel being home? They were never close – Cecily is five years older than Isobel, and they're completely different characters – but she must have felt her sister's absence somehow. For a second, I wonder if I should have called before springing Isaac on her, but Cecily is strong, stable and unflappable. When I rang her from my hospital bed after my stroke fourteen years ago, she hopped on the first flight from Asia, where she was travelling at the time before starting her dream job in Hong Kong. She came straight to my bedside, helping out at the school and keeping my health scare under wraps.

My recovery took more time than planned, but thankfully Cecily stuck around. I may have put a little pressure on her in the beginning, but the longer she stayed, the more settled she seemed. She must like it, because all these years later, she's still here, and she's as eager as ever to carry on once I retire.

'Ah, good morning, Cecily.' I enter the main office with Isaac to find her locked in her daily battle with the photocopier. When she started as deputy head, she carved out her own space in the secondary-school wing where the sixth form is, but I wanted to stay here. I like to be close to the entrance, where I can keep an eye on the comings and goings. Cecily starts off her days here, too, before heading upstairs. We work well together, but I know she also treasures her independence.

She lifts her head, her normally pale face red and sweaty with her exertions. 'Get that fringe out of your face,' she snaps at Isaac, whose hair has defaulted to falling in front of his eyes again. 'For goodness' sake, tell your mother you need a trip to the barber. *Tonight.*'

Isaac glances at me, and I can see from his expression that he doesn't know how to respond. This isn't quite the cosy meeting with his aunt that he probably expected.

I lay a hand on Cecily's arm, surprised at its softness. She used to be all skin and bones, but then she's not a teenager any longer. She's in her mid-thirties now, and sometimes she can be a little... brittle. 'Cecily, this is Isaac. Your nephew.' I pause, watching her mouth drop open. 'Isobel's son. She's come home.'

The words loom large in the small room, expanding until it seems like they've taken all the space. Cecily stares from me to Isaac, then back to me again, her face frozen. I realise that even after all these years, Cecily and I never talk about Isobel. It's like she's been dead to us. I can't blame Cecily for acting as if she's seen a ghost.

A memory runs through my mind of the day I'd called Cecily to see if she knew anything about her sister's disappearance. Her voice was so cool and distant, and sadness had filtered through me that the two of them were like strangers. No, it was more than that: there was a kind of resentment, something I'd hoped would fade but never had. Isobel's unexpected birth had changed things in our family. It had changed Alan from a happy man to one that was tired, irritable and acting as if he was in jail. You'd think Isobel was more of prison sentence than a child, and Cecily clearly sensed it.

And then Alan left – nothing to do with the children and everything to do with not wanting to be tied to the Square. I knew Cecily blamed Isobel, but I was too overwhelmed with everything else to deal with it properly. I'd hoped she'd outgrow it.

'Isobel just... showed up at the house?' Cecily says, still not moving any closer to Isaac. My heart goes out to him. 'When?'

'Last night,' I say softly. 'They need a place to stay, so she and Isaac are with me for a bit. I thought it would be a good idea for him to start today at the school, and Isobel is going to be working with me here in the office to earn some money.' Finally, all of us will be together. I can hardly believe it.

Cecily blinks, and I try to read her expression. But then, I was never good at reading my eldest. While she and her father were always on the same wavelength, I often hadn't a clue what either of them was thinking. Which is obvious, given I was hugely surprised when Alan left me. I'd thought I could read Isobel, but then she left too. It seems that when it comes to my family, my vision is impaired.

But maybe – just maybe – it will be different with Isaac.

Finally, Cecily smiles at her nephew. 'It's very nice to meet you,' she says, reaching out for an awkward hug. My heart twists as I watch his arms tighten around her, and I wish now I'd been able to do that too. If Isaac's going to stay, he needs to feel accept-ed... loved. I take in a breath at the word. Can I do that? Can I start to expose my heart again; to make space for something besides the school? I think of the earlier moment on the steps – of how good it felt to be there for my grandson when he needed me – and I realise that despite myself, I may have begun to do just that. 'I'm sorry, it's just such a shock. I'd no idea you existed! I'm Cecily.'

Isaac nods, his cheeks colouring. I can see all of this is becoming a bit much for him, and it's time to get him settled.

'Cecily, can you do me a favour?' I ask. 'Isobel's going to be starting today, and she needs some appropriate clothes to wear. Would you mind nipping home and selecting a few things until she can go shopping? She's about the same size as you.' Truthfully, she seems much thinner, but at least Cecily's garments will fit.

'Sure.' Cecily looks anything but happy, but she shrugs on her coat and grabs her bag. 'I'll be back in thirty minutes or so.' She lives just around the corner from the square. I'd asked if she'd like to stay with me when it became clear she was here for good, but she'd wanted her own place. I'd thought it was better for her too – I'd hoped she'd meet someone, have kids, make a life... but for some reason or other, she never did. 'We'll chat more later, Isaac.' She touches his fringe. 'Sorry to snap at you! But you really do need to cut your hair.' She smiles again, and I can't help grinning at Isaac's protest that it isn't that bad. It's hideous, but I've learned over the years that young people often have no idea how ridiculous they look. Thank goodness for uniforms.

A bell sounds, and I see Isaac tense. 'Let me take you to your class,' I say as Cecily ducks out. 'And remember, if ever you feel nervous or shy, remind yourself that you belong here. No one can take that away.' *Not even your mother*, I say in my head.

I walk him to his class and introduce him to the form teacher, watch him sink into a desk, then head back to my office. I click open my email to see if the builder has sent through the estimate he promised for the roof repairs in the secondary-school wing. It's been leaking so much that I've had to close the top floor, and I pray it won't cost the earth to fix. Ah, here it is.

My heart sinks as I scan the words. It's not just a simple repair:

the whole roof needs replacing. It's not stable, it could be a safety issue if not done in the next month or so, and... *wow*. My jaw drops open as I take in the figure at the bottom of the email – a huge number, much larger than the amount I had earmarked to fix the school's security system as well as finally purchase that new air filtration system the parents have been harping on about. I swallow, remembering the form rep meeting where one mum claimed that 'every other school in London' had one, and that I'm putting their children's lives at risk by holding off. I'd promised to implement it this term, but what good is an air purifier if the whole building collapses?

I lean back in my chair as my chest tightens. Once again, that strange feeling sweeps over me that the school is mocking me, *testing* me. Am I clever enough to find a way to keep it going, or will I let it cave the same way the roof has? Fixing the roof will prop up the school for now, but what about maintaining its stellar reputation? My father always said that reputation is the most important asset any school possesses – intangible, yet invaluable. And once that starts to slip, it's almost impossible to get back.

Am I going to be the one to fail? To let it down just as my grandson has finally returned to take his rightful place?

An idea filters into my head, and I click through my inbox. Last week, a private equity firm got in touch, wondering if I'd consider outside investment. That's not uncommon: over the past decade or so, several firms have either invested in or started their own schools outright. I've received my fair share of offers over the years, although they've trickled off recently. I've never been interested because we could always do things on our own. But times have changed, and there's no harm in checking things out, is there? Seeing what they might be able to offer?

Because this isn't only about the school. And it's not only about our legacy either. This is about my grandson too... about Isaac. I picture his eagerness to become a student here and his wonderment when he entered the building, and determination rushes through me. Isobel may have rejected this world, and I may never know why. Isaac didn't, though, and, like I told his mother, he does deserve a place to shine. He deserves a *life*, as part of something so much bigger than what he left behind.

I find the email from Lovell Capital and pick up the phone. As I dial, I can almost sense the school smiling in approval.

SEVEN

ISOBEL

Isobel sipped the last of her tea, anxiously waiting for Cecily to arrive. In the otherwise silent house, the clock in the lounge sounded like a ticking time bomb. Just the thought of Isaac entering the school without her made her vibrate with tension. She couldn't believe her mother had taken off with him! She'd been in the shower and she hadn't even heard them leave.

Her mobile pinged and she grabbed it, freezing when she saw a message from Silas. Before she could tell herself not to, she clicked it open, nausea rising at the torrent of abuse and threats to come find her if she talked. His rage-filled face flashed into her mind, accompanied by an absolute certainty that he wouldn't hesitate to follow through on anything he'd said. She'd seen evil, both past and present, and she recognised it now. If only she'd recognised it sooner, she thought, guilt and sadness pouring into her. She could have saved herself. She could have saved her *life*.

Heart pounding, she set the phone down and sank onto the bed. As much as she hated coming back here, she'd done the right thing. Silas had no idea where they were. He couldn't, since she'd never mentioned her past. She was safe – *Isaac* was safe. And as soon as she had the money, they'd be out of here. In the meantime... she cringed, thinking again of Isaac at the school.

He'd be fine, she told herself. He didn't know what had happened there. He'd never know. And he wanted to go. Still, she couldn't wait to check on him and make sure he really was okay. At least being the head's grandson would help pave the way. It certainly had for her. She'd never had a tight-knit group of friends, but no one ever bullied her. No one had dared, except—

'Hello? Isobel?'

Isobel jerked at the sound of her sister's voice. It had been ages since she'd heard it, but she'd never forgotten it. When Isobel was a child, she'd been fascinated by Cecily, watching for hours as she straightened her long blonde hair and swooped mascara on her lashes, making her light-blue eyes look enormous. Isobel would watch her on the phone, talking and laughing to her friends with an animated tone, or spy on her as she walked home from school, flirting with the boys clustered around her. Cecily had never seemed to care about her little sister, but Isobel reckoned that was par for the course with most siblings. They might never have been close, but Isobel had longed for a shred of affection from her with every fibre of her being.

What was Cecily like now? Isobel wondered. In her mind's eye, she saw a successful woman with two perfect children and an adoring husband, living in a nearby townhouse, with a rescue Labradoodle and fresh veggies in the huge back garden. In short: the exact opposite of Isobel's life.

'I'm in here,' Isobel said, taking in a breath as she prepared to see her sister for the first time in years. She turned, surprise washing over her. The person standing in front of her was neither the young woman she remembered nor the woman she'd imagined. Her blonde hair was streaked with grey, cut in a bob that ended just below her ears. The light-blue eyes had darkened, and her sister's slim frame had filled out. Cecily was only thirty-six, but she had a definite air of middle age about her.

But it was more than that, Isobel thought, meeting her sister's gaze. She'd always been so alive, so full of life – as if something exciting was going to happen. Now she seemed faded, like that life had drained from her. Isobel took an uncertain step towards her sister, but Cecily stood without moving.

Was she angry Isobel had left without a word? Isobel wondered, eyeing her sister's stony face. Had she expected Isobel to reach out at some point? They'd never been close, but they *were* sisters, after all. Even though she'd tried not to, Isobel had thought of Cecily every year on Valentine's Day, her birthday. Their father had always sent her a huge bouquet of glossy red balloons, along with a massive box of chocolates. Isobel had swallowed back jealousy – she was lucky if she got a card in time for her big day – and made herself sick on the chocolate Cecily would deem too fattening to pass her lips.

'You're back.' Cecily handed over a stack of cellophane-wrapped clothes still on their hangers. Isobel couldn't help noticing that she wasn't wearing a ring. Maybe she was divorced? Men had always chased her sister, and it was hard to believe she'd never married. 'How long are you here for? It's just that it's such a busy time at school right now. We're doing mocks and some modular exams, and I really don't have time to train up someone new.'

Isobel drew back at her sister's words. Was that all she was? Just an annoyance to 'train up'? They hadn't seen each other for years, and her sister was worried about her interfering with mocks? But she was the one who'd left, Isobel reminded herself. And she didn't want to be welcomed with open arms anyway. The more tightly closed everything stayed, the better.

Still, she couldn't help feeling stung at Cecily's brusqueness.

'We won't be here long. Just a few weeks,' Isobel responded, taking the garments. 'Thanks for these.' They faced each other awkwardly, Isobel scrambling for something more to say. 'Did you meet Isaac?' Hopefully Cecily had been warmer than their mother, although judging from what Isobel had just seen, she doubted it.

Cecily nodded. 'I did. He seems like a nice boy.'

Isobel smiled, pride flooding through her. 'He is.'

'Right, well, I'd better get back to the school.' Cecily slid a key from her key ring and handed it to Isobel. 'You can lock up here with this. I'll see you soon.'

'Okay.'

Cecily nodded again, then crossed the room and went out the door. Isobel watched from the window as Cecily hurried down the pavement towards the Square, thinking how strange this all was. She'd walked back into her old world, and while the surroundings seemed the same, everything else had shifted... as if she was looking in through a warped window. Life had gone on without her, effectively erasing her planned place here, time seeping in to fill any gap she'd left. And now that she'd returned, there was no space for her any longer – even if she'd wanted one.

Isobel peeled off the cellophane from the clothes Cecily had given her, cringing at the contents: a white blouse, navy blazer and matching navy trousers. God, she was going to look like a flight attendant. She undressed and stepped into the trousers, grimacing as she pulled them up. They were way too big on her waist, but she managed to cinch them in with the narrow belt. She shrugged on the crisp white shirt, tucked it in, then slid her arms into the blazer. Then she tugged the hair-tie from her messy topknot, gathered her wayward brown hair into a low bun at the base of her neck, and secured it. Holding her breath, she padded over to the mirror in the hallway.

Oh my God. It was her mother, staring back at her. Isobel let out a yelp, rammed her eyelids shut, then slowly opened them again. Okay, maybe it wasn't her mother, but she did look like she'd aged about twenty years in these clothes. They fit – barely – but she felt like she was playing dress-up. Was this how she would have looked if she'd stayed? It was like seeing herself through that warped window.

Right. Time to go. She tore her gaze from the mirror and glanced out the window at the school, gulping back rising dread. She slid on the low heels that Cecily had left, then picked up her phone and the key, locked the door, and headed down the stairs. Each step felt like she was descending further and further into the past, ever nearer to the memories that had plagued her. Across the street, she could sense the Square watching her, tracking her every move, like a predator eyeing its prey. A shiver went through her, and she forced herself forward.

Sun streamed from the sky and the air was fresh, but the closer she got to the school, the more the light leached from the day... as if she was entering a long, dark tunnel. By the time she arrived in front of the building, she could barely breathe, her brow was covered with sweat and her heart pounded so loudly she could almost see the vibrations in the heavy air around her. She'd spent so long erecting a wall between what had happened here and the life she'd made, and now she was about to go straight into it – straight into the core of everything she'd tried to forget.

She could do it, she told herself. What had happened was behind her, surviving only in her head. It didn't exist in the here and now... not like her son. And he was what was important in all of this. He was what mattered. She had to be there for him.

As if moving in slow motion, she reached out and pressed the buzzer. 'It's Isobel,' she said when the secretary asked who was there. She cleared her throat, conscious her voice was trembling. 'I'm, um, Mrs Cosslett's daughter.' It had been so long since she'd described herself like that. It had been so long since she'd *felt* like that. She shoved away the thought.

The front door clicked open, and Isobel pushed hard against it. The familiar smell of polish and dust hit her nostrils, and a million images swam through her head as the door thudded shut behind her. Coming here with her mother, and spending endless hours colouring and drawing during the holidays while she worked. Skidding down the corridor with Cecily to see how far they could slide. Her first day as a student and how proud she'd been to finally be a part of this place – to finally start on the journey that would take her all the way to where her mum was now. She'd been so excited that she was shaking.

She was shaking now too, but it wasn't from excitement.

Isobel tried to move her legs forward, but her gaze caught on something: a cracked display case with rows of pictures featuring students and staff, past and present. One face loomed towards her, and instantly, she felt a crack judder through the wall she'd erected, as if she was a reflection of the case in front of her. She backed away, but it was too late. The darkness had already found its way in.

A hand in her hair. A body on hers. The whistle as he walked away from her, leaving her silent on the floor.

She shook her head to clear the image, but instead more memories rushed in. Memories of those heady days and weeks when she'd met Isaac's father. Memories of when she'd been foolish enough to think he'd actually liked her.

She'd been in the science lab late one afternoon trying to finish up an experiment when he'd come in from French club. All the girls in her form had signed up for it – not to learn French, but to stare at him and flirt. Isobel had thought he was handsome, too, but he was a *teacher*, for goodness' sake, and she could barely say hello without blushing. He'd started talking to her in French, and she'd stammered out a few words, thrilled that he'd taken the time to stop and chat. He'd kissed her on both cheeks – like the French do, he'd said – and then went off, whistling down the corridor. She'd never forgotten that tune. It had haunted her dreams so much that one day she'd looked it up: 'Non, Je Ne Regrette Rien'. Nausea had swirled inside as she'd thought of how very fitting it was.

She'd started staying late every Wednesday to spend time with him, although she knew she was being ridiculous. Even if by some miracle he did like her, the barrier between them could never be breached. He'd smile and kiss her cheek, squeeze her arm or touch her hand. She knew he was just being friendly, but she couldn't help but fall into daydream after daydream of the two of them together. There was nothing wrong with dreaming, right?

Then one Wednesday, she was staying late as usual. He came into the classroom, closed the door, and without saying anything, kissed her on the lips. Isobel had stiffened in surprise, wondering if this was really happening or if she was in one of her daydreams. Before she could absorb that it *was* real, he'd snaked his arms around her back and pulled her close. She'd tried to enjoy it like she'd imagined she would, but all she could think about was how her mother would kill her – kill them both – for what it would do to the school if anyone saw them. She was so caught up in her fears that she didn't notice him sliding his hand up her skirt until she felt her knickers being tugged down.

'What are you...?' she tried to ask, but he covered her mouth with his as he manoeuvred them gently to the floor, his hands roaming her body. She blinked, her mind racing. Surely, he didn't think they would—not here, not in the classroom just down from the main office. But then he'd peeled back from her and got a condom out of his pocket, and she could barely believe her eyes. Had he thought this was what she was waiting for? All those kisses on the cheek and after-school conversations... did he think this was what she wanted? It hadn't been – had it?

But what would he think if she didn't? That she was just some young, dumb girl who wasn't mature enough? That she wasn't special after all?

She lay there, her thoughts still whirling, as he eased up her skirt and pushed into her, trying not to wince at the pain as he panted into her ear. After a few minutes, he'd rolled off, zipped his trousers, and stood up. Isobel had scrambled to her feet, pulled up her knickers, and tugged down her skirt, unsure how to feel about what had happened. It was... okay... but not exactly what she'd envisaged. She'd forced a smile at him, though. He'd kissed her cheek, then hugged her and walked away, whistling.

Maybe it was just the first time that hurt so much, she'd thought. Maybe it was so fast because he'd been worried about her mother. The next time would be better. Maybe they'd go on a date or something? Okay, so dating a teacher was wrong, she knew that. But if he really liked her, then perhaps it was all right? And he must really like her if they were having sex. Having *sex*! She'd wrapped her arms around herself, shaking her head in disbelief.

She'd heard Cecily and the girls in her form talking about it, but she'd always felt so far removed from their world. Not now, though.

But despite her hopes, the next few weeks followed the same pattern. He'd come into the classroom, close the door, and a few minutes later it would all be over. It wasn't really enjoyable yet, but it wasn't terrible either. And she kept hoping that one day, they'd move from beyond the school to the real world.

Everything changed, though, when she'd found out she was pregnant.

Her eyes flew open and she grabbed onto the wall for support, feeling as if her legs were about to give out. He wasn't here any longer, she told herself, gasping for air. He couldn't hurt her any more – at least not physically. She straightened up, remembering when she'd heard that he'd been killed on holiday just a few years after she'd run away, in a case that made national news. She'd thought it would make her feel better, but the dreams that plagued her had only got worse. She would never be free, she'd realised then. He might be dead, but he lived on in the darkest part of her.

'You're here.' Cecily appeared in the foyer, and Isobel hauled herself back to the present. She didn't want to remember more. She *couldn't*, or she would never be able to stay. Isobel swallowed, staring over Cecily's shoulder into the empty corridor. She could almost hear the whistle echoing down it.

'You coming?' Cecily's impatient tone bit into her reverie, and Isobel met her sister's eyes. *Was* she coming? Was she really going to walk inside here? Walk down that corridor; past the classroom where—

'I'm coming.' She wasn't going to let him stop her. Not now. Not ever again. She wiped the sweat from her face, then straightened her blazer. 'Lead the way.'

'Great.' Cecily shot her an inquisitive look, but she didn't say more. 'I'll give you a quick tour. We've changed so much since you were here last. It's practically a brand-new school.'

If only. Isobel let out her breath and followed her sister deeper inside.

EIGHT

RUTH

Excitement swirls through me as the clock in my office ticks closer to eleven... closer to my meeting with Alex Lovell from Lovell Capital. When I spoke to him a couple of days ago, he was so enthusiastic that he wanted to come in as soon as possible. I didn't want to wait either, if I'm being honest. Ever since I rang him, my mind has been buzzing with everything we could do here – of how I could cement the Square as *the* top private school – if only we had a little extra money. I need to stay calm and think carefully about the next steps, though. I need to make sure this firm is the right fit for us. I've done a quick Google search on them, but apart from a slick website with several photos of their Mayfair headquarters, I can't find out much.

'Here you go.' Isobel places the yearbooks that I'd asked her to grab on my desk. There's nothing better to showcase our illustrious past, and everyone loves staring at school photos of our most famous alumni. One recently won an Oscar, and we had the tabloids onto us for days trying to get old photos. Of course we said no. We always protect our students' privacy from the paparazzi. We honed that skill when we had a member of the royal family attend our prep school a few years ago.

I blink up at Isobel, still unable to believe she's really here –

that this is my daughter, in the school, before me now. She's wearing Cecily's ill-fitting clothes, and although she's been working here for a few days now, the school seems just as ill-fitting... as if pulling on this place that's her birthright irritates every nerve-ending. At home, too, she skulks around the rooms like she can't let down her guard, staying silent and sullen as Isaac and I get to know each other. She's only been back a short time, but she's certainly not settling in easily. Maybe she would if she actually *let* herself, but she's made it clear that's the last thing she wants. I don't think she's even unpacked all of her things yet.

'Is there anything else you need?' she asks, cutting into my thoughts.

'No. Thank you.' The light catches the dark circles under her eyes, and I tilt my head, biting back the question *Are you all right?* Whatever's going on inside of her – whatever she's facing – she's obviously not keen to talk about it. An image of our former heart-to-hearts comes to mind, and I push it away. Those days are over, and Isobel's not the eager girl who looked at me with so much love. And I... I swallow as the scar inside me throbs. I'm not that woman any more either.

'Are you finding things okay here?' I ask finally. 'Cecily's familiarising you with everything?' My mind flips back to yesterday, when Cecily was showing Isobel the computerised attendance system. There'd been no hint of sisterly affection; Cecily had sounded just as businesslike as I do now. But how can I expect anything different? They are strangers.

And my daughter is a stranger to me too.

Isobel nods, her eyes on the door as if she can't wait to get out of here. 'Oh yes, she's been very helpful. Anyway, admin is hardly rocket science. I'm used to dealing with disorganised contractors. This is a walk in the park compared to that.'

I gaze at my daughter, realising that I'd no idea what she did back in Brighton. 'Isaac has settled in like a duck to water,' I say, eager to emphasise the positives. 'I put him with our very best form tutor, Mrs

Nowak. She's also the art teacher. He's really enjoying it.' I smile, remembering his excitement when he filled me in on his first day. The art room, the computers with Photoshop, an actual darkroom... and the hot lunches that consist of something other than chicken nuggets and rubbery burgers! He seemed in awe, yesterday practically jumping from his bed without Isobel having to get him up. He cut his fringe too, and although it's a bit of a hatchet job, I have to give him credit for effort. The past few days have proven I was right: he's adjusted with such ease, it's clear that he belongs here. *This* is his world.

He's slid into my heart with the same ease too... so quickly that it's taken me by surprise. He seeks me out each night in my office, chattering about his day and showing me his latest photos. They could do with refinement and more technique, but I love the quirky angles and fresh takes on everyday objects. He wants to photograph me, and despite my busy schedule and aversion to sitting still for longer than five minutes, I couldn't help but say yes. I worried that I might not be able to find space in my life, but I didn't even have to try. I'm enjoying getting to know my grandson so much that it's far from a struggle.

Isobel's face tightens, and I can see that she's still anything but thrilled that Isaac's slotting into this life so easily. Isaac's shown he can stand up to her though, and if she does try to drag him away, he won't go without a fight. I won't let him.

'Right, I'll just...' Isobel doesn't bother finishing her sentence as she hurries from the office.

The buzzer for the front entrance sounds, and I stand. Is that Alex Lovell? I smooth down my hair, then glide through the corridor. I could get the secretary to buzz him in, but I love to see people's expressions when they enter our impressive foyer.

'Oof!' I bump into Cecily, and my heart sinks. *Shoot.* I'd thought she'd be safely tucked away in the secondary-school wing. This investment, well... this is a course I need to navigate on my own. The school's financials have always been in my hands, and the last thing I want is to get her hopes up about all we might be able to do – or to worry her about what might happen in the future if we don't secure extra funds.

The buzzer rings again, and Cecily's brow furrows. 'Meeting with a parent?' she asks. I shake my head.

'No, it's an educational consultant I've invited to work with me for the next little while,' I say breezily, wondering where on earth that lie sprang from. I've never been a particularly quick thinker.

'Educational consultant?' She tilts her head. 'You never told me about that. I thought you said you'd reviewed the curriculum and everything was up to date? Why do we need a consultant? Anyway, shouldn't I meet with him? I'm sure you have other things to do.' Cecily's been taking on more and more of the academic responsibilities lately, and she's constantly pressing me to give her more. I like that she's so eager, but I'm not ready to relinquish too much just yet.

'That's fine.' I wave a hand, wishing she'd leave. Alex is going to get tired of waiting on the steps outside. 'Don't you have a class starting soon? I'll take you through it all later.' There might not be anything in this anyway. Cecily nods but doesn't move, and when the buzzer rings again, I've no choice but to open the door. On the other side is a handsome young man wearing an expensive-looking grey suit, paisley silk tie and very polished black brogues. He looks every inch the successful investment banker, and exactly how I'd like our students to turn out.

'Alex Lovell,' he says, holding out a hand. Relief floods through me that he hasn't said where he's from. Given my lie to Cecily, that would prove quite difficult to explain.

'Nice to meet you.' I shake his hand, approving of the firm grip. 'Please, come in.'

'Hello, I'm Cecily Cosslett, the deputy head here.' Cecily steps forward and gives him her hand, her face flushing a little. He *is* very handsome. 'I'd love to stay and join your meeting, but I'm afraid I'm meant to be covering class right now. Very nice to meet you and I hope to see you again soon.' Her cheeks go redder still, and I can't help smiling despite the tension of the situation. It's nice to see her soften a little... nice to see her come *alive*, just for a second.

'Come through to our meeting room. We can talk there,' I say, ushering him in.

I watch his face carefully as we head into the foyer, where I make a show of pointing out the antique chandelier overhead. We go down the corridor and into the wood-panelled room that's like something from a Harry Potter film – or so the kids say. Most people can't help but be impressed, but Alex's expression doesn't change. He's either very good at keeping a poker face or he went to a school that's equally impressive. If he did, it can't have been in London. We have been the pinnacle for years.

Determination floods through me, and I clench my jaw. We'll be the pinnacle for years to come too.

'Have a seat.' I gesture to the padded armchair across the polished mahogany table. 'So how did you hear about our school?' I ask, diving right in. 'Why would you like to invest?'

'Everyone knows about the Square,' he responds, and I nod with pride. Of course they do; it's renowned worldwide. I'd once been on a trip with Alan to Iceland, before Cecily was born, and even the owner of the B&B we'd stayed in had heard of our school. She was a voracious reader of *Today!* magazine, an outlet that stalked many of our famous students for years, but still.

'The private education sector has been growing year on year – it's a solid opportunity for investors,' he continues. 'And with a reputation like yours, what better school to invest in? We've been eyeing you for some time. I'm so pleased you're considering it. I know the school has been in your family for years.'

'It has, yes,' I say, my chest tightening. He's right. Am I really thinking of giving up a piece of this very special place? I draw in a breath, telling myself that nothing's been decided. This is purely to feel each other out. 'But we're always open to new ways of doing things.' I pause. 'Can you tell me a little about your firm? Why should we consider accepting an investment from you?'

'Oh, of course.' Alex leans back. 'Just like yours, it's a family business – my father started it with money made by his grandfather. I've only recently taken it over. I'm looking to diversify our portfolio, education being one of the areas I'm investigating.'

'Well, I think that's a very good choice.' I smile, unable to help being won over by this charming man. I love that his firm is a family business, too, with a history not dissimilar to the school's. It seems like a perfect match... *if* I decide I can do this.

'I have some brilliant ideas of how we can leverage the Square's brand,' he says. 'You've got such an amazing reputation here in London. Like I said, everyone knows about you. So why not make that national? Or international, for that matter?'

'International?' A thrill goes through me. He's certainly got my attention.

'Why limit such high-quality education to London? Why not offer it to children in New York, Singapore, Hong Kong... I can think of so many places around the world where parents would kill to have something like the Square.'

I tilt my head, loving his vision. I can already see the campus in New York, the school flag flying out front. I'd never thought beyond this site, but maybe...

'But look, I'm getting way ahead of myself, aren't I?' He smiles. 'I know this is only our initial meeting, and there's a lot to think about. But the potential is huge.'

It is, I think excitedly. It's bigger than I ever imagined. We could do more than just fix the building, maintain our reputation, and secure our legacy. We could expand. We could make the Square global. My father never could have *dreamed* of this. But...

'What percentage of the business would you be looking at in exchange for such an investment?' I ask. I don't want to jump the gun by talking numbers, but as heady as his vision is, it also sounds costly. If he wants too much, then we might as well stop talking. It's one thing to give away part of the school and another to relinquish control.

'We're not prepared to talk specifics until we have more insight into the business,' Alex responds. 'But I know the school has been in your family since it started, and, coming from a family business myself, I appreciate how important that is. We wouldn't want to take that away from you.'

I nod, happiness rushing through me that the vision he just set out could still come true.

He slides a glossy folder across the table towards me. 'Everything you need to know about us should be in there, but please do call if you have any questions.'

'I'll have a read through and let you know,' I say, thinking now's the moment I should give him all our information. I swallow, remembering the mediocre financials inside my folder. I don't want to dilute his enthusiasm by handing those over; don't want to end this before it's begun. Maybe... I blink as an idea hits.

'The school is having a drinks reception next Wednesday in the assembly hall. I'd love it if you could attend. I'll get together everything you need to know about the Square and share it with you then.' This place never looks better than in the twilight, with tables creaking with wine and champagne (donated by a student whose parents own a vineyard) and the best canapés, organised by the famous chef at the delicatessen around the corner.

I'm not naïve enough to believe that good food and drink will make up for our spreadsheets, but maybe, just maybe, the glamorous parents and prestige of the school will help gloss it over. Like Alex says, it's all about reputation, and I'm quite certain that the calibre of our students' families – from the lead actor in one of Britain's top TV dramas to a former cricket star – will make a positive impression.

'I'd love to,' he says, and I smile again.

'Come around seven before all the champagne is gone,' I say. 'You've never seen how quickly dozens of bottles can go until you've met our parents.'

'Looking forward to it.' He stands and shakes my hand with that nice firm grip of his.

'Oh, and if you wouldn't mind, could we keep this conversation and our business quiet?' I ask. 'I hate to be so secretive, but if any of our parents hear that we're speaking to a private equity firm, they may start to get a little antsy... wondering if there's something wrong, if things will change, et cetera, et cetera. You know how it is.' I let out a little laugh to try to sound casual, but I'm watching him closely. 'Part of what makes us special is the fact that we aren't a large firm, and it doesn't take much for gossip to get around in these parts.'

'Of course,' Alex agrees easily, and relief seeps into me. 'Don't worry, I'm good at keeping secrets. And you're right: your personalised approach is what makes this school's brand so special. *You're* what makes this school so special.'

I try not to blush, feeling ridiculous as my cheeks burn. There's just something about this young man. Although actually, he's not that young – early-thirties, I'm guessing? A year or two older than Isobel.

He gets to his feet, and I do too. 'Well, it was lovely to meet you, and I'll see you on Wednesday.'

'Yes, Wednesday. I'm very much looking forward to it.' I see him out, then stand in the foyer as the sounds of the school echo around me, almost like it's cheering me on.

Hope and excitement stir inside, and I straighten my spine. I *have* risen to the challenge. I have proven I can find a way forward. And while I may have just taken the first step towards letting someone else into this business, I'm anything but upset. If we go through with this, it's not just a new chapter.

We could be writing a whole new book.

NINE

ISOBEL

Isobel lay on a bench in the square's private garden, looking up at the sky. It was a clear night, but she couldn't make out a single star, unlike back in Brighton where at least a few were visible. It was a reminder of how far she was from where she wanted to be – not back in Brighton since Silas was still bombarding her with texts she didn't dare open. But somewhere she could breathe... somewhere she didn't have to hold herself so tightly. Somewhere the hulk of the school didn't loom over her, casting a dark shadow wherever she turned.

Somewhere she didn't jerk awake at night, heart beating fast from the sensation of a hand on her throat; her arm.

Because as much as she'd tried to hold them back – as much as she'd prayed that they wouldn't come – the nightmares had returned with a strength she hadn't suffered since she'd fled. She'd manage to drift off to sleep only to awaken minutes later, eyes wide open but still trapped in the past. She'd lurch to the window, her gaze drawn to the Square, then yank the curtains closed more tightly and crawl into bed. But even burrowed under the thick duvet, sleep was impossible.

When she'd been young, her mum would come and soothe her after scary dreams. Isobel would throw herself into her mother's arms, holding onto the feeling of love, warmth and safety long after her mum had returned to bed. Despite the time that had passed, Isobel could still feel that warmth. And though she knew it wasn't real, the memory would finally lull her back to sleep.

No wonder she couldn't relax, she thought now, sitting up and looking over at the school through the trees. No matter where she went, she could still feel that bloody building staring out at her. It was impossible to lower your guard so much as an inch when you felt like you were being watched.

The sound of laughter and clinking glasses floated from the school's open windows, as if to reinforce its presence. At least she'd managed to escape the drinks night. Her mum had railed at Isobel, saying she needed to attend now that she was school staff... and, more importantly, that she was representing the family. She'd dug up an old dress for her to wear, which funnily enough was now the height of fashion. Isobel's eyes had widened as soon as she'd seen it laid out on the bed because she remembered it clearly. Her mother had worn it to an event like this when Isobel had been about ten. Isobel had stared at the deep blue colour and silky material with envy and awe, thinking how one day, she'd wear something like that too. She could just imagine her mother sweeping through the school's hall, regal and graceful with all eyes on her, and despite her shyness, she couldn't wait to be that woman.

Sadness had engulfed her as she'd stared at the garment all these years later, thinking of everything she'd lost to protect her mother... to protect the school. She'd pledged never to tell her mum that she was pregnant; to keep everything quiet. Isobel couldn't have borne the disappointment in her mother's eyes, or what the resulting scandal would have done to the Square. And even if Isobel had decided not to have the baby, she knew she could never have stayed; never have walked the school's corridors each day with *him* still there, with that whistle ringing in her head, and the fear and shame swamping her.

There was no way she could put that dress on now, after everything that had happened. The vision she'd imagined would be fake and hollow, echoing with emptiness and pain.

So she'd told her mother in no uncertain terms that although she might be home, she wasn't 'part of the family'. That she had her fill of the school during the day and that it wasn't going to take over her evenings too – not that she did anything in the evenings now. Back in Brighton, she and Isaac used to flop down on the sofa, Isaac flipping through his photos as they chatted about their days. But here, Isaac usually disappeared upstairs into the study with her mum. Isobel would go into her room and try to settle with a book, but the laughter and animated voices put her on edge.

Last night, Isaac and her mother had been giggling about some Latin words Isaac was trying to pronounce. *Latin!* Isobel had shaken her head, wondering what the hell had happened to her son. He used to say learning French was torture, and now he was into Latin? But that wasn't really what was bothering her, she knew. It was how quickly Isaac had connected with his grandmother. Had he been that lonely with 'just the two of them'? Or had Isaac and her mother simply clicked?

Listening to them together made her yearn for the relationship she'd once had with her mum – the closeness she knew she could never have again. Even if Isobel *had* wanted that, her mum didn't seem interested anyway. She hadn't asked Isobel why she'd left, treating her daughter more as a house guest than a long-lost family member. Clearly, Isobel's rejection had done too much damage – not that Isobel could blame her. Isobel knew it was for the best and that they would be leaving soon, but no matter how much she hardened herself against it, still the longing rang through her.

Isaac had clicked with the Square too, slotting straight into place despite starting midterm. He was inside the school right now, helping to serve drinks and canapés along with other students. Isobel hadn't known he was going until she'd seen him cross the square with her mother, and by then, it was too late to drag him home again. He'd climbed the steps to the school with his shoulders straight and hair neatly combed, almost unrecognisable from the shaggy shy boy she'd brought here. A chill had washed over her as she watched him go inside, as if the building was devouring the boy she'd known and replacing him with a stranger.

The sky was darkening and the autumn air cool, and Isobel slid her hands up and down her bare arms to try to warm them. The cheap thin T-shirt she'd bought from Primark ten years ago and the now almost-translucent leggings weren't exactly made to ward off the cold. She got to her feet and pushed open the gate, then started down the pavement towards home. A noise behind her made her turn. In the gloom, she could just about make out the figure of a man on the nearby corner, standing still, as if watching her. She quickened her pace, then looked over her shoulder, alarm rising as the man turned in her direction, still staring.

She hurried faster. Her heart raced and fear surged through her, despite telling herself there was no reason to worry. This was the safest part of London. The nightmares and the school, combined with Silas's threats to track her down, had unnerved her, nothing more. Still, she couldn't help breaking into a run, her breath tearing at her lungs. And when she finally dared to look back again, the man had crossed to the other side of the street and was now turning the corner away from the square.

Isobel slumped down on the front steps of her mum's house while her pulse slowed. This was stupid. No one was watching her. She was fine. She was safe. But as much as she tried to convince herself, the unsettled feeling remained.

She got to her feet, staring at the glowing lights of the school as if defying it to look away first. Would she ever really feel safe? Would she ever truly believe it? Before she could stop herself, she crossed the street to stand in front of the school, peering up at the windows to try to catch sight of Isaac. It was stupid, she knew, but she'd feel better if she could see him... if she could know that, even if he was inside the place of her nightmares, *he* was safe, like she'd always pledged to keep him.

As she gazed into the school, she remembered when she'd first realised that she wanted to keep the baby growing inside of her.

She'd only been in Brighton for a day or two, and she was exhausted, worried and scared. Unsure what else to do, she'd wandered down to the beach and bought some chips to fill the ache in her stomach. The air had been chilly, but she'd taken off her shoes and gingerly crossed the pebbles to the water, feeling the delicious cold fizz around her ankles. She'd opened the greasy bundle and started eating the chips while still in the water, each bite tasting better and better as she stared at the horizon. The emptiness stretched in front of her, unmarked by any trauma or pain. It was a blank slate – hers to fill however she wanted.

Although she'd left behind everything and everyone she'd ever known, she hadn't felt alone. She had someone: she had her child. Nothing bad would ever happen to him; she'd never let anyone damage him the way she'd been. She'd give him a life full of love, even more than she'd had. Money had been tight and there had been many days she'd struggled, but she'd never once regretted her decision to have Isaac. He'd given her a purpose and a reason to create a new world. From the moment he was laid in her arms, he was an antidote to the past.

Isaac was the future. He was *hope*.

'Are you all right?' A man with dark hair, a high forehead and kind eyes was coming down the stairs. She started, realising that with her ragged clothes, the way she was lingering in front of the building probably seemed suspicious.

'I'm fine. Just looking for my son. He's helping out at the reception tonight.'

'Oh, he's a student at the school?'

Isobel nodded. 'He is. He just started there.'

'And does he like it?' The man tilted his head, and it struck Isobel that he actually seemed interested in the answer rather than simply being polite. He held out a hand. 'I'm Alex, by the way. Alex Lovell.'

'Isobel Cosslett.'

'Cosslett?' Alex's eyes widened. 'Are you related to the headmistress?'

Isobel nodded again, still unused to being back in a place where she was defined by her mother. 'I'm her daughter.'

'Is your son Isaac? He told me his grandmother owns the school.'

Isobel cringed. He was so proud of that fact. She had been as well.

'I enjoyed talking to him,' Alex was saying. 'He's really into photography, by the sounds of things. We had a good chat about it. It's one of my hobbies too.'

'Yes, that's him. Do you have a son or daughter at the Square?' He must. She couldn't imagine another reason he'd be attending.

'Actually, no. I'm a consultant. I'm doing some work for the school and your mother, and she invited me tonight.'

'Oh.' Isobel lifted her eyebrows, surprised she hadn't seen him around. But maybe he'd been there before she started.

'Right, I'd better make a move. Much as I love a good glass of champagne, I have to admit this really isn't my scene. I mean, what do you say to someone who's won the Nobel Peace Prize?'

Isobel smiled, feeling a connection between them. 'It's not my scene either.'

He held her gaze. 'Listen, Isaac told me he's been taking photos on a very old camera. It's excellent practice for him, but I do have a few digital cameras kicking around at home that I rarely use. They're all in great condition and fairly recent models. He's welcome to have one, if he likes?'

'Oh, that's really kind,' Isobel said. 'But we can't accept that. We barely know you!'

'Okay, he can borrow it then.' Alex smiled. 'He really made an impression on me with his passion. He seems a special young lad.'

'He is.' Isobel could feel herself softening. 'All right. Thank you. He'd love to borrow it, I'm sure.'

'Great. I'll bring it the next time I'm in school. Well, have a good evening. I'm sure I'll see you around.' He paused. 'I hope so anyway.'

Isobel nodded and walked down the street a bit, turning back to see him climbing into an expensive-looking black Jaguar. Whatever kind of consultant he was, he must be doing very well.

'Mum!' Isaac came down the steps looking handsomer than ever, and instantly any lingering unease vanished. She stared at her son, pride rushing in. He seemed to have grown older in just the few short hours he'd been inside. 'What are you doing here?' His gaze swept over her, and she could spot traces of embarrassment on his face. That was new, she thought, her heart twinging. He'd always been happy to see her. *Was* the Square changing him already? 'Er, you're not coming in, are you?'

'No, I'm not coming in. Are you done?'

'Almost, but can I stay a bit longer? Mrs Nowak's showing some older kids a few advanced darkroom techniques, and she said I could watch once I finish. Is that okay?'

'That's fine,' Isobel answered, although all she wanted was to drag him away right now, back to a place where they could slough off this world and be themselves once more.

Soon, she reminded herself.

'Great, thanks.' Isaac disappeared inside the school, and Isobel turned from the glowing lights and headed back into the darkness.

TEN

RUTH

I must be getting old – no, scratch that, I *am* old – because at the end of these school events now, I'm bone-tired. My feet hurt from the high heels I've jammed them into, my back aches from standing too long, and my eyes are bloodshot from the one glass of champagne I've allowed myself. Granted, this wasn't just a normal drinks night; there was a lot riding on it. Because ever since I met with Alex, I can't stop thinking about the future he outlined: the international schools, the top-notch campuses. With every second, I want it more and more... for Isaac, for the Square. Yes, I'll be giving away part of the school, but what we'll be getting in return more than makes up for it.

'Right, the caterers have put all the leftovers in the kitchen, and Isaac's collecting any unopened bottles for the supplier to pick up tomorrow,' Cecily says, appearing at my side. 'I think everything went smoothly.'

'It certainly did,' I respond, remembering Alex shaking my hand and saying that he'd be in touch once his team reviewed the files I gave him. Even with our less-than-stellar financials, how could he say anything but yes after being here tonight? Unlike the last time he came, his face changed when he entered the assembly hall, and he stopped to take everything in. With dim candlelight and our best music student – a finalist in the BBC's Young Musician of the Year, no less – playing Chopin on the grand piano, it *was* beautiful. Inviting him here was a brilliant move on my part.

'Thank you for all your help, as usual.' I may be the stalwart figurehead, but Cecily did all the hard work behind the scenes. Usually, she's too busy to relax and enjoy herself, but I spotted her talking to Alex several times this evening with an expression like the one when they first met: eager and flushed, as if she was glowing. For a second, she reminded me of the teen she once was before she grew into this surprisingly sombre woman.

'Tell me about Alex,' Cecily says suddenly, as if she's read my thoughts. 'What's the name of his company? I have some questions I'd like to ask about the coming mock exams. I tried to tonight, but he said he didn't like to talk business when there were more interesting things to discuss.' Her cheeks go a deeper shade of red.

I breathe a sigh of relief that he kept the ruse going. I feel guilty keeping this from Cecily, but I don't want to raise her hopes. This school is her future, and to be given a glimpse of such a stellar one... 'Let's talk tomorrow, okay? I'm exhausted.' It's true – I am. 'Are all the students gone?'

Cecily shakes her head. 'Mrs Nowak took a few up to the darkroom. The Group of Six, or whatever they call themselves.'

I nod, smiling at the name. They're all good kids in the upper years who've taken to hanging around the art room, forming a tight little clique. We had some of their work on show tonight, and it's absolutely stunning. One of them is gunning for a scholarship to the UK's most prestigious art school, and my connection there tells me he's a shoo-in.

'Is Alex coming again next week?' Cecily asks, bringing the topic back to him despite my attempts to shut it down. I can tell that she's trying to sound casual, but her high voice gives her away.

I lift my eyebrows, turning to look at her. I can't remember Cecily ever being interested in a man. It's funny because as a teenager I had to practically beat them off with a stick – it helped, of course, that I was their headteacher. But ever since she came back to the Square, she's been on her own... as much as I'm aware anyway. For all the insight I have into Cecily's personal life, she could be having nightly orgies in her flat.

Somehow, though, I doubt it.

'He might be,' I say, hoping that he will – hoping I can lock this thing down and tell her who he really is. I gaze at my daughter, drifting into a daydream where we secure the investment, Cecily marries Alex, and the school is once again all in the family.

'Great.' Cecily pauses. 'Why don't you head home? Isaac and I will finish up here, then I'll get the kids from the darkroom and lock up. I'll see you tomorrow.' For once, her tone is warm, and I feel a thread of connection between us. Since her return, our relationship has been complicated, laced with guilt on my part for interrupting her life, and a kind of coldness, almost, on her side. I don't think she resents me, but... sometimes, I do wonder if this is the life she wants, despite her pleas for more responsibility. Does she *really* want to run the school, or is she doing it because she's worried about me?

Maybe now, with Isobel home, I can start to ease the burden on Cecily – to let her know that she doesn't need to carry the weight alone... or at all, if she doesn't want to. I know Isobel *says* she's not staying, but with Isaac settling in so well, perhaps she'll finally act in his best interest. Surely, she must see how happy he is and what a change he's undergone in such a short time, all thanks to the school. And however much it pains her to be here, it can't be worse than what she's left behind. She's woken me several times this week with her shouts at night – she must be having terrible nightmares – and I dread to think what she fled.

Her cries wound their way into me, reaching under the scar and touching something deep inside... an instinct to soothe and protect my child, no matter what. I almost went to her, like I used to when she was young, before reminding myself she wouldn't want that. For goodness' sake, she's barely looked at me since she returned, let alone accepting my comfort. I lost her long ago, and although she's back in the house, she's not *home*. But despite knowing that, still the urge persisted. It took all my strength to stay in bed and not check on her, and I couldn't go back to sleep until everything stayed quiet and I knew she'd drifted off.

'All right,' I say. 'Thank you.' I put on my coat and pick up my bag, about to head home when I notice a window hasn't been closed properly. I trudge across the floor, my feet protesting every step, and reach out for the heavy brass handle. Wait, is that... is that Alex and Isobel, chatting on the pavement outside? What on earth is she doing? She told me that she wanted nothing to do with this night, and now here she is... sporting an extremely unattractive outfit that looks like it's been salvaged from a landfill site.

I shake my head, thinking of the silk dress I laid out on her bed earlier tonight. She's the same size I was at her age, and for some reason, I'd wrapped this dress in tissue, saving it for... well, for her, I suppose. I'll never forget the night I slipped it on, then turned to see her in the doorway. She said I looked like a princess – or a queen, maybe, since they were older. I'd asked her to help me put on my necklace and allowed her a rogue spray of perfume, leaving the house that night filled with love and warmth.

When I unwrapped the dress earlier today, those same emotions arose from the fabric, swirling around me. But then... then Isobel saw the garment on her bed. When I told her why I laid it out, her face hardened, she turned away, and instantly everything inside me went dark. It was another reminder that my daughter was gone. The woman before me was someone else – someone who rejected this life.

I watch as Alex touches Isobel's arm and smiles, and uneasiness threads through me as I recall Cecily's interest. The last thing this family or our school needs right now is a love triangle. I laugh at myself, pushing away the ridiculous thought. Nothing has happened with either of my daughters, and Alex is a professional through and through. There's no room for emotion when it comes to business.

I'm certain Alex would agree.

ELEVEN
ISOBEL

Isobel pushed back from the desk, stifling a yawn. Thank God it was 5 p.m. and she could go back to her mum's before she collapsed. After two weeks, the lack of sleep was starting to take its toll. She'd lain in bed for hours last night, afraid to close her eyes. And when she'd finally succumbed, she'd awakened shaking and cold, the covers cast aside, her hands held out as if she was warding off that same old invisible intruder. She must have called out loudly, too, because her mother had thrown open the door and snapped on the light.

'You're okay,' she'd said from the doorway. 'You're safe here. You know that.'

Isobel had blinked at her mum, wondering for a second if she'd gone back in time. In her nightgown, with her hair messed and without her specs, this was the mother of her memories, who'd say those exact words whenever Isobel was scared. The urge to throw herself into her mother's arms swept over her, but she steeled herself against it. She wasn't a child any longer and, judging by the fact that her mother hadn't come inside the room, she wasn't here to comfort her.

Her mother was wrong anyway. Isobel might be safe physically, but the memories and secrets she'd kept would always pursue her, no matter how far she ran... always threatening her, no matter where she was. Her reaction to the man in the square last week was a harsh reminder of that.

'Your ex doesn't know where you are,' her mother had continued. 'He can't find you.'

'It's not about him,' Isobel had mumbled, realising she hadn't heard from Silas for a few days now. One less thing to worry about, thankfully. Her mum had nodded, then closed the door behind her, and Isobel had only been able to go back to sleep by reminding herself that when she got paid at the end of the month, she and Isaac would be out of here.

Because they *were* leaving – soon – despite her mum giving her more responsibilities; despite the constant entreaty that this was Isaac's legacy. Maybe Isobel wouldn't be safe from her subconscious anywhere, but at least she could get away from the very place that had caused these nightmares. She'd get paid in another week or so. Then she should have enough for a rental deposit somewhere far away.

She sighed, dreading the moment she'd have to tell Isaac they were leaving. They hadn't been here long, but – far from her hope that he'd reject this world – he seemed to disappear further into it with every passing day. He'd even started going into school early and staying late, brushing off her questions about what he was doing there. Her mum had assured her he was usually in the art room, working on his photos with the teacher and some students, and a pain had shot through her that the son who used to share everything now told her next to nothing. Sometimes, when she looked at the school and pictured her son inside, it felt like the building was sneering down at her, asking how she could have been so stupid to think that anyone could resist its lure.

And it wasn't just school. The longer they were here, the stronger Isaac's connection with her mother was growing. It wasn't only evenings in her office now; her mum had started taking Isaac to museums and galleries too. Isobel swallowed, remembering Isaac's happy face and excited voice when he'd returned from a trip to Tate Modern with her mum last Saturday. Isobel hadn't known they were going, and they'd spent hours afterwards dissecting every artwork they'd seen there. That same longing she'd felt earlier had risen up, and she'd had to go out for a walk to escape their chatter.

Isaac had been getting to know Alex too. He'd been so good with Isaac, not only following through on his promise to lend him a camera, but showing him how it worked, and taking him around the square on an impromptu photo shoot. Isobel had tagged along, curious to learn more about this man who'd give a kid he'd just met an expensive camera – and, after all she'd been through, wanting to make sure she could trust him with her son.

'Thank you so much for doing this,' she'd said, as they stood on the pavement watching Isaac snap the school. She'd shivered at the look of admiration on her son's face as he angled the camera for the best shot. She'd felt that way about the school too.

'Cold?' Alex had his blazer off and slung around her shoulders before she could say no. She'd gathered the soft fabric around her, loving its fresh clean scent.

'Do you want to have a go, Mum?' Isaac held out the camera, and she backed away from it.

'No, thanks.' She had enough images of the Square in her mind to last a lifetime.

'Go on. Don't worry about breaking it. You can't really mess it up.' Alex smiled, gesturing towards the camera, but she couldn't help backing away.

'No, no. That's okay. I just...' She shook her head, unable to continue, and Alex put a hand on her arm.

'You don't have to. That's fine.'

She nodded, her cheeks colouring. He probably thought she was being silly. But when she met his eyes, she felt that same connection as the other night, and she sensed that even if he didn't understand, it didn't matter – he wouldn't push it. They'd wrapped up their photo session and headed to the café around the corner for hot chocolate to warm up, chatting and laughing until Isaac said he had homework to do.

Next week, Alex was going to show Isaac some of his favourite locations in London, so he could get to know the city better and practise with the new camera at the same time. Alex had asked Isobel if she wanted to come this time too. She'd almost said yes, but Isaac had told her she'd just be bored and cold, and that he was fine on his own. She'd turned to look at Alex, her mind spinning. He might seem gentle and kind, but he was still a stranger, and she knew only too well how deceptive appearances could be. But Isaac wasn't a child, and this wasn't the past. He had his mobile, and he knew to call if he needed her... he knew he could call her for anything. Anyway, she'd rather read a good book in front of the fire than shiver by some mouldy wharf, no matter how atmospheric the scene. She just might join them for the after-shoot hot chocolate, though.

Isaac had known this would be temporary, but was she really going to tear her son from the first place where he seemed at home – where he seemed *happy*? She sighed, shaking her head. She didn't want to, but... Maybe at the very least, Isaac and Alex could keep in touch. Listening to them chatter over art and technology, they seemed to have really connected. Isaac could do with a good male role model, and although she'd only known Alex a short time, his generosity and kindness touched her.

'Are you heading back to the house?' Cecily poked her head into the office. 'I need to get some papers from the office there. And since you still have my key...'

Isobel nodded, thinking how strange it was that Cecily never referred to the building they'd grown up in as 'home'. It was always 'the house' as if all those years she'd lived there meant nothing.

'Let's go,' she said, grabbing her handbag and shrugging on her coat. She followed Cecily's brisk walk through the school, then down the steps, breathing in the fresh air after being inside the stale office all day. Although it was late afternoon, the sky was dark and the street lamps were on already. The square was deathly quiet, its residents tucked away against the autumn chill, and a thick mist made it impossible to see more than a few feet away. An image of that man on the corner sprang into her mind, and though she knew it was nothing, Isobel couldn't help shivering. Thank God her sister was here.

'Have you seen much of Alex lately?' Cecily asked, her face tense despite the casual tone. 'I heard him ask you out the other morning.'

'He wasn't asking me out. He's taking Isaac on a photo shoot and he invited me along.' She eyed Cecily curiously, remembering how she'd seen her blush one day when Alex had come into school, then chit-chat with a tone that bordered on flirting. Isobel couldn't picture the two of them together, but she was happy to see Cecily interested in something other than the Square. Her life seemed to have shrunk in the years since Isobel had left, not expanded like she'd thought Cecily had wanted. Maybe that was why her sister seemed to have so little joy in her.

'Why don't you ask him out for a drink or something, if you're interested?' Isobel asked. She certainly wasn't. She liked Alex, but romance was the last thing on her mind. He seemed to sense that, staying strictly friendly and nothing more. It was part of the reason why she felt so comfortable with him.

Cecily's cheeks flamed and she dropped her head. 'I didn't say I was interested. And I don't need any advice from you about my dating life, thank you.' Isobel bit her lip, regretting her words. Despite all the time they'd spent together recently, she and Cecily never talked about their personal lives. Cecily had never once asked why Isobel left, and Isobel had never asked her why she'd stayed. The only thing Cecily *had* asked was when she might be leaving since she'd need 'to fill the position'. Isobel had just said the end of the month, holding back the response that she'd get out of here as soon as humanly possible.

'Okay.' The two of them rounded the corner, and Isobel squinted at the pavement in front of their mum's. Something glinted in the street light... was that broken glass? She stared up at the huge bay window, her mouth dropping open as she took in the damage. The middle pane was shattered, leaving a gaping hole in its centre. The darkness inside leered out at them, and Isobel put a hand to her chest.

'Oh my God.' Cecily hurried towards the window, the glass crunching beneath her feet. 'What the hell?' She swung to face Isobel, still frozen on the pavement. 'Check the door. Is it open? I don't think anyone could have got in through the window, but...'

Isobel climbed the steps, legs shaking as she tried the front door. Thankfully, the heavy wooden door didn't budge. 'It's still locked. I don't think we've been burgled.' She shook her head. 'But why... To just break a window and leave... it doesn't make sense.'

'I don't know.' Cecily's eyes were wide. 'This has never happened in the square before. Who on earth would do this? And why Mum's house?' She swung to look around the square, then back towards Isobel. 'All the other houses seem okay.'

Isobel held her sister's gaze as a name flashed into her mind. *Silas.* Oh, God. Could this have been him? He'd been so angry – all those texts and voicemails had been drenched in rage. But despite his threats to come find her, he didn't know where she was. Did he? She thought of that man on the corner once more. *Could* that have been him, after all? Had he managed to track her down and been hanging around, waiting to see where she lived?

But how had he known she'd come here?

A memory of a woman she'd met in a hostel in Brighton floated into her head, and fear juddered through her. The woman had fled all the way from Scotland in the dead of the night and she still looked over her shoulder. This was her second time trying to leave: the first, her husband had found her and dragged her home. She'd told Isobel never to underestimate the fury and determination of a man who felt diminished by a woman... how he'd stop at nothing to prove his power.

It looked like she might just be right.

'It could have been my ex,' Isobel said in a dull voice, hating how weak all this made her look to her strong sister. 'He's... he's not exactly a good guy.' That was putting it mildly. 'He was so angry that I left.'

Cecily's eyes softened. 'Mum told me what happened. It must be him then. I can't think who else would do this.'

Isobel nodded, still unable to believe Silas had found them, but it didn't matter how. All that mattered was that she and Isaac weren't safe here now – they weren't safe from *reality*, never mind threatening memories. If Silas had done this, who knew what he might do next? Maybe this was simply a reminder not to report the missing money, but Isobel wasn't taking any chances. Anyone who would take the trouble to track you down and throw a brick through your window was likely capable of more, and she wasn't going to stick around to find out what that 'more' might be.

She'd take the money she'd earned so far and run. Isaac wouldn't be happy, but he'd understand. And in a strange kind of way, Silas had done her a favour: at least she didn't have to feel guilty now for tearing her son away from here.

'We need to leave,' she said, wrapping her arms around her body. 'I can't stay now that he knows where we are.' She shivered, wondering if Silas was watching them this very moment. Thank goodness Isaac was safe at the school.

Cecily walked up the steps and put a hand on her back. 'Come on. We can talk about all of this inside.' She took the key from Isobel, unlocked the door, and ushered her in, then locked it behind them again. The house was freezing, a chill wind moving the thick curtains as it blew into the room. They went into the lounge, both staring at a heavy brick resting on her mother's rug. Isobel shivered, thinking she could feel the anger emanating from it.

Cecily steered her back into the kitchen. 'Let's get a cuppa and sit down, think things through,' she said, her tone practical and businesslike. For once, Isobel was grateful. 'Where could you go with no chance of him finding you? Somewhere with absolutely no ties to anything in your past. Somewhere you and Isaac could really settle and make a life; be happy.'

Isobel met her sister's eyes, surprised to see worry and concern there. Maybe she cared more than she let on.

'Look at the *window*. Oh my goodness. What on earth is going on?' Isobel heard her mother's incredulous words from outside, then her footsteps march up the steps and the door opening. 'Isobel? Are you in here? What happened?'

'Mum?' Isaac's anxious voice rang out.

'In here,' Cecily called.

'We're both fine,' Isobel added, not wanting her son to worry. They sat in silence until their mother and Isaac joined them, Isaac going straight to Isobel's side.

'Well?' her mother said, her eyes moving back and forth between them. 'What happened?'

Isobel swallowed. 'Someone threw a brick through the window.' Legs still shaking, she gestured towards the lounge. 'I'm pretty sure it was Silas,' she said. 'It had to be. I don't know how he found me, but—'

'It's because of me,' Isaac interrupted in a low voice. 'I'm sorry. I had some photos at home that I really wanted. I left a message asking Silas to post them to the school... not here.' He dropped his head. 'I didn't think he'd actually try to find us. I didn't think he'd do *this*.'

Isobel put an arm around her son, holding him close. She hadn't, either, until that day he'd grabbed her arm and shaken her. Then she'd seen what he was really like. 'It's okay,' she said, a few minutes later when she felt her son finally calm. 'We'll find somewhere else to go. This was never going to be permanent anyway.'

'Mum, no.' Isaac's eyes glistened. 'Please. I don't want to leave. I want to stay. I'm so sorry, I never thought—'

'You two aren't going anywhere,' her mother interrupted. 'We'll call the police and let them know what we think happened; give them Silas's details. Not that they'll probably do much, but at least they'll have it on record.'

Fear ballooned inside Isobel at the thought of Silas's reaction if the police did get in touch, but she tried not to show it in front of

Isaac. 'Mum, don't worry. There's no need to call the police. Isaac and I are going.' She turned to her son. 'Isaac, start getting your things together, all right? We'll check into a hotel tonight.'

'No.' Her mother shook her head. 'I won't let you. You can't keep running from this dreadful man, or you'll never be able to settle. This is your home. He might know where you are, but throwing a brick through the window... that's the action of a coward, I can tell you that much. And you're safer here with us than somewhere alone if he does try to find you again.'

Isobel listened in surprise. Part of her had suspected her mum might find this whole thing embarrassing: a brick through the head-mistress's window was definitely prime curtain-twitching material. But her mother didn't appear to be the least bit concerned about that. All she seemed to worry about was Isaac and Isobel.

Her mum crossed the room and put a hand on Isobel's arm. 'Stay. Please.'

Isobel almost shied away, but the heat from her mother's hand on her cold skin seeped in, chasing away the chill lodged inside. As she met her mum's eyes, for the first time since returning home, Isobel could see a flicker of emotion... a flicker of the woman from her childhood. The one who'd hugged her when she'd been scared; the one she'd loved with all her heart and soul.

Her *mother*.

Isobel held her mum's gaze, unable to stop herself from drinking in the comfort and strength. Maybe she and Isaac could stay a while longer. Her mother was right: it was safer. Silas might have found them this time because of Isaac, but if the woman from the hostel was right, he would find them again. Isobel shuddered at the thought of all that rage directed at her. They were better protected here with people around them, at least until Silas's anger burnt itself out. Yes, the spectre of the past still haunted her dreams, but it could only touch her mind. It couldn't hurt her or Isaac, not like Silas could. Right now, the danger of the present loomed larger.

'All right.' She nodded. 'We'll stay. Maybe until the end of term… to give Silas a chance to calm down.' That would give her time too – time to save up; maybe get a much better flat in a better area.

'Wonderful. You sit down and rest now.' Her mum smiled, and Isobel sank into a chair at the kitchen table between Isaac and Cecily. Her mother sat across from her, and Isobel drew in a breath as she glanced around the table. She'd rarely been alone since she'd returned, but she'd still felt that way… still felt like a stranger, an interloper. But as she sat here now, she felt a part of something – part of a family.

And though she knew she should fight it – though she *knew* she was leaving – she couldn't resist relaxing into the soothing warmth encircling her.

TWELVE

RUTH

I lean back in my chair and close my eyes, smiling as I listen to Cecily and Isobel debate the least offensive item in the cafeteria. Their voices mingle, fading in and out, and it takes me back to a time when they both lived at home. Isobel would sit at the foot of Cecily's bed, watching her get ready for whatever night she'd planned. Who'd have guessed that all these years later, they'd be together again? Now that Isobel's staying until at least the end of term (longer, if I have my way), I've spoken to Cecily about including her in more decisions – to help her feel ownership of the school and reclaim her place, but also to ease the load on Cecily.

I send up yet another prayer of thanks for Isobel's despicable ex. He hasn't returned since the incident last week, and Isobel says she hasn't heard from him. The police have come up with nothing, no one saw anything – all the pensioners who live in the square were probably taking afternoon naps – and to be honest, I don't really care. I'm grateful to him: first for leaving her no choice but to come here and then for scaring her into staying.

And also... I swallow, emotion rising. Also, for helping my daughter and me come together a bit. When I asked her to stay that night, I admit I was thinking more of Isaac. I couldn't let her take him away from everything here – away from all I can give him. Not now, before I've even got started. I wanted her to be safe, of course, but I never thought she would start to come around to this world... or to me. Something shifted in the way she looked at me, though. It was almost like she needed me again – needed her mother – and that urge to protect and comfort her stirred once more, so strongly I couldn't begin to hold it back. And this time, she let me in. This time, she *stayed*.

I don't know if I can ever forget the hurt and pain her leaving caused – if I can let all that love I buried pour out again – but something changed in me too. Something softened inside... already primed, maybe, by the tender part of me exposed by meeting Isaac. Isobel and I have reverted to our nightly cuppa by the telly, and if I close my eyes, it almost feels like she never left... like she might just stay for good. And despite the many unanswered questions and secrets still separating us, I sense she might feel the same way.

And my grandson, well, he's coming alive here more every day, in this place where he doesn't have to hide to read poetry, with people around him he can trust... with family. In fact, he's glowing so much I've begun to suspect there might be a girl in the picture. I tried to gently pry during one of our photo sessions, and his cheeks turned bright red, poor lad. I wonder who she is? I know these things don't last, but I can't help hoping that he does get into a relationship. It will make it that much harder for him to go if Isobel does decide to leave in the end.

My heart twists when I think of them going, and I push away the image. Everything is unfolding perfectly, and if things keep following this path, leaving will be the last thing on their minds. Now I need to keep moving the investment forward. Alex has been into the school several times, and together we've drawn up a list of what needs to be done, starting with the roof and moving onto my wish list. We've also delved into what international schools would entail; he has a contact who's an expert. It seems to be all go, but we've yet to start hammering out the investment agreement – like exactly what percentage of the business we'd be expected to give up and exactly how much they'll give us in return. I don't want to rush him, but...

I shake my head. I'm worse than a child. This is a big step – a huge step. It's right that it takes time.

I wander into the assembly hall and stare at the huge painting of my grandfather, thinking of the empire we could build. It's important not only for the future: I also owe it to the past, to everything my grandfather and father have done to breathe life into the school. The Square has the potential to be bigger than they ever could have imagined... an entity beyond their wildest fantasies.

And while they might not be here any longer, I'll do whatever it takes to give them – and the family around me now – exactly that.

THIRTEEN

ISOBEL

Isobel hummed as she made tonight's meal – a roast chicken, more in line with her mother's traditional tastes than her usual fare. She'd watched with amusement while her mum struggled through the more outlandish meals she'd prepared. It had become a personal challenge to find something that might defeat her. She'd underestimated her mother, though: she'd managed to finish the vindaloo with extra Scotch bonnet peppers that even Isaac, who adored spicy foods, had found too much. Isobel had reached across the table and laughingly shaken her mother's hand in admiration, as tears streaked from her mum's eyes. The spices had warmed her inside out, but Isobel knew it wasn't just that. It was having people around her – people who cared. Ever since Silas had thrown the brick through the window, it seemed like the mum she'd remembered had returned... or maybe she'd always been there, and Isobel hadn't let herself see it until that night. And though she knew she should try to keep some distance, with every day that passed, Isobel felt more and more like the years between them were fading away.

Like maybe, just maybe, this place could be home again.

That was impossible, though, Isobel told herself for the millionth time as she slid the chicken into the oven. Staying here meant facing every day what had happened, and though she could cope during the day, the nightmares were so bad that she could barely close her eyes before being jerked awake. Knowing her mother was there helped, but... Isobel blinked as a thought jolted through her. Her mother *was* there. Maybe Isobel didn't need to carry all of this alone. Maybe she could finally tell her mum about Isaac – about what had happened. Maybe the nightmares would stop if she did... if she had someone on her side, propping her up against the past.

Could her mother give her the strength to find the words? The strength to face the horror of it all? If anyone could, it would be her, Isobel thought with a tiny smile, remembering her mum's fierce words about Silas.

At least Isobel didn't have to worry about him any longer. He'd gone quiet since that night. She had hunkered down at home for a few days, scared to go out in case he was waiting – in case the police had infuriated him further. But eventually, she'd ventured out with her mother by her side, crossing the square to the school and back again. Her phone had stayed silent and Silas out of sight, and although she still felt fearful, she knew she was better off here than alone.

She lifted her head as she heard her mother and Isaac coming through the door.

'Hello!' her mum said as she entered the kitchen. Isobel glanced up from the onion she was chopping for the gravy, thinking her mother looked pale and tired. She did work hard and she wasn't getting any younger. At some stage, she would have to slow down and let Cecily take over. Cecily certainly seemed to be chomping at the bit to do everything. Despite their mother asking her to share more with Isobel, she said she had it all under control. From what Isobel had seen, she definitely had that. Thankfully, Cecily hadn't asked her more about Alex, but then she never talked to Isobel about anything other than school anyway. After the closeness of that fearful night, the two of them had reverted back to a business relationship.

Would that change if she stuck around? Isobel wondered. Cecily had shown she *did* care. If Isobel stayed, would her sister let down her guard? Would she let her into her life?

'Hi!' Isobel gave the onion a final chop, then slid the pieces into the frying pan, enjoying the sizzle.

'That's such a satisfying sound, isn't it?' her mother said, closing her eyes. Isobel smiled, thinking yet again how much she and her mum were alike. It was uncanny how Isobel would be thinking something and her mother would echo that thought. 'Right, I'm going upstairs to get changed and finish some work. Let me know when dinner is ready. It already smells delicious.'

'Isaac?' Isobel called. 'Did you have a good day?' She sighed when he didn't answer. Probably had his headphones on again.

'Isaac!' She raised her voice. 'Take off your uniform and get started on your homework, okay?'

'Oh, is Isaac not home?' Her mother paused on the stairs. 'He's not with me. I thought he'd come back earlier. The school was empty when I locked up.'

'No, he's not here. I thought he was with you.' Worry shot through Isobel, and she took a deep breath. 'Maybe he went up to the shops or something?' He loved his fizzy drink, and her mum never bought any. 'I'll give him a call.' She grabbed her mobile and hit his contact, trying to stay calm. His voicemail clicked in and she hung up, then rang again. Once more, there was no answer. She tried again and then again, her heart picking up pace. Why wasn't he answering?

'Maybe he lost his phone?' her mother suggested, coming back down the stairs to the kitchen. 'Kids seem to go through them like hotcakes. There are always at least a dozen in the lost property box at school.'

Isobel nodded, but she didn't think that was it. Isaac hadn't had his mobile handed to him like the other kids here, to be replaced easily when it got lost. It was nowhere near the latest version of the popular brands, but he'd worked hard for that mobile, saving up his meagre pocket money for months until he had enough. At his school in Brighton, he'd kept the phone in his hand at all times in case someone tried to steal it. He'd never be so careless.

The acrid smell of burning onions filled the air, and Isobel leapt up to turn off the burner. 'You know, I think I'm going to take a quick look in the garden,' she said, knowing she was being ridiculous but unable to help it. 'He mentioned wanting to take some photos there when it was getting dark. The "magic hour", or whatever it's called.' She paused. 'You're sure you didn't see him at the school? You know how involved he can get when he's working on something. He might not have heard anyone calling or locking up, especially if he had his headphones on.'

Her mother tilted her head. 'I'm almost certain, but I suppose it's possible I missed him.' She got to her feet slowly, wincing as if the effort was almost too much. 'Let me go back and check.'

'No, no, that's fine,' Isobel said, touching her mother's shoulder and pushing her back down gently. God, she looked absolutely knackered. Funny how Isobel always used to think of her as indefatigable. 'I'll look in the garden first, then run up to the school. You keep an eye on supper, okay? I'm sure we'll be back soon. You know how hungry Isaac gets – he wouldn't miss a meal!'

Isobel braced for an argument, but instead her mother nodded and handed over a huge ring of keys for the school. Isobel shrugged on her jacket and boots, grabbed her phone, and headed out into the dark. Silas's face slid into her mind, and a tiny finger of fear prodded her. She paused on the pavement, looking up and down the empty street, cursing him for making her afraid. She jammed her hands in her pockets to keep warm as she hurried across the street to the garden gate. Everything seemed quiet and still, but she fit the key in the lock and went inside, cocking her ears for voices.

'Isaac?' she called as she crunched down the gravelled path that lined the garden's perimeter. There was nothing but the sound of the wind in the large trees framing the night sky, and Isobel continued down the path. 'Isaac? Are you here?' She stopped, her heart jumping as she heard something rustling in the bushes. 'Hello?' *Silas?*

A bird hopped out from under a bush, and Isobel rolled her eyes and laughed, the sound loud in the darkness. God, what an idiot she was. Only residents with keys could access these gardens anyway, she reminded herself. Silas couldn't get inside.

Well, there might be wildlife here, but there didn't seem to be any trace of Isaac. She completed her loop, then went back out through the gate and across to the school. She stood for a moment, feeling even smaller as it towered over her, like Goliath staring down at David. The darkened windows gazed out, daring her to come inside, and she took a deep breath. In the light of day, she could just about manage, but now...

Don't be silly, she told herself as she forced her legs up the steps. *It's just a building. A building, and that's all. Nothing can hurt you now.* The automatic light turned on, and she put her key in the lock, then pushed open the heavy wooden door and went inside, jumping as it clicked back into place behind her. Quickly, she flicked on the long row of lights, eager to banish as much of the darkness as she could.

'Isaac?' she called, her voice ricocheting eerily down the corridor. God, this place was creepy without students. How did her mother spend so much time here alone? 'Isaac!'

There was no response, so she hurried down the hallway, trying to ignore the whistle echoing in her memory. She rushed up the stairs towards the art room on the second floor, hoping Isaac was there and that he'd just lost track of time as she'd said to her mother. They'd have a good laugh and head home together, back to the warm meal awaiting them and away from the darkness.

Isobel held her breath as she rounded the corner, praying to see light, but the corridor ahead yawned black and silent. But... her heart lifted when she noticed the door to the art room was slightly ajar. She quickened her steps towards it as relief filtered through her. God, *Isaac*. She was going to kill him, giving her a scare like that! She shook her head, irritation now replacing the relief.

She opened the door and glanced inside the room, eyebrows rising in surprise at the darkness. He *was* here, wasn't he? She flicked on a light, scanning the space. It was a bit of a mess with paint streaking the tabletops and brushes on the floor, but there was no sign of her son.

She bit her lip, noticing a door in the corner. Was that the darkroom? Could he be in there? Maybe that was why he hadn't heard her mother locking up or noticed the lights flicking off. That must be it. Isaac was going to be so surprised when she told him that he'd been locked in and he hadn't realised! She crossed the room and knocked hard on the door, annoyed but not wanting to ruin any developing photos by letting in light. There was no answer, so she rapped again – harder this time, in case he was wearing his headphones. Then harder still, so much that her knuckles smarted.

Right, well, if he couldn't hear her, then she had no choice but to open the door. She pushed against it, squinting into the red light while her eyes adjusted. 'Isaac?' Her voice was loud in the small space, and her heart sank as she scanned the room. It was empty, except for... she narrowed her eyes. What was that? It looked like... she froze.

It looked like a leg, sticking out from under the table.

She shook her head, laughing at herself. It was just her mind playing tricks on her. Isaac wasn't here; no one was. But despite her words, her heart pounded as she edged her way forward towards the corner of the room where the table was.

Oh my God. There was someone there. She knelt down quickly, letting out a cry as the face slid into focus in the dim light. *Isaac.* Her son. Lying here, alone, on the floor. She put a hand to his head, heart pounding when it came away covered in blood. What the hell had happened?

'Isaac!' His eyes were closed and his face was pale. Terror seized her when she couldn't tell if he was breathing. She moved her face close to his, sagging in relief when she felt a faint breath on her cheek. Mind spinning, she grabbed her phone and dialled 999, giving them the school's address. Then she hunkered down beside her son, taking his hand and praying for him to be okay. He had to be – there was no other choice. He was her life, the reason she'd kept going in a world so far from the one she'd known. She couldn't imagine being without him.

In the silent school, the clanking pipes and creaking walls seemed as if they were jeering her, triumphantly signalling that they had finally managed to devour her son. She gripped Isaac as tightly as she dared, nightmarish thoughts swarming through her head as they lay in the dark for what felt like forever. Maybe she'd been wrong. Maybe the school *could* hurt them. Maybe it wasn't just a building, after all, but a place that gained power by consuming others. A place that—

She lurched to her feet when she heard the paramedics banging on the front door, then raced down the stairs to let them in. 'This way!' she shouted, leading them back up the stairs to the classroom. She opened the darkroom door, beckoning them over to where Isaac was lying.

'Can you tell me what happened?' a burly man asked, panting from the run through the school. 'Has he been here long?'

Isobel shook her head, still unable to believe her son was unconscious. 'I'm not sure,' she said. 'An hour, maybe? He's bleeding.' She showed him her hand. 'I didn't want to move him too much.'

'Very good.' The paramedic grunted his approval. 'Right, this is very tight quarters, and we need to get him out with as little movement as possible. Could you step outside?'

'He'll be okay, right?' Her voice trembled, and the man looked at her kindly.

'It's hard to say until we can fully assess his injuries, but we'll do our best.'

Isobel swallowed and nodded, forcing herself to back away. Outside the small room, the cooler air made her shiver, although she couldn't say if it was from the temperature change or from fear for her son.

She caught her breath as the paramedics carried Isaac into the light. His hair was matted with blood, and one eye was so swollen she could only see his dark lashes protruding. An angry bruise had already formed on his arm, and his white school shirt was splattered with red. She stared down at him, unable to move, longing to gather him in her arms again, but terrified she'd hurt him more.

'Looks like someone did a real number on him,' the paramedic said as they started to manoeuvre him down the stairs.

'Someone... someone did this to him?' The question left her mouth, but she'd no idea how she'd formed it.

'You don't get trauma like that just from falling over.' The paramedic winced under the weight of her son. 'I'd wager he has internal injuries too. They'll do a scan at the hospital.'

Internal injuries. Oh, God. Isobel sank back against the wall, trying to comprehend the words. Someone had attacked her son. Someone had beaten him unconscious. Here, in a place he loved... a place he was proud of and that belonged to him. A place he'd thought he was safe.

A place she hadn't protected him from, even though she knew what evil could happen here.

Her legs gave way and she sank to the stairs, images flooding her head.

Hands on her throat. Bruises blossoming on her arms. The whistle echoing down the corridor as she slumped to the floor, trying to breathe...

Blood on her hands. Blood on his face. Dark red staining a bright white canvas.

Fear burst inside and she jerked to her feet, then rushed down the stairs and out of the school, away from the memories and towards her son. This wasn't the past. She couldn't let it overwhelm her now, not when Isaac needed her most. Whatever had happened to him was nothing like what had happened to her. *Nothing.*

Because he wasn't alone – not like she had been, with only her fear for company... with only her nightmares. She would stay beside him every step of the way, for whatever he needed to recover. She would help him leave all of this behind, so it would never *touch* his life. This place would never devour him, not like it had her.

'I'm here for you,' she whispered to her son, leaning over the stretcher. 'I'm here, and I'll never let you go.'

FOURTEEN

RUTH

The timer for the roast chicken goes off, and I look up from my work in surprise. Where on earth are Isobel and Isaac? Isobel must have left almost thirty minutes ago now – it shouldn't take that long to walk around the square and check out the school. I get to my feet, sighing with exhaustion, then turn off the oven. Hopefully, they'll be back soon because tonight I just need to eat dinner, have a hot bath, and fall into bed.

I take off my glasses and rub my eyes. I'd be more worried about Isaac, but I know teenage boys. Isaac may be one of the more conscientious ones, but the last thing they think about when they're with their friends – or girlfriends – is time. Wherever he is, I can guarantee he's fine and having fun.

I glance at my phone, eyebrows rising when I see a message from Cecily. It's rare we talk outside of school; we get our fill of each other during the day. I slide on my specs again and open the text.

Is something happening up there? I just saw an ambulance with flashing lights go by. Looked like it stopped in the square.

My heart stops as a thought enters my head. Could this be

something to do with Isaac? Is he hurt? Is that why he hasn't returned? I run to the window, fear coursing through me when I see the red and blue lights reflecting on the white facades of nearby houses. I tell myself to calm down: the ambulance is probably here for one of the square's many geriatrics. Faces peer from the windows, gazing out towards... I squint. Towards the school? I can't see clearly from here, but the ambulance looks like it's parked right in front of it.

I slip on my shoes and rush into the night. The cold air wraps itself around my bare arms and slides down my neck, but it doesn't register. Inside, everything is on fire. I've got to get to the school. I have to see what's happened.

It's only the other side of the square, but every step feels like wading through treacle. My chest squeezes so much I can barely catch a breath. The road in front of me waves up and down as if I'm staring into a funhouse mirror. I should stop to rest, but I can't. Panic grows when I see that, yes, the ambulance *is* in front of the school, and I try to move faster.

I reach the steps just in time to see a stretcher being levered into the ambulance. I rush over, praying it's not a student.

Praying it's not Isaac.

But everything inside me freezes when I spot the face because my prayers have not been answered. It's my grandson, lying there so pale and so still. His hair is stiff with blood, and one eye is so swollen that I can't see it, but it's him. I feel myself start to sway as my legs weaken beneath me. Is he dead? He can't be dead. He can't be. I've only just found him. I can't lose him now. Not now... now that I've discovered what a joy it is to have a grandson; to have him in my life.

'Mum!' Isobel appears at my side, wild-eyed and anxious, gripping onto my arm as if I'm the only thing that can hold her up. I turn towards her and take a deep breath. I need to be strong now – for her. No matter what happened, I need to be stronger than I ever have been.

'Is he...?' I can't say it.

'He's alive,' she says, and my insides uncoil. Thank *God*.

'Everything will be all right,' I say firmly, putting my hand on her arm. 'I'm here now, and everything will be fine.' I have no idea if those words are true, but I know that's what she wants – needs – to hear. I can feel her body shaking, her breath tearing at her lungs. And then she throws herself against me, just like when she was young. I pull her into my arms and hold her tightly as the love I'd laid to rest roars to life, sweeping away any remaining pain and distance between us. No matter how she hurt me – no matter how she rejected me – I'm her mother.

I'm always her mother.

'He's in,' one of the paramedics shouts to her. 'Come on, let's go.'

Isobel turns from me and clambers into the back of the ambulance.

'Wait!' I yell. 'Which hospital? I'll meet you there.'

'St Mary's,' the paramedic calls out. Then the door slams and the ambulance shrieks away.

I hurry home to get my things and go to the hospital. So many thoughts and feelings are flying through my head that I can't keep hold of any. Worry for Isaac, and so many questions. What *happened*? How long was he in there?

Did I lock up while my own grandson was lying in a classroom, bleeding and unconscious?

No.

Inside the house, I grab my handbag and mobile. Then I head back into the night and up to the main road where I hail a taxi and tell it to go to St Mary's. I get out my phone to ring Cecily to ask her to make sure the school is secure. The latch on the door is fixed now and it should lock automatically, but I was in such a hurry that I didn't think to check.

'I was about to call you. What's going on?' Cecily's voice comes through the handset. 'I got a text saying the ambulance is in front of the school? And that they've taken someone away on a stretcher?' Her voice rises in disbelief, and I shake my head. I can barely believe it myself.

'Isaac has been hurt.' I swallow, trying to hold back the tide of emotion. 'They're taking him to St Mary's now. I'm in a taxi on the way there.'

'Hurt? At school?' Her tone is incredulous. 'What happened? Is it serious?'

'I'm not sure. He wasn't conscious when they took him,' I say, my voice low as the image of Isaac lying on the stretcher comes into my head. 'He looked awful. Isobel found him when he didn't come home for supper.' I still can't grasp it all.

'Oh my God.' I can tell from Cecily's tone that she can't either. 'But he'll be okay, right?'

'I hope so.' *Please, God.*

'I'll come to the hospital,' Cecily says. 'I'm coming now. I—'

'Actually, could you head to the school and make sure everything's locked up?' I ask. 'I left in such a hurry – I just wanted to get to the hospital. And get a good night's sleep because I'm likely going to need you to step in for me tomorrow. I may be at St Mary's for some time.'

'All right,' Cecily says. 'Please, let me know if there's anything I can do. And give my best to Isobel and Isaac. Tell them... tell them I'm thinking of them.'

'Will do. I'll let you know how Isaac is as soon as I find out more.' In the midst of all this, Cecily's desire to rush to her sister and nephew straight away is a bright light. I know she and Isobel have never been close, but in times of crisis, it's good to see that Cecily wants to be there.

'What should I say to everyone who's asking about what happened?' she asks. 'I have about fifty messages on my phone.'

I breathe in. Of course. The school is the anchor of the square, and plenty of our students live nearby. This is big excitement, and people will be chomping at the bit to find out more. 'Just say a student took ill, and we thought it best to ring an ambulance to be on the safe side,' I answer. 'By tomorrow, I'm sure the whole thing will be forgotten.'

I hang up and shift in my seat, trying to loosen the knot in my chest. Isaac will be fine, I tell myself. What I've instructed Cecily to say has to be what happened: Isaac took ill. If he fainted, then maybe he hit his head when he fell – that would account for all the blood. It looks bad, but head wounds always do.

We've had a scare, but everything will be okay.

I won't allow it to be anything but.

FIFTEEN

ISOBEL

Isobel slumped in a chair in the corner of the hospital ward, her hand clutching Isaac's. Thankfully, his face had a bit more colour now. He'd even opened the one eye he could for a second, then sunk back to sleep. The doctor had given him an alarming number of painkillers and sedatives, but he'd said Isaac *should* be all right... despite a potential eye haemorrhage and two broken ribs, all caused by what the medic had termed 'blunt force trauma'. For one heart-stopping moment they'd thought his spleen might have ruptured, but scans had shown only a bruised kidney and no internal bleeding. He'd be in pain for weeks, and there could be long-term complications she'd need to watch out for. But in time, he should recover.

She'd finally been able to breathe again until she remembered the paramedic's words that this wasn't an accident... that someone had done this to him. Then anger surged through her so strongly it almost lifted her off the chair.

Who would do this? And *why*? To beat a boy so badly, it had to be someone full of venom. Someone violent. Someone with a reason to target him. Someone... She shivered, her mind flashing back to the man on the corner. To the brick through the window; to the constant feeling she was being watched.

Silas.

It must be him. Who else could it be? Maybe Silas couldn't get to her, so he'd settled for damaging the one thing he knew meant the world to her. He knew where they were now; Isaac had given him the school's address. He must have got inside somehow, and then... She shook her head, unable to imagine the scene.

Isobel sat up straight as a thought hit. *Had* that rustle in the bushes been Silas? Had he been hiding there, waiting to see what unfolded? It wouldn't take much to scale the garden fence if you really wanted to. Anger enveloped her at the thought of him crouching in the darkness, watching everything with a leer, and she grabbed her phone. He may have thought he'd triumphed, but he was wrong.

No one would hurt her son and get away with it.

She looked up the number for the police station near the Square. 'I want to report an assault,' she said, her voice shaking. As quickly as she could, she gave the officer Isaac's details, the school's address, and Silas's information, telling them why she suspected him and about the previous incident.

'Isaac's on a lot of sedatives at the moment,' she continued. 'He's asleep, but I wanted to give you this information as soon as possible so you can question Silas.' Guilt gripped her so strongly that she could barely breathe. Isaac hadn't been harmed because of the school. He'd been harmed because of *her*... because of her bad choices; her mistakes – again. She'd pay the price for that forever, and the least she could do was make sure Silas was punished too.

'We'll call you as soon as Isaac's awake.' She jotted down the crime number the office gave her, then hung up, some of the horror inside easing slightly. When Isaac finally awoke, she could tell him that he'd nothing to fear – that the police were already on it. Maybe they'd have caught Silas by then. Isaac would get better, and the incident would hopefully recede in his mind, like a ship disappearing over the horizon. If not, she'd encourage him to talk and help until it did.

'Isobel?'

Isobel blinked at the sound of her mother's voice, wondering if she was imagining it. The nurse had forbidden any visitors on the wards, but her mum had texted to say she was waiting outside and that she'd stay as long as she needed to. Despite the panic and fear of the night, just knowing her mother was near had made Isobel feel better... as if she could still feel the warmth of her mum's embrace. She hadn't thought twice before throwing herself into her mother's arms; it was purely instinctive. In the midst of this living nightmare, she'd needed her mum's comfort more than ever. And she knew her mother would be there for Isaac, too, just like she had been for Isobel with Silas.

'Mum.' Isobel was silent for a second, drinking in her mother's steady strength. 'I'm so glad you're here.' She drew in a breath. 'They've done some scans. Isaac has two broken ribs and a bruised kidney.'

'Oh my goodness.' Her mum put a hand to her mouth. 'Broken ribs? Bruised kidney? But... how? Has he told you what happened?'

'He hasn't been awake. But...' Isobel hardened herself against the words she was about to say. 'From his injuries, it's obvious he was attacked. Someone did this to him.' Fury stirred inside again as she met her mother's shocked gaze. It *was* unbelievable. 'I'm sure it was Silas,' she continued, wanting to get it all out. 'He was so angry. He knew where Isaac went to school. He must have slipped in somehow. I've already called the police and told them what happened. I'm hoping they can track down Silas and put an end to all of this – fast.'

'Silas.' Her mum's face twisted, and Isobel nodded.

'I can't believe he did this,' Isobel said, tears streaking down her cheeks now as guilt hit her once more. 'I should have known what he was like. I should have—'

'Stop.' The word was gentle but firm, and Isobel met her mother's gaze. 'This isn't your fault. How could it be? You can't control the actions of other people.' Her eyes narrowed, and she put a hand on Isobel's arm. 'You've already rung the police, yes? We'll make sure they find him. To break into the school and assault a young boy so brutally...' Her grip tightened. 'He won't get away with this, I promise you. I'll make sure of that, no matter what.'

Isobel nodded, gratitude sweeping through her that despite her mistakes, her mum didn't blame her; didn't think all this was her fault. She wasn't sure she could ever agree, but she drank in that reassurance, feeling it course through her veins.

She'd been wrong to run away, Isobel realised suddenly. She should have told her mother she was pregnant – what had happened – instead of drowning in shame, guilt and fear. She should have trusted her mum: trusted the strength and love she'd shown; the strength and love that proved she'd do whatever it took to keep her family safe... to keep *Isaac* safe.

Exactly like her daughter.

When all of this was over, Isobel would say why she'd left. With her mother standing by, she'd have the courage to face the past. She'd tell her mum she was sorry for the hurt and pain she'd caused, and hoped that they could start again. For now, though, she just wanted to focus on her son... with her mother by her side.

This *was* different than what she'd been through. This time, Isobel wasn't alone.

SIXTEEN

RUTH

For the first morning in years, I'm not crossing the square to the school. Instead, I'm sitting in the waiting room of St Mary's. I barely slept a wink after talking to Isobel. Every bit of me aches, but I can't go home. I need to be here for my family. Thankfully, Isaac's all right – if you consider a bruised kidney and broken ribs 'all right'. I could kill Silas with my bare hands. I was right about him being a coward. Imagine attacking a child... in a school of all places.

In *my* school.

Anger floods into me and my chest squeezes, as if an invisible hand is gripping my heart. It feels like a sacred place has been violated – a sacred place that was under my protection. An intruder slipped in on my watch, and my grandson... I draw in a shuddery breath as my mind flashes back to Isaac on the stretcher, bloody and bruised. In some strange way, Isaac's attack feels like a punishment for failing to keep the school safe.

How the hell did Silas get inside? Could the latch have played up again? It's fine, though, I'm sure of it. I suppose he could have snuck in with another student, then hidden somewhere until he spotted Isaac. However he gained entry, if this gets out, it will be more than damaging. A stranger, entering a 'secure' site with children, then beating one of them unconscious... *Christ*. When Sheffield House had a near-fire in the science lab one year, there was a petition to shut the school down. I can only imagine what parents would say if they knew a student was attacked.

If there's one thing to be thankful for, it's that all of this happened within the family. It'll be easy to keep under wraps. Rumours can spread at the speed of light, and any negative publicity would be a death knell to the investment. That sounds horrific, I know, and I wouldn't wish an attack on anyone, let alone my own grandson. But it *has* happened, Isaac will recover, and we need to deal with it as quickly and quietly as possible.

My mobile bleeps and I draw it from my handbag, a bit of tension easing as I read that Cecily's opened up the school, blocked off the art room in case the police need to see it (we'll tell the kids there's been a leak or something – goodness knows that's believable), and organised everything for the day ahead. I know several officers at the station around the corner from the Square quite well – we always have them in to give safety talks – and I trust them to keep things under their hat. Besides, it's not like there will be much of an investigation. We know who did this, and once Isaac confirms it, it will be an open-and-shut case. If he wakes up soon, then perhaps the police won't need to come to the school.

As I stifle a yawn, a memory flashes into my mind of when I gave birth to Isobel here, in this hospital. I hadn't intended to get pregnant again. I'd taken over the school when Cecily was just three, and there was no room in our lives for a new baby. Things weren't great between Alan and me either: before my dad died, we'd planned to take a year or two off and travel, once Cecily got older. Then my father passed and the school engulfed me, and the life we'd wanted grew distant. I tried to get Alan involved in the Square – tried to bridge the widening gap between us – but he resisted, preferring to stay home than attend events by my side. I didn't mind too much at first. Alan doted on Cecily, and I knew that if I was working late, I'd come home to a happy and cosy house full of giggles, the scent of lavender baby bubble bath, and Alan's smiling face.

Then I fell pregnant with Isobel, and something shifted. Alan started getting restless as if my growing belly was weighing him down. I told myself things would be back to normal once the baby arrived, and arrive she did... four weeks early, as if she sensed the disquiet and couldn't wait to come help. She was small and they whisked her away to the neonatal unit, but when I finally held her in my arms, I felt an overwhelming urge to keep her close – a sense that in this moment, she was everything to me; the only thing that existed. I would have done anything to keep her safe. I feel that same urge once more, towards her and Isaac, coursing through me with a power that almost takes my breath away.

Right, enough's enough. I need to see my family. I get to my feet and scuttle down the corridor towards Isaac's ward. I shouldn't be doing this – I'm lucky I got away with ducking in there last night – but being older has its advantages. Nobody notices you, and if they do, they never think you could be up to anything suspicious.

My heart lurches as I spot Isobel slumped in a chair by the bed, her hand touching Isaac's shoulder as if she's shielding him, even in slumber. Thankfully, Isaac has more colour in his cheeks than last night. But his eye is still swollen shut, the skin around it the shade of a ripe aubergine. Anger curls through me once more, and I curse Silas for doing this.

I need to find him.

I need to make things right again – for the school, and for my grandson.

'Mum?' Isobel stirs, turning towards me. 'You're still here? What time is it?' She rubs her eyes and looks over at Isaac, adjusting the covers around him.

'It's morning – just after eight,' I whisper, touching her arm. 'How was the night?'

'He slept straight through.' She gets to her feet, stretching. 'I think the drugs knocked him out. But he's moving around a bit more, so they're starting to wear off. Could you sit with him for a sec? I'm bursting for the loo.'

'Of course.' I watch as Isobel hurries out of the ward, then I sit in the chair. As I stare over at my grandson, my mind flashes back to the first day I saw him, all scruffy with that terrible fringe and black nail varnish, hunched over at the door. So much has changed, and yet he still couldn't outrun the world he was born into – the world Isobel chose. I'm not sure I really meant what I said earlier, to be honest: that this isn't her fault. Because actually, it partly is. If she hadn't left and made a life in such a rough environment, none of this would have happened.

Everything could have been so different.

But she did come back, and she brought me my grandson. They are here now, in my world, and I'll do everything I can to make sure they're safe.

To make sure they never need to be afraid again.

SEVENTEEN

ISOBEL

Isobel hurried down the corridor towards Isaac's bed, fatigue weighing on her. He'd slept deeply, but she'd only dozed fitfully in the chair by his bed. The shock of finding him, of waiting for the ambulance in that dark, stuffy room as she held him in her arms like a baby, afraid she'd lose him, still jarred her. Knowing her mother had been there had made a big difference, though. She couldn't believe her mum had stayed the whole night. The fact that she'd remained here rather than opening up the school was huge, reinforcing what Isobel had felt last night: her mother would do anything for her family.

Isobel's mobile rang and she glanced at the screen. The police. Had they already got Silas and were ringing to confirm with Isaac? She jabbed 'answer' eagerly.

'Hello?'

'Hello, is this Isobel Cosslett? This is Sergeant Martin from the Metropolitan Police.'

'Yes, speaking.' Her heart was pounding.

'I'm calling about the incident you reported last night.'

'Yes?' Impatience flared inside. *Get on with it.*

'We managed to track down Silas Farmer,' the sergeant said, and Isobel sank into a nearby chair, relief flooding into her. Thank

God. 'However, he couldn't have been involved. He was in a cell last night in Brighton police station for antisocial behaviour. That's an airtight alibi if ever I've seen one.'

What? Isobel sat up straight as his words hit. It wasn't Silas? She shook her head. It had to be. It *had* to. Who else could have done this to her son? 'Are you sure?' She couldn't resist asking.

'Very.' Silence fell between them as her mind spun.

'Is Isaac awake yet?' the sergeant asked. 'We'd like to speak with him to get his version of events.'

'He's still sleeping,' Isobel responded. 'The doctors gave him some pretty strong painkillers. But I'll make sure to call you as soon as he's awake.'

'Great.' The sergeant hung up, and Isobel leaned back in the chair, relief and confusion making her light-headed. It *wasn't* her fault Isaac was hurt. It wasn't because of the mistakes she'd made. But if it wasn't Silas, then who had beaten her son? And why? She swallowed, recalling her strange thoughts in the darkroom: that the school had done this. That the school…

She shook her head, forcing away the notion. The school didn't have power. Her mother did. And Isobel didn't doubt for a second that once Isaac woke up and said what happened, her mum would do whatever she needed to punish the person who'd done this.

She hurried into Isaac's ward and over to his cubicle, where her mother was still sitting by the bed. Isaac's eyes were closed, but he stirred when she came in as if he felt her presence. His eyes slowly opened, and he gazed around the tiny space.

'It's okay. You're okay. You're in hospital,' Isobel said, watching as understanding sunk in. She smiled, gingerly moving his fringe off his forehead. 'How are you feeling? You're pretty banged up, you know. Broken ribs and a bruised kidney, the scans said.'

'I feel like shit,' Isaac croaked. 'Sorry, Gran,' he added when he spotted her, and Isobel's heart squeezed that, even in his current state, he was worried about offending his grandmother. 'Can I have some water?' He gestured to the glass with a straw that a nurse had left by the side of his bed. Isobel grabbed it, then turned back towards him, every bit of her tightening in anger when he winced with pain as he tried to sit upright.

'Here, let me help you.' She took the glass and gently manoeuvred him into position, wanting to *kill* the person who had done this to her son. Isobel passed him the water, trying to be patient while he took a few sips. Finally, he lowered his head back onto the pillow.

'So.' She swallowed, her heart pounding. 'Can you tell us what happened?'

'I... I...' Isaac's face twisted, and he closed his eyes, turning away from them. Isobel met her mother's gaze over the top of his head. Did he remember? Was he scared of whoever had done this to him?

Scared like she had been?

'We know Silas attacked you,' her mother said. 'We know, and you don't need to be afraid.' Isobel shook her head, but her mum was staring at Isaac so intently that she didn't notice. 'The police are already tracking him down. He'll be punished. He won't hurt you again, I promise.'

But Isaac didn't respond, and Isobel turned towards her mother. 'It wasn't Silas,' she said quietly, not wanting to agitate Isaac. 'The police just called to say he's in jail in Brighton right now. There's no way it could have been him.' Her mother's mouth fell open, and Isobel looked back at her son. His eyes were still closed, but she knew he was listening.

'I know it's hard to talk about. I know it's scary.' She put a hand on his arm, thinking she knew that better than anyone. 'But we need to find whoever did this to you. Can you tell us who it was?'

'No one did this,' Isaac's voice was low, and for a second, Isobel wasn't sure she'd heard him. He couldn't have said what she'd thought.

'Sorry?' She leaned closer, and Isaac struggled to sit up.

'No one did this. It was an accident.'

Isobel shook her head slowly. An accident? With broken ribs and a bruised kidney? No. It wasn't possible. She could understand why he wouldn't want to talk about it, but they couldn't let his attacker simply walk away. This wasn't a schoolyard tussle. This was an assault that could have killed him.

'It's okay to tell us, Isaac. You don't need to be afraid. We—'

'I said, it was an *accident*. I... I tripped and hit my head on the counter and then I must have fallen into the table or something. I can't remember too much.' Isaac lay back down. 'When can I go back to Gran's? I really want to get out of here.'

'Isaac, please. Just tell us the truth.'

'I did!' He groaned as he jerked away from her, and a monitor started beeping.

'Isobel.' Her mother put a hand on Isobel's arm, and Isobel tried to calm down as a nurse came in. She pressed a few buttons and the monitor quieted.

'There are too many people in here,' the nurse said. 'One of you will have to leave. This boy needs his rest.'

'I'll be in the waiting room.' Her mother got to her feet. 'Let's let Isaac get some sleep.'

Isobel sighed, thinking her mother was right – as much as she wanted to find whoever had done this, she shouldn't push, not now. Isaac had been through so much, and he was probably still in a lot of pain – and, after all the painkillers and sedatives, maybe not quite lucid. She'd give him a few more hours to rest up. In the meantime, the sergeant could head to the school to question students and gather whatever evidence he needed.

She sat in silence for a few minutes, watching as Isaac's breathing evened out and he fell asleep again. When Isobel was certain he was out, she crept to the waiting room and over to where her mother was sitting. She sank into a chair, rubbing her throbbing head, then gazed tiredly at her mum.

'Isaac's obviously too scared right now to say what really happened. And with all the medication...' She drew in a breath. 'The school has cameras, right? CCTV images?' She'd seen the security cameras dotted around the building. 'Is there one inside the art room, or in the corridor outside? It should be easy enough to see who came in and out of the room when Isaac was there. We can take that to the police now.'

'That system hasn't worked for a few months,' her mother said slowly. 'I keep meaning to get it fixed, but the bill was huge and I was planning to spend the funds on new smartboards before our old ones blew a fuse.'

'Oh.' Isobel's heart dropped. 'Well, I'm sure the police can talk to the students; find out if anyone saw something. Someone must have. It's a school, for God's sake, not a deserted car park. Once word starts to spread, someone will come forward.' She paused, thoughts tumbling through her mind. 'You know people at the station, right? Do you think you can get them to come in straight away? The more evidence we can gather, the less pressure Isaac will feel – and the easier it will be for him to open up.'

She waited for her mother to nod and swing into action like she always did. Instead, she just reached out for Isobel's hand. Isobel held her mother's steady gaze, impatience flaring. She wasn't going to tell her to wait, was she? Because Isobel didn't want to wait. The more they could do now, the better.

'It's awful, what Isaac went through... what we've all gone through in the past twelve hours,' her mother said. 'But it's nothing as horrific as what we thought, and that's a good thing. It wasn't Silas, and it wasn't an attack. Isaac might be a little woozy, but he was very certain of that.'

Isobel's mouth dropped open. 'Don't tell me you *believe* him?' She knew it was an awful thing to absorb, but surely her mother could see the obvious. 'A bruised kidney and broken ribs just from falling over? That's ridiculous.'

But her mum shook her head. 'I know you've been through a terrible scare, but it's over now, and there's no need to worry. Nothing happened. The school is safe.' Her mother squeezed Isobel's hand. 'Let's stand down our emotions and focus on getting him better. Isaac can call the police once he's awake, and then our family and the school can get back to normal. We can put this all behind us and forget it ever happened.'

Isobel drew back like she'd been slapped. Forget it ever happened? When the person responsible for almost killing her son was still out there? While Isaac was lying, bruised and battered, too terrified to say what had happened? Because it *was* an attack. Anyone could see that it had been, despite Isaac's denial. Her mother had thought it was, too, when they'd suspected Silas. Why was she suddenly so eager to believe the opposite? It made no sense.

She stared at her mum as a thought entered her mind. It made no sense unless that was what you *wanted* to believe... wanted to believe because it was easier to accept than someone in the school community being responsible. She could understand that. Her mum gave everything to the school, and this was a betrayal. But Isaac was her grandson, and Isobel knew she loved him. The only way to put it all behind them was to find out who had done this.

And Isobel knew only too well just how unsafe the school could be.

'I know it's hard to accept that someone at the school could have attacked Isaac,' she said. 'I don't want to think that either.' She shifted on the chair, feeling the past echo within her; the phantom conversation she'd never had with her mother ringing in her ears. 'But we can't just pretend it was an accident.' Her mum would agree. She simply needed a second to absorb everything. She wouldn't let her grandson's assault go unpunished, just like Isobel knew she wouldn't have let her own abuser go free, if only she'd known.

But her mother shook her head once more. 'This isn't about pretending, Isobel,' she said calmly. 'I'm simply listening to Isaac. And if you want what's best for him, you will too.'

'If I want what's best for him?' Isobel stared, incredulity flooding through her. Her mum didn't actually think they could forget this, did she? She *couldn't*. 'What's best for Isaac is helping him face his fears. To talk about what really happened, and make sure he knows that the person responsible has been caught.' God, how she wished that she'd trusted someone to do that for her.

'Living in fear never leaves you. Ever.' Her voice was low. 'Mum, we have to find who did this.' She held her breath, knowing as difficult as it was, her mother would accept the truth. She'd nod and say that of course Isobel was right. That together, as a family, they'd do everything they could to uncover the attacker. The strength and love Isobel knew ran deep would come to the fore once more.

But cold started seeping in when her mother remained silent. She didn't nod, and she didn't say Isobel was right. Instead, she held Isobel's gaze, like she was waiting for her to back down. With every second that passed, Isobel felt darkness creeping in, as if she was moving further and further away from the light... as if the features of the woman in front of her were blurring, obscuring that love she'd seen. Why *wasn't* her mum nodding? Why wasn't she saying Isobel was right?

'You're not thinking clearly,' her mother responded finally. 'Take some time. Get some sleep. Things will be better tomorrow. You—'

'*No.*' Isobel jerked away, anger mixing with disbelief that her mother was prepared to brush aside an attack on her grandson. It wasn't because her mum needed time to accept it – she'd had enough time now. It wasn't because she believed Isaac either. How could she?

Isobel swallowed, words ringing in her ears once more. *Our school is safe. Our family and the school can get back to normal.* There was only one explanation; only one thing that made sense. Her mother wanted to believe it was an accident because it was better... not for Isaac, like she'd said, but for her and the school. No investigations, no questions, no gossip – no loss of reputation and status that her mother held so dear.

How could she do that? How could she put the school over her own grandson? Over *family*?

Isobel flinched as a thought hit. Would her mother have done the same all those years ago? If Isobel had gone to her and told her the truth, would she have turned a blind eye then too? Pain sliced through Isobel so strongly she could barely breathe. She'd just been telling herself she was wrong to run – that her mother loved her more than anything. She'd finally been planning to say why she'd left; to maybe start rebuilding her life here... her *son's* life here. She'd known how important reputation was – that was part of the reason she'd left – but never in a million years had she imagined her mother wouldn't have believed her... wouldn't have supported and protected her.

The jeering sounds from last night and the whistle that had haunted her for years echoed in her mind, and white-hot anger rushed through her. She got to her feet, towering over her mother, whose expression had hardened into that unreadable mask Isobel knew terrified students. It had never terrified her, though. She'd known her mum loved her more than anything, and she'd loved her fiercely in return. She'd had to push down those emotions after leaving just to survive. But she realised now that she'd been mistaken: that love was an illusion. The woman in front of her only cared for the Square, and nothing else. She wasn't the mother Isobel had believed in; the woman she'd sacrificed her future for. And this place wasn't Isobel's home – this world wasn't hers. How could it be, when the very person holding it together turned out to be a stranger?

What had happened wasn't an accident. Isaac may not want to tell the truth now, but he would. He'd tell the police, and then her mum would have no choice but to see what was right in front of her... and to deal with the consequences. This time, Isobel would *gladly* watch the school suffer.

She turned away and strode down the corridor, back to Isaac.

Her son – her whole world. The only world that mattered to her now.

EIGHTEEN

RUTH

'We're here, madam.'

The black cab driver's voice cuts through my haze of exhaustion, and I force my eyes open as he stops in front of my house. It's just gone ten and the square is peaceful, but my mind is anything but. How could Isobel say I'd rather pretend my own grandson wasn't attacked than accept someone within the school did this? She must know I'd do anything for Isaac – and for her. The way she gripped me outside the school, and how she leaned on me at the hospital... She's finally allowing me to help; finally able to accept my love... the love I can feel flowing through me now. So how could she think that?

Yes, it's better for the school if it's an accident. I don't dispute that. Anything else could ruin us, and I nearly collapsed in relief when Isaac said what happened. Even Silas was a threat to both our reputation and investment, although at least if it had been him, it would have been an open-and-shut case. But Isaac's handed us a clear pass from any potential harm. What he's said gives him and the school a solid future. Besides, why would he lie?

And to think that someone in our very own school community could have done this... Well, that *doesn't* make sense – not at all. I'm not in denial. It's just that it's simply not possible.

I climb from the cab and stand for a moment, looking across at the Square. I fill my eyes with its graceful lines, breathing in deeply. I didn't let it down, after all. I didn't allow an intruder. Isaac's attack wasn't a punishment. It wasn't an attack full stop.

'Thank you,' I whisper, though I'm not quite sure why. I feel like I've been awarded a second chance, and I'm more determined than ever to give the school and my family the future they deserve.

I go inside the dark house and climb the stairs to my office, my chest squeezing as I plot the day. Isobel's already called the police, so I'll need to ring them too and get ahead of the game; tell them I was in the school when the accident happened and I didn't notice anything unusual. That's true anyway. I cast my mind back to that day, scouring it for anything different, but there's nothing.

The school *is* safe. Bad things don't happen there. Sure, the older students might have an argument or two, but that very rarely escalates to aggression. And yes, we have the odd pupil who causes problems sometimes – we've had a few incidents over the years, like most schools do – but they're taken care of swiftly and everything returns to normal, proving it was *them* that was the issue and nothing to do with the Square itself.

I walk to the bookshelf, absently taking down a stack of yearbooks and flipping through them. I'm not quite sure what I'm looking for. I just want to cocoon myself in the world of the school. Face after smiling face peers out at me: staff who are vetted to within an inch of their lives; attractive and well-groomed children who I can proudly say turned out to be doctors, lawyers, journalists, authors and musicians. A few are even MPs – I smile when I catch sight of them on the television news every once in a while. None of them could have done anything as horrific as what Isobel is suggesting. I *know* that.

I pause my page-flipping, staring down at a face in front of me. A young man with dark hair and an easy grin gazes out from the book, and I hold it closer. With his high forehead, dark eyes and open face, this boy looks a bit like a young Alex Lovell. I don't have to look at the name beneath the photo to know that it can't be, though – this boy and his sister both 'decided' the school wasn't for them, never to return. Talk about problem students.

I close the book, turning my mind back to Isobel. Why is she insisting that Isaac was assaulted? The paramedic might have made an offhand remark, but that's hardly proof. Isaac's explanation makes perfect sense, accounting for his head injuries and broken ribs – if he hit the counter, then fell into the table with force, he's lucky he didn't suffer worse damage. I recall Isobel's angry face when she told me it was Silas who did this, and I sit up straight as her voice echoes in my head. *Living in fear never leaves you. Ever.* Sympathy and sadness float through me when I think of her tortured tone. I suppose if that's your life, your mind becomes accustomed to anticipating the worst... the unthinkable. If I'd been through what she has, maybe I'd believe Isaac was attacked too.

I shake my head. If only our CCTV was working, then I could show her it's okay to step down from crisis mode. It's okay to believe her son.

She will, I tell myself. Once she calms down, she will. In the meantime, I'll stay strong. I'll keep reminding her that she is safe here, just like I told her that night in her bedroom. I'll be there for her and Isaac, doing all I can to keep their future secure until they're ready to take it on.

NINETEEN
ISOBEL

Isobel sat by her son's bed later that morning, watching him sleep. The doctor had said that if everything looked all right, he could be released this afternoon. But where would they go? She couldn't stay with her mother. Just the thought of being anywhere near her made Isobel shake with rage. All that time her mum had spent with Isaac – the laughter, the chatter, the trips to the galleries – had any of that been real? Did she care at all about her grandson? Or... Isobel swallowed, the pain rearing up again as she remembered how her mother had held her last night; how Isobel had needed her. For her *daughter*?

Isobel shook her head, shoving the emotion aside. The answer was clear, and there was no point dwelling on it. She'd closed off that part of herself once already, and she could do it again. It'd be much easier now that she knew the truth about her mother. The most important thing was getting away from her. Isobel should have enough money for a deposit for a flat, but she couldn't even start to think about where she and Isaac might settle. All they needed was somewhere temporary to crash for a few days while Isaac recovered, and then she could contemplate the future.

A hotel might be an option, but it wasn't exactly the most restful environment. Besides, Isobel didn't want to blow her hard-earned pounds before she'd had a chance to find a flat. The only person Isobel really knew was Cecily and staying there was out of the question – although they'd worked closely together for weeks now, Cecily hadn't invited her or Isaac over once.

Maybe Alex? Isobel hadn't seen him since their last post-shoot hot chocolate, but she knew that Isaac still met up with him for photo sessions. He'd come home with his cheeks flushed from the chill, buzzing with excitement. She'd ask him what he'd learned, but he'd be in too much of a hurry to answer, racing up the stairs to download his photos. Alex had been a great mentor to Isaac, and her son looked up to him – she'd seen the admiration in his eyes and the way he hung onto Alex's every word. Yes, her mother had hired Alex as a consultant on the curriculum or something, but he'd told her his work was pretty much done on that front. She still didn't know him well, but there was something there... something that put her at ease.

It was a huge imposition to foist a teenager and his single mum onto someone she'd only just met, but somehow, she didn't think he would mind. It wouldn't be long anyway. She'd call him now, while Isaac was still sleeping. Hopefully when he awoke, at least they'd have a safe place to stay.

She went out to the corridor and hit Alex's contact on her mobile, praying he would answer.

'Hello?' Just the sound of his warm friendly voice made tears come to her eyes. Funny how an almost-stranger could make her feel so much better, while her mother... She pushed the thought from her mind.

'It's Isobel. I need your help.' She realised that she'd never actually asked anyone that, in all her years alone. Even with Silas, she'd always been the one to sort things.

'Of course. What can I do for you?'

'Isaac and I need a place to stay for a few days. Would it be all right if we stopped at yours? It shouldn't be too long, I promise, just until—'

'Isobel.' His voice cut into her exhausted babble, and she

slumped over. 'You two can stay as long as you like. I have plenty of space, but I have to warn you that I live in East London, not west. It might be quite a journey to the school. If you can cope with that, then you're both more than welcome.'

'Isaac won't be going to that school any more,' Isobel said, her voice strident. 'Neither will I, for that matter.'

'Why? What happened?'

Isobel shook her head, barely able to believe yesterday's events. 'Isaac was attacked.'

'Attacked?' Alex's voice was shocked.

'He didn't come home for supper last night, so I went out to find him. I thought maybe he'd lost track of time up at school, so I went to see if he was there.' She shut her eyes against the images that flooded into her head. 'He was lying on the floor in the darkroom, unconscious. Someone had beaten him so badly that his ribs are cracked, his kidney is bruised, and his face is so swollen I can barely recognise him.'

'Oh my God.' Alex sounded horrified. 'Is he okay?'

'He will be.' Isobel let out her breath. 'He's still in hospital. They wanted to keep him overnight for observation, but he should be released in a few hours.'

'That's good to hear.' Alex paused. 'Did he say who attacked him?'

'No. Not yet. At first I thought it might have been my ex...' Isobel swallowed. 'He's the reason we had to come here, to get away. But I told the police I suspected him, and they've been able to rule him out.'

'The police are involved?' She could hear him trying to absorb everything. All of this was so horrific.

'They're going to talk to Isaac later today, when he's more alert. He was still pretty out of it with all the medication this morning.' She crossed her fingers that when he did speak to the police, he'd be able to tell the truth. She'd be beside him every step of the way.

'What does your mother say? She must be furious. I can only

imagine her interrogating everyone until she finds out who did this.'

Anger shot through Isobel again, and she let out a strangled laugh. 'You clearly don't know my mother.' She paused, thinking that she hadn't either. 'She's very keen to sweep it all under the carpet... even if it did happen to her own grandson. She's insisting it was an accident. Of course nothing terrible could happen at her precious school.' Isobel shook her head, firmly pressing down on the pain that threatened. 'That's why we can't stay with her any longer.'

'I'm so sorry to hear that. It must be very difficult.' Alex's voice was sympathetic. 'Well, you're welcome to stay with me as long as you need to.'

'You're finished working with my mother, right? I won't be putting you in an awkward place?'

'Don't worry about it. Happy to have you both here.'

'Thank you.' Tears ran down her cheeks, and she swiped them away. 'I'll come by in the next couple of hours, if you're going to be around? I'd like to get Isaac's things from my mum's so when he gets out of the hospital, he has everything he needs.'

'I'll be here,' Alex said. 'Let me know when you're about to leave and I'll give you the address. Talk soon, okay?'

Isobel nodded and hung up, relief flooding through her that they had somewhere to stay – the further from home, the better. And now that his work was done, Alex was removed from the school too. He had nothing to do with her mother or that world.

She made her way back to Isaac's room, her heart feeling lighter at the thought of space and distance from the square. It had been a mistake to stay... a mistake to believe that her mum cared for anything but herself and the school.

And she wasn't going to let her son suffer the consequences of her mistakes any longer.

Back at the Square, it's almost easy to believe that last night's events never took place. I've done what I can to minimise any potential damage: told the police I spotted nothing unusual while locking up, relayed what Isaac said, talked the officer through Isobel's history and why she believes it's an assault, then got the caretaker to tidy up the art room and reopen it to classes. Isobel would be furious at everything I've done, but I'm only taking the necessary steps to protect us all. Our future... and our family. Once the shock of everything wears off, she'll come to see that.

The lunch bell rings, and my heart sinks when I realise I've left my lunch at home. I could partake in today's meal of fish and chips, but I can't face the crush of the lunchroom right now or the cloying smell of frying. I push through the crowded corridors and over to Cecily, who's standing at her usual post, telling students to tuck in their shirts. 'I'm going home for a second,' I say. 'I'll be back soon.'

'Why don't you take the afternoon off?' Cecily asks, her voice full of concern. 'You look exhausted. I've got everything covered here.'

'I'm fine,' I snap, and she draws back like I've slapped her. 'I'm sorry. I am tired, you're right, but I think some fresh air will do me good.'

She nods, and I walk down the steps. The bright November sun makes me squint, and I almost stumble, cursing myself for losing control back there. Cecily's by my side whenever I need her, and she doesn't deserve my impatience. But the last thing I need is time to myself. I don't want to think; to rest. I want to rededicate myself to the world of the school and do everything possible to make this investment happen. In light of last night and Isobel's accusation, it seems doubly important now... a way to show how much I love my daughter and my grandson by offering them a world they never could have dreamed of. I'll grab my lunch, hurry back, then work on our business plan. If I can find a way to beef up the numbers, maybe that will move things along.

My brow furrows when I fit the key in the door and realise it's already unlocked. Is someone inside? Fear shoots through me as I remember the brick through the window, and I think of Silas once more. *Was* that him? Or was it a burglar who got scared off? A burglar who's back?

'If anyone is in here, I'm calling the police!' I yell, trying to make my voice sound firm. Instead, it emerges shaky and weak, like an old woman.

'Wait!' Isobel's voice floats down, and I take a step back. 'It's just me.' She comes out from the bedroom and peers down the stairs. 'I thought you'd be at school.'

'I was,' I say. 'I just came back to get my lunch. How's Isaac doing?' It's only been a couple of hours since I left the hospital, but it feels like days.

'He's the same.' Her tone is cold and distant, and my heart sinks. As much as I'd thought I'd connected with my daughter, right now it's like looking into the face of a stranger again. 'Still sleeping. But the doctor says he can be released later today.'

'Oh, that's wonderful news,' I say, happiness flooding through me. 'I'll put some fresh sheets on his bed and open his window. There's nothing like crawling into clean linen, especially after that dreadful hospital stuff. And...'

My voice fades away as Isobel puts up a hand.

'We're not coming back. We won't be coming back ever again... to here or the school.'

My mouth drops open, and I shake my head. *Not coming back?* I hold her gaze, panic seeping into me. No. She can't mean that. She can't leave. I know she's angry at me, but she needs to listen. This isn't just about her future. It's about her son's too. And she can't take him away from it... away from a spectacular life, once the investment goes through. I need to give him that. I need to give her that. This is my chance, finally, to make sure she's in the right place.

And I... I can't bear to lose her, not again. I can't bear to lose Isaac either. I've just let them in. I'm not sure I can take having to close the door again. I'm not sure I can bury that love once more.

They have to stay. They have to.

'Isobel...' I draw in a breath, struggling to find the right words. 'You've been through a lot with Silas. What happened with him was awful. It must be hard to let go of that sense of danger. But please don't let that influence what you think happened to Isaac.' I pause, praying I can get through to her. 'He's settled in so nicely, both at school and at home. He has a family. Don't destroy all of that because of something in the past.'

'Because of something in the past.' Her face twists as she echoes the words, and fear curls inside. Perhaps I was a bit too glib, but I want her to see that she shouldn't let it have power over her. Instead of reaching her, though, I've angered her more. 'I'm not the one destroying this family. You—' She's about to say something else when her mobile rings, and she picks it up. I hear her echo an address, then say: 'Thank you, Alex.'

I pause as the name hits. *Alex?*

'You talked to Alex?' I ask. I know he's close to Isaac, but...

She nods. 'Isaac and I will be staying with him until we find a place of our own,' she responds defiantly, as if she knows how much this will grate on me. She doesn't know the half of it.

'Did you... did you tell him what you think happened?' I try to keep my voice calm as thoughts spin around my head. If Isobel said

Isaac was attacked at the school, what on earth must Alex be thinking right now? I grip the banister, attempting to stay steady on my feet.

'It's not "what I think" happened. It's the *truth*. And yes, of course I told him. He's as horrified as I am.' Before I can respond, she ducks into the bedroom, then comes out hauling two huge carryalls. She drags them down the stairs and past me on the landing. Without saying goodbye, she opens the door and slams it behind her.

And with that, she's gone.

The sound of the door closing echoes through the empty house, and I slump in the chair in the corner. She's *not* gone, I tell myself, trying to calm down. Not this time, not like before. I know why she left, I know where she is, and I know she'll be back. I can't believe she talked to Alex, though – she has no idea how damaging what she told him could be. I need to deal with this before it goes any further. I need to make sure he knows that it *was* an accident... that Isobel's past is colouring her present.

Actually, perhaps it's not a bad thing that Isobel's staying with him. She must trust him, to ask if they can stop there. She doesn't know that he has a stake in all of this, so maybe she'll listen to *him* if he says it must have been an accident. Because he will, of course, once I fill him in. And maybe space will be a good thing. It'll give Isobel a chance to think clearly.

Finally, the weight on my chest shifts enough so I can move without feeling like I'll pass out. I head up the stairs and into my office, then sit down at the desk, preparing myself for the phone call ahead.

TWENTY-ONE
ISOBEL

Isobel rushed onto the Tube and sat down, hauling two huge carryalls onto the seats beside her. Thankfully, the train was only half full. She hadn't been on the underground for ages, but she remembered the special kind of hell that was the Central Line when it was packed.

Her muscles ached and her head hurt after the broken night in hospital by Isaac's side, but rage propelled her forward. For her mother to claim that Isobel was letting her own trauma rip apart Isaac's present, to try to blame *her*... She rubbed her face fiercely. It wasn't Isaac's present her mother was worried about: it was her own. Isobel had kept quiet for her mother once, out of love.

Not this time.

The train pulled into Liverpool Street station, and Isobel dragged the bags up the escalators and out to street level, checking her phone to see the location of Alex's place. The busy street lined with metal and glass skyscrapers was a world away from the quiet gleaming squares of West London, and for a second, Isobel felt like she'd travelled to another planet, not just a different part of the city.

Right, now where was Alex's flat? She pivoted in what she hoped was the right direction and started walking, the straps of the bags biting into her shoulders. Despite the pain and fatigue, she couldn't help staring around her in interest. Old red-brick facades mixed with sleek new builds, rubbish swirling around the street as a parade of buses blew by. She followed the signs to Spitalfields Market, as Alex had said, then wandered through a glass-covered passageway, past some stalls, and turned left. She carried on until she saw the sign for Folgate Street, then walked down it until she came to number 27.

Her mouth fell open as she stared up at the facade. How much money did educational consultants make anyway? The rest of the street was lined with modest terraced houses, but number 27 looked like it had been dropped from a different world. While three-quarters of it paid homage to the surrounding red-bricked fronts, one corner was made only of tinted glass that reflected the street it sat on. The effect was striking: it was the perfect combination of old and new, sleek yet understated at the same time. Isobel couldn't wait to see inside.

She shifted the bags on her shoulder and rang the buzzer, relief rushing in when she saw Alex's face. She was away from the square – away from her *mother*. And while she still may not know Alex well, she knew instinctively that he'd support her and Isaac, and someone on their side was exactly what she needed right now. Her gut clenched when she remembered how she'd believed her mum had been just that.

'Hello!' He took the bags from her and motioned her in. 'Welcome! Come on through.'

'I can't thank you enough for having us,' Isobel said, wiping the sweat from her face. 'Especially at such short notice. I promise we won't be here long.' She breathed in, thinking again that she had no idea what the future held. Where would they go after this? She pushed the thoughts from her head, telling herself to take it one step at a time. First things first, she needed to get Isaac out of hospital, have him tell the police what really happened and then she could think about the days ahead.

'Follow me. I'll show you where you can get settled.' Alex beckoned her forward, and she padded after him, trying to stifle her gasps of appreciation as she took in her surroundings. Her mother's house was huge, but this... this was in a whole other league. A sun-drenched lounge filled with greenery opened out onto a kitchen, through which she could see what looked like a landscaped garden. A metallic staircase wound its way up from the far corner of the lounge to the first floor, where a cosy snug was dominated by a huge sofa surrounded by piles of books and cushions, with a door leading off to what looked like a massive bedroom on one side and an office on the other. Alex took her up another flight of stairs to the top floor of the house, with a bedroom on either side of the corridor.

'You and Isaac can stay here,' he said. 'Choose whichever room you think suits you best. They both have en suites, so you won't have to fight over the loo.' He made a face. 'My sister and I used to have some fierce battles.'

Isobel laughed. 'Me too.' She met his eyes, realising that she knew next to nothing about his past and he knew little of hers. She liked that, actually. They connected in the present, and that was what mattered. 'I'll take that one,' she said, motioning to the right. Alex nodded and set the bags on the floor.

'This house is incredible.' She gazed at the huge bed and the floor-to-ceiling glass window that slid open to reveal a balcony overlooking the back garden. She tilted her head, wondering yet again how he could afford such a property as an educational consultant.

'My father was really into architecture,' Alex said, as if he'd heard her thoughts. 'He made an obscene amount of money and wanted to do something with it, so he indulged his passion. He was just getting started on this when he fell ill and couldn't continue. So he handed it over to me, and I was able to change a few of his designs to something that suited me a bit better.' His face twisted, and Isobel reached out to touch his hand.

'I'm sorry to hear your father's been ill,' she said. 'Is he okay now?'

'Not really.' Alex shrugged, as if he was shaking off emotion. 'But we aren't close anyway. That's what happens when you ship your kid off to boarding school, I guess.'

Isobel nodded slowly, thinking she could never, not in a million years, send Isaac away. 'I wasn't close with my father either.' Understatement of the year. She'd barely known him at all after he'd left when she was only two. He'd moved to Australia, sending cards only at birthdays and Christmases until those had tapered off too. She didn't think even her mother was in touch with him. She'd never really understood why he'd left, but then she'd never thought much about it. Her mum had been the centre of the family; the centre of her world. Everything else was just... peripheral. Pain curled inside as the realisation hit that she hadn't been the centre of her mum's world at all. The school had held that place. It still did.

'Would you like a cup of tea?' Alex asked. 'You must be absolutely knackered.'

The thought of a warm brew in this relaxing, calm place was almost irresistible, but she shook her head. 'I need to get back to Isaac.' She looked at her watch. 'He should be ready to be released by now. The doctor just wanted to do a final scan to check on his spleen. God, I hope he'll be okay.'

Alex touched her shoulder. 'I'm sure he will be. He's young and strong. Kids like him always bounce back quickly.'

Isobel nodded, swallowing down the emotion that threatened to spill over.

He *would* be fine, she told herself as she travelled back to West London on the Tube. He'd recover, and no scars would mark him – physically or emotionally. He'd tell the police the truth when he realised there was nothing to fear; that he wasn't alone. He'd bounce back, like Alex had said.

She was about to enter the hospital when the phone rang. She glanced at the screen, sighing when she noticed her sister's name. The last thing she needed right now was someone else insisting what had happened was only an accident. Isobel shook her head, remembering the warmth inside when she'd thought she had family around her for the first time in years. She couldn't have been more wrong.

'Hello?' Might as well get this over with while she was too tired and angry to really care about mincing her words, not that she'd ever need to with Cecily.

'Isobel.' To her surprise, her sister's tone was more sympathetic than Isobel had ever heard. 'How's Isaac?'

'He's fine. Well, he will be. He's pretty sore and bruised at the moment, but they're releasing him now. I'm just on my way to pick him up.'

'Mum said he was in quite a state.' Silence fell between them, and Isobel braced herself for her sister's next words. 'So... you don't believe what he said about it being an accident? Mum seems certain of it.'

'Mum would believe dinosaurs still roamed the earth if it made things better for the school.' Anger surged inside. 'Of course it's not true. And anyway, his injuries...' Isobel winced just thinking about it. 'But you know, it's not just me who thinks he was assaulted. The paramedics who found him said that someone did a real number on him. If they'd hit him just an inch lower, his spleen could have ruptured. He could have died.'

'*Wow.* That's awful, Isobel. I'm so sorry. I just... I can't believe it. Who would do such a thing?' Cecily sounded horrified, and Isobel's eyebrows rose. She'd expected her sister to firmly dispute any hint of an attack, just like their mother.

'Do you think he'll say what really happened?' Cecily asked. 'Do you think he'll say who did this to him?'

'He will.' He had to, so the person responsible could be punished and they could move on. 'We're going to call the police as soon as he's out of hospital.' She wanted him settled into Alex's first, feeling safe and secure.

'Why don't I come with the car and get you both back to Mum's? I can duck out of here for an hour or two, and anyway, I'd like to see Isaac.'

Isobel bit her lip, guilt swirling inside. Maybe she'd misjudged Cecily, lumping her unfairly with her mother. They might both be invested in the school, but perhaps Cecily was more human. Perhaps she actually *cared* about others. 'That would be nice, but we're not staying at Mum's. I've moved our things over to Alex's.'

'You're going to stay with Alex?' Isobel could tell her sister was trying to sound casual, but her tone was tight. She knew Cecily was interested in Alex, but from what she could see, the feeling wasn't reciprocated. He was always pleasant towards her, but nothing more.

'Just for a few days, until we find a place of our own,' Isobel said carefully.

'You could have stayed with me, you know,' Cecily said, and Isobel raised her eyebrows in surprise. 'You still can. I have a spare room Isaac can bunk in, you can take my room, and I'll stay on the sofa. I barely sleep anyway.' There was a tone in her voice that Isobel couldn't identify – something like loneliness – and sympathy swept through Isobel. She had been wrong about her sister. Underneath the serious exterior was a person who did want to have a relationship.

'Thank you,' Isobel said in a soft voice. 'But I think it's better if we're away from the square just now. I really appreciate it, though.' Despite everything, that warm feeling filtered in again.

'Do you think Isaac's up for visitors this evening?' Cecily asked. 'I can come round to Alex's.'

'Maybe tomorrow?' Isobel said. 'He'll probably be so tired tonight that he won't even notice you're there, and his painkillers might be wearing off. I'm not sure he'll be up to seeing anyone.'

'Okay.' Isobel could hear the disappointment in her sister's voice, and she made a mental note to reach out to her more. 'I'll give you a call, okay?'

They said goodbye and hung up. Isobel went into the hospital, thinking that while she may never have had a mother who cared, perhaps her sister did, after all.

TWENTY-TWO

ISOBEL

Isobel opened her eyes, staring up at the white ceiling for a minute until she remembered where she was: Alex's house, in another world across the city. She sat up on the low-slung bed, so different from the old-fashioned one at her mum's house where her feet could barely touch the floor. Exhaustion slid over her, and she wiped her eyes, then stared at the clock, surprised to see it was 6 p.m. She hadn't meant to pass out, but the journey from the hospital to Alex's had tired both her and Isaac out – not to mention the sleepless night and emotional day.

Isaac had protested every step of the way, asking over and over to go back to his grandmother's. Thankfully, he hadn't the energy to fight her, and she'd managed to bundle him into a taxi where he'd dozed off. He'd barely glanced at Alex before crawling into bed and closing his eyes again. She'd waited a while for him to wake up so they could call the police. But when he hadn't awoken, she'd crawled into her own bed to rest her aching muscles.

She heard Isaac stirring now and she stood up. This was it: she'd talk to him, find out what really went on, and they'd ring the police together. She crossed the hall and went into his bedroom, relief flooding through her when she saw him sitting up with his phone. Despite the horrific bruising and an eye that was still swollen shut, he must be feeling better.

'How are you doing?' she asked gently, sinking down beside him. Her gut wrenched as she thought of what the doctor had said: if he'd been hit one inch lower, he could have died. 'How's the pain?'

'I'm okay,' Isaac said, and Isobel nodded. He did sound better: his voice was clearer, more like himself now. 'Mum...' He turned to face her, and she tried not to flinch at his injuries. 'I don't understand why we're here. Why couldn't we stay at Gran's? Can we go back there? I just want things to be normal again.'

Isobel's heart sank as she stared into her son's eyes. How could she tell him that his grandmother cared more about the school than finding and punishing the person who had done this? How could she say that coming back had been a huge mistake and that they'd never see her or live in the square again?

She couldn't do that. Not now.

'After what happened, I thought a change of scenery might do us all some good,' she said finally.

'Nothing happened, Mum!' The words left Isaac's mouth in an angry hiss unlike anything she'd heard from him before, and she jerked back in surprise. 'I told you, it was an accident. Why won't you believe me?'

Isobel took her son's hand, clenched into a fist. 'I know you're frightened,' she said. 'I know it's hard to talk about something so scary, and that it's easier to pretend it never happened.' God, did she ever. She'd never spoken to anyone about what happened to her. She couldn't believe she'd ever considered telling her mum.

'But if you don't face it straight on, well... it never goes away,' she continued. 'It's best to talk about it, get it out in the open. The sooner you do that, the better you'll feel.' She held her breath. 'I promise.'

'It's fine, Mum. I'm fine.' Isaac dropped his gaze, and she shook her head. He was anything but fine. 'You don't understand.'

I do, better than you think, she thought, wishing she could tell him why but knowing that secret had to stay hidden. She never wanted her son to discover what his father really was.

'What don't I understand?' she asked. 'You can tell me anything, you know. Anything at all, and I'll be here for you.' She looked at him, bruised and beaten yet still so brave, and a memory of herself all those years ago came to mind. She'd been brave, too, but she hadn't realised how hard things would be – how much the past would plague her despite her best efforts.

Silence fell and Isobel prayed her son would open up, but he continued staring down at the crisp white duvet. Just as she was about to prod him more, her mobile started ringing. She glanced at the screen. *Shit* – the police. She ducked from the bedroom and into her own, thinking that perhaps she could put them off. Isaac clearly wasn't ready to talk.

'Hello?'

'Hello, this is Sergeant Martin again, calling to speak to your son Isaac about the assault you reported last night. The hospital told us he was released, and we're keen to talk to him. Is he able to speak now?'

'He's still sleeping,' she said in a low voice. 'And he's in a lot of pain. He—'

'Mum?' She spun around to see Isaac hunched over in the doorway. 'If that's the police, I can talk to them now.'

She waved him back, but the officer on the phone had already heard.

'It seems he's awake, if you'll just put him on.' Isobel had no choice but to hand over the mobile, praying Isaac would tell the truth.

'Hello?' Isaac said, his voice gravelly.

Every inch of her body strained towards her son, desperate to know what he'd say.

'No, my mum wasn't there. She didn't see what happened. It wasn't a fight or anything like that.' Isaac turned away from her, and Isobel's stomach twisted. Oh, God. 'I was in the darkroom at school and I tripped over something. I fell and hit my head on the counter, and then... then I don't remember anything after that. I must have hit some other stuff on the way down.'

Isobel rolled her eyes as she heard the story once more. The police couldn't believe that, surely. They must know there was no way Isaac sustain such serious injuries just by falling down. She jiggled her leg as she waited for the sergeant to question Isaac.

'No one else was there. Yes, I'm sure. Okay.' Isaac was nodding. 'Yes. All right.' He looked over at Isobel and held out the phone. 'They want to talk to you again.'

Isobel's eyebrows flew up. That was it? They weren't going to ask any more questions? She took the mobile, her hand shaking.

'Hello,' she said, trying to stay calm as she watched her son limp back to his room. She closed the door behind her. 'I'm sorry about that. He's been through a lot, and he's obviously not ready to say what really happened. Can you call again tomorrow? I'll have a word with him.'

'Look.' The sergeant's voice was gentle. 'I know it's hard, but unless your son says he was assaulted, then there's nothing more we can do. We've spoken to the school. As far as they're concerned, given the lack of evidence, it very well could have been an accident.'

Yes, Isobel thought bitterly. *I know.* 'But what about his injuries?'

'I'm afraid those really aren't enough to justify an investigation when the victim won't say it was a crime,' Sergeant Martin continued. 'It may seem unlikely, but it is possible he could have received them the way he stated.'

She shook her head, unable to believe what she was hearing.

'They're all good kids up at the Square,' the sergeant said. 'I know Isaac has transferred from a different environment, perhaps where something like this might be more likely. But in all my years in the force, we've never had any incidents at the school – or even with one of the kids, after school. Your mother would murder them, and they know that. And for someone to set upon her grandson, well...'

Isobel felt rage boiling. *Never had one incident at the school.* If only they knew.

'Anyway, feel free to call again if your son does want to change his statement or if he thinks of something else. I'm happy to help any way I can.'

Isobel nodded and hung up, everything inside vibrating with anger. What was she going to do now? She could hardly force Isaac to say what really happened. They'd been so close – he'd told her everything – until this. And now... now when he needed her most, he wasn't talking.

Give him time, she told herself, taking deep breaths. It'd only been a day since the attack, and he'd just come out of hospital. Maybe after a good night's sleep, he'd feel able to face the truth. He'd be able to confide in her once again.

Unable to stay in the room, caged in with her thoughts, she went down the stairs, the metallic railing cool and smooth under her hot hand. She stood in the middle of the open-plan room, breathing in the airy space and the scent of greenery. God, she loved this house. It reflected its owner perfectly: casual yet warm; stylish yet homey.

'You look like you could use a cup of tea. Or maybe something stronger?'

Isobel turned around at the sound of Alex's voice. 'Yes, please. Something stronger, definitely.'

He nodded and took down two tumblers from a glass shelf with lights that made the crystal sparkle like jewels. Then he poured a generous slug of whisky in each, crossed the room, and handed one to Isobel.

'Cheers.' Alex lifted the glass to his lips.

'Cheers.' She took a big sip, savouring the smoky sting in her throat as she swallowed. When was the last time she'd had whisky? A memory flashed into her mind of a rare time she'd actually seen her father when he'd visited. She must have been... maybe seven or eight? Her father had invited her and Cecily out for supper before his plane left in the morning, to a restaurant on Portobello Road.

Cecily had been dying to get their mother to take them there, but she never would, claiming it was more of a bar than a place to eat. One mention from Cecily, though, and her father had agreed without hesitation, saying it sounded like fun.

Isobel had hated the loud music and flashing lights. She'd been looking forward to talking to her dad about the book she'd read on Australia, and maybe asking when she could visit. With the booming beat, she couldn't hear one word he and Cecily were saying, and her father didn't make an effort to include her. The one time he did pay her any attention was when he'd reached across the table and told her to try his drink, looking at her with mischievous eyes as if he knew he was doing something wrong and was daring her to join him.

She hadn't wanted to. The liquid inside the glass looked like wee, and it smelled horrible too. But she'd smiled at her dad and taken a huge gulp, coughing and spluttering as he and her sister laughed. She hadn't had whisky since.

'What's going on?' Alex motioned her towards the sofa, flicking on a light that bathed the room in a soft glow. Isobel sat down, curling up against a pillow and taking another sip, loving how the whisky warmed her stomach. She could almost see why her father enjoyed it so much.

'The police just called to talk to Isaac.' Her gut clenched again.

'And?' Alex leaned forward.

'And instead of saying what really happened, he told them the same story: that he tripped and fell.' Frustration swept over her. 'It's obviously a lie, but the police said without any more evidence, there's nothing they can do.' She thumped the pillow.

Alex swivelled to face her. 'Look, don't take anything from this other than a question from a friend who cares, but is there any way this *could* have been an accident? I know Isaac's injuries are quite severe, but you did find him under a table, right?'

Isobel tilted her head, pondering his words. She would have eviscerated anyone else who dared to question events, but she knew Alex meant well. He didn't have a stake in the school or anything that could be damaged by all of this. She stared at him, for the first time really considering his question. Was her mother right? *Was* she letting her own past influence her now?

'No,' she said finally. 'I really don't think it could have been an accident. The extent of his injuries, well... that simply doesn't happen from falling down. Something went on in that room. I just need to convince him that it's okay to talk about it.'

'You will.' Alex put a hand on her arm. 'He's lucky to have a mother like you.'

'I'm not sure about that!' Isobel laughed, but tears came to her eyes. She'd made so many mistakes in the past, but she would always be there for her son as she'd promised... making sure he *did* bounce back and that he wasn't swallowed by darkness like she had been.

Somehow, she had to get him to tell the truth.

TWENTY-THREE

RUTH

I cross the square to a dark, empty house. For a moment, I wonder where Isobel and Isaac are, before remembering that they're gone – for now anyway. It's been three days since the accident, and despite the weekend alone, I still haven't readjusted to the quiet. I shrug off my coat and turn up the heat, then slot some bread in the toaster. It's hardly a sustaining meal, but I can't get used to cooking for one again. My mind flips to a few days ago when I came home to the smell of roast chicken with all the lights glowing, and my heart lurches. I need my family back here, cosy and warm. I miss them. I miss who I am with them: a mother again, a grandmother. I'm still those things, of course. I always will be, but without them here, my heart feels emptier than ever.

Soon, I tell myself, trying not to think of Isobel's cold, distant face when she told me they were leaving. Alex must be making some inroads on my daughter by now. When I called him after the accident to explain why Isobel might think Isaac had been assaulted, he'd immediately seen the truth in what I was saying and agreed to have a word with her to try to calm things down. I'd hung up, relieved the investment wasn't threatened; confident my daughter would see sense... that this time, she'd return. If anyone could convince her, Alex could. He has such an easy, rational way about him.

But I've heard nothing yet. Everything in my world has returned to normal. The police have closed the incident file, the ambulance has long since been forgotten, and kids have stopped asking how Isaac is. All that's missing is my daughter and my grandson.

I head up the stairs to my office to grab some papers to review while I'm eating. If my mind is occupied, the silence doesn't seem so deafening. I'm just about to go back down when the mobile rings. Alex's name shows on screen, and I pick up the phone, praying he's calling to say that Isobel's calmed down and that she and Isaac are on their way here right now. 'Hello?'

'Ruth.' Alex's warm tone comes on the line. 'I have some very good news.'

My heart leaps. They're coming back. I knew it!

'This is getting way ahead of ourselves, but we're so excited here that I couldn't resist calling. As you know, I've been working with a contact who has experience in international schools. He's been investigating the cost of expansion, and he came across a perfect site for the new campus in New York. It's ideal, apparently. Have a look at your email when you get the chance. I've sent you over some photos and possible development plans.'

'Oh.' My heart drops. 'That's wonderful!' My voice sounds hollow, even to me, and I try my best to muster up excitement. Because this *is* exciting. It's a gigantic step to become international! But I'd hoped... I'd thought...

'How's Isaac?' I ask, unable to stop myself. 'And Isobel?'

'He's pretty battered, but he'll be okay. Isobel, well...' His voice drifts off, and I get to my feet and put on my cardigan, as if trying to protect myself from his next words. 'She's still convinced it wasn't an accident. I did try to suggest it very well could be, but she's having none of it at the moment.'

My chest tightens. 'All right. Thank you.'

'Ruth, before we *do* get too far ahead of ourselves, I'd like our team to start drawing up the equity documents for you.'

I let out a breath. Finally.

'I know we haven't discussed expectations until now,' Alex says, 'but I wanted to have a solid idea of the school's valuation and what its potential could truly be. I've been impressed with what I've seen so far.'

I can't help smiling. Of course he has.

'To that end, would 40 per cent of the business for £24 million be acceptable to you? That would value your business and premises at just over £60 million, which we believe is a very fair valuation.'

I nod absently, thinking it's not the valuation I have a problem with. But 40 *per cent*? That's almost half, and while it's not a majority, it would still give Alex's firm a significant stake not only in the ownership of the company, but also in any decisions we make. Still... £24 million! My mind spins with all we could do with that amount; so much more than fixing the roof and getting the school back up to scratch. How long would it take to secure that New York site? I smile, picturing Isobel and Isaac's stunned and excited expressions when I tell them our plans. There's no way they could turn their backs on this... on me.

'I know the percentage might be a little more than you expected,' Alex continues, 'but for the level of investment we're prepared to offer and all our plans for future expansion, we need to make sure our interests are protected. I'm sure you can understand that. You would still have control over the day-to-day running of the business, of course. If you agree, I'll have our lawyers get the documents to you as soon as possible. If things move quickly, we might be able to start on building repairs over the Christmas holidays.'

I'm silent for a minute, my heart beating fast. Part of me wants to drive him down, more towards what I'd anticipated. But the sooner this is signed off, the better... the sooner we can move past Isaac's accident, and the sooner I can show Isobel what awaits. And while 40 per cent is a huge chunk – much more than I envisaged – it's worth it, given what we'll get in return. Alex and I want the same thing: for the school to grow even better; even bigger. Any decisions we make in the future will be mutually beneficial. 'That all sounds good,' I say, keeping my tone steady and strong.

'Wonderful.' I can hear the excitement in his voice. 'I want you to know how much I admire your commitment to the school and this investment. Less dedicated people might want to further investigate an incident where their grandson was injured, but you understand how these things work... how they can damage a school. Seeing your commitment has only solidified my sense that we certainly chose the right institution to invest in. We did have several we were feeling out.'

I gulp at the thought of some other school getting this windfall. 'I'm pleased you chose us.' This might be a choice for Alex's firm, but it isn't for us, I remind myself, as '40 per cent' rings in my ears. We need this money, now and for the future.

'I am too.' His tone is warm. 'Enjoy the rest of your day and have a look at those photos I sent you.'

'I will.' I hang up and open my email, tapping my fingers as the photos download. I stare at the screen, but as I take in a gorgeous brownstone on a New York street, a sign reading 'Burlington Square School New York' photoshopped onto the building, and drawings of children scurrying up the stairs in our smart uniform, I still can't get Alex's voice out of my head. *Less dedicated people might want to further investigate an incident where their grandson has been injured, but you understand how these things work.*

He meant it in a good way, but the words have unnerved me. Does he think there's more to investigate and I'm simply holding off out of worry – 'commitment' – for the school? Does he think, like Isobel, that I'm willing to sacrifice my grandson for the Square? I shuffle some papers, and my fingers touch the black-and-white glossy photo that Isaac took of me a couple of weeks ago... one that touched me so deeply that I had to shove it away for fear I'd embarrass myself in front of him.

I slide it out now, my heart filling as I run my eyes over it. I'm not sure how, but in this picture, he managed to capture that part of me I didn't know was still there until he and Isobel came home. I'm gazing at the lens – staring at him – with a look of such warmth... such happiness. In this photo, I'm not the stern head-mistress I've come to embody so well. I'm a grandmother who loves her grandson more than anything.

A finger of doubt prods me as I stare at the picture, and I remember how I took his arm on the steps his first day of school. I *am* his grandmother, and not just the Head. Should I have investigated more? But investigated what? Isaac himself has said it was an accident, and there's not a shred of evidence otherwise. If there was, I'd be on it in a heartbeat.

I sigh, tearing my gaze from the portrait and back to the photos of the New York campus. This is what will bring us together. Our family *is* the school, and what's good for it is good for us. If I focus on that – on securing the investment and everything that comes with it – I can get through the days until Isobel and Isaac come home again.

TWENTY-FOUR

ISOBEL

Isobel sat up and rubbed her eyes, thankful it was finally time to get out of bed. The few precious hours of sleep she usually managed had disappeared since Isaac's attack. She'd toss and turn for ages, anger lifting her lids every time she thought of her mother. Every time she remembered the sergeant's words on the phone, saying there was nothing they could do; saying there'd never been an incident at the school. Every time she thought of her son, refusing to talk. *Still* refusing to talk, after five days.

And the longer he refused, the harder it would get... the more the darkness would threaten. No one knew that better than her. Her nightmares were worse than ever now, filled with images of not just her but also her son, lying helpless as a faceless man battered him. She'd try to reach out to him but the man would grab her throat and squeeze until everything went black and she sank into nothingness, unable to scream as Isaac disintegrated in front of her.

Sighing, she got to her feet and went across the hall to his bedroom. He hadn't left the room since he'd got here, getting up only to go to the toilet. He'd barely eaten the plates she prepared, pretending to sleep whenever she came to collect them. She knew he was awake – she could see by the light on his mobile that he'd been using it. Alex had tried to tempt him downstairs by saying he had a new photo book by Isaac's favourite photographer, but Isaac had only turned away. Forget talking about what happened: her son wasn't talking, full stop. Clearly, the attack was having a huge impact.

Because it *had* been an attack. She'd had a few rogue doubts after Alex's suggestion that what had happened could have been an accident; that maybe Isaac's injuries could be caused by falling. Even after dismissing Alex's question, his words had drifted through her head. But witnessing her son's behaviour these past few days, she was surer than ever that he'd been assaulted. After her attack, she'd climbed into herself too. It had been the only safe place until the nightmares started.

She sat down on Isaac's bed, brushing aside a lock of hair from his forehead and wincing at the angry purple bruise extending its tentacles from under his eye towards the rest of his face. One eye was red from broken blood vessels, and Isaac still couldn't see much through it. Thankfully, though, the swelling in his face had gone down, and apart from the bruising, it looked almost normal.

That was the thing, she thought. Bruises may fade and wounds may heal, but it was the emotional injuries that scarred... that lingered, tormenting with a pain that was worse than anything physical.

What was she going to do? She needed to get him to talk. *He* needed to talk.

Absently, she reached out to the bedside table and picked up the camera that Alex had given Isaac. She'd discovered it on Isaac's bed back at home and rammed it into their bags – Isaac was rarely without it. It had been around his neck when she'd found him that day, she remembered now. Someone must have come across it at school and returned it to her mum. Maybe Isobel could suggest he get outside today and take some photos? The fresh air would do him wonders.

Her eyebrows rose as she noticed the cracked lens, and she winced, envisioning the blows raining down on him. On a whim, she flicked on the camera. She scrolled through the random photos of houses and cityscapes, unsure what she was looking for, but...

She squinted as the last photo came into view. It was taken at a strange angle, clearly not something her son had meant to snap. She drew it closer to her face, making out a figure wearing dark clothes. He had dark hair, too, but his face was blurry, as if he was in motion. Heart beating fast, she checked the time and date stamp, letting out her breath slowly when she saw it had been taken the day of the attack... at 5:07 p.m., just an hour or so before she'd found Isaac.

She set down the camera, staring at her son again. For the first time, she had proof that Isaac's story wasn't true. He hadn't been alone in the school, like he'd said. Someone else had been there... someone who had almost killed him. Someone who deserved to be punished. Isaac may not want to talk, but this could be the prompt he finally needed to face the truth.

'Isaac.' She said his name softly. 'Wake up.'

'Go away.' The words were muffled.

She reached out and took the camera from the bedside table. Slowly, she turned it to face him.

'You need to see this,' she said, crouching down to his level. 'This was taken on the day of your accident, at 5:07 p.m. Isaac...' She drew in a breath, praying he'd open up now. 'I know someone else was there in the room. Someone did this to you, and you need to tell me who.'

'Give me that.' He grabbed the camera. Isobel moved back, surprised at the sudden burst of energy. Then everything seemed to drain out of him, and he leaned back in bed. 'I don't know what that is, Mum. I didn't take it.'

Frustration swirled inside. What the hell would it take for him to say what happened? 'It's a person,' she said, trying to keep her tone neutral. 'It's someone who was with you. You had your camera that day – it was around your neck when I found you.' She squeezed his hand. 'If you're afraid of whoever this is, then don't be. I'm here for you. I always will be. We'll start again, somewhere miles from all of this.'

'*I'm not afraid.* I just don't want to talk about it.' Anger twisted Isaac's face, and he jerked his hand away. 'And I don't *want* to be miles from the square,' he said. 'I like it there. I like having somewhere nice to live – a decent bedroom that doesn't reek of mould. I like having Gran around... having family, finally. And I like living in a place where I don't trip over puke on the street or some drunk hanging around on the steps.' Isobel cringed at his description of where they'd lived. She couldn't deny it had been awful, but at least they'd had each other; at least they'd been safe. Well, until Silas anyway.

'We'll find another place,' she said. 'A *better* place. Maybe out in the countryside. We can get that dog you always wanted, and—'

'I'm not a baby, Mum. I don't want a dog.' Isaac spat the words out. 'I have friends here. Friends who are interested in the same things I am, who can talk about paintings, and art, and everything else without calling me horrible names. Coming to the Square... it saved me. God, you really have no idea, do you?' Pain flashed across his face, and he turned away.

No idea? Surprise shot through her. What did he mean? 'Tell me then.'

He met her eyes once more. 'I hated my old school. *Hated* it. Did you know that? Every day was hell.'

What? She pulled back. 'I know the first few weeks were tough, but it got better. Right?'

He shook his head. 'No. I just stopped telling you about it. You couldn't do anything, and anyway, you only made it worse. The teacher told them to lay off after you talked to him, but he was a joke, and no one listened. They kept on for years, and then I... I couldn't take it any more.' He stared at her. 'I stopped going, did you know that? Did you know I hadn't been there for weeks?'

'Isaac...' Shock swept over her as she listened to her son. He hadn't been there in *weeks*? How could she not have known that? Where had he been then? She pictured him wandering the streets of Brighton, all on his own, and sadness curled through her. She'd thought she'd known everything about him; blamed the attack for the distance between them. How could he have been suffering so much for years and she hadn't noticed? 'I'm so sorry,' she said. 'I'm sorry you didn't feel like you could talk to me. I hope you know that no matter how difficult, you can tell me anything. I *want* you to tell me everything. I'll always be here for you. I'll always love you.'

A look Isobel couldn't identify slid over his face, then he stared down at the sheet for a minute. 'Just like you tell me everything, right, Mum?' he said, glancing up again. 'Like you told me about this whole world, this school we own, my grandmother... like you've told me about my father?'

Isobel's gut clenched. *His father.* 'All of that was in the past. It had nothing to do with you. With *us*.'

'Well, what happened to me has nothing to do with you.' Isaac held her gaze defiantly. 'I don't want to talk about it. I *won't* talk about it. Just... just leave me alone. Let me get through this – on my own. I can deal with it, the same way I've been dealing with everything else.'

Isobel swallowed, pain flaring inside at the thought of him navigating years of torment alone. How could he not have said anything? But even if he had managed to bear it, this attack was hardly the same thing. It had almost killed him, and now she was more determined than ever not to let him suffer in silence.

'Right, well, maybe you don't want to say anything,' she said, her voice shaking. 'But I will. Now that we have proof you weren't alone, the police will have to act. Do you want to come with me to show them this photo, or shall I go myself?'

Isaac reached up to grab the camera from her, but the sudden movement must have pulled at his injuries, and he fell back into the bed, crying out in pain. Tears sprang to Isobel's eyes at her son's distress. She hated to do this to him, but she had to. If he wasn't strong enough to stand up for himself, then she would be.

She'd show him she *was* here for him and that she could make things better. He'd see that in the end, and then they'd build a new world once more... together.

TWENTY-FIVE

ISOBEL

Isobel sighed as she opened the door and slipped back inside Alex's house. She'd rushed out as soon as Alex had returned from a meeting, eager to show the photo to the sergeant at the police station around the corner from the school. She might as well not have bothered, though. The sergeant had taken one look at the picture on the camera and shaken his head.

'This proves there was someone else there,' Isobel had said, trying to stay calm. 'This shows that it wasn't an accident.'

'It could, but...' He peered at it again. 'All it really shows is that your son wasn't alone sometime in the period his injuries occurred. We might be able to find out more if we could see who it is, but unfortunately there are no distinguishing features. We will keep it on file, though.' He tilted his head. 'Look, I understand you want to find out what happened. I'm a parent, and I get it. But if it really wasn't an accident, well... have you ever thought that your son doesn't want to talk about it because he might be implicated in something?'

Isobel drew back. 'You think he might have done something wrong?'

The sergeant shook his head. 'I'm not saying that, exactly, but when it comes to these kinds of things, sometimes it's best to let sleeping dogs lie. Kids can get up to all sorts they may not want their parents to know about – even good kids – and it might have got out of hand. A little horse play gone wrong, or... I don't know. At this age, is it really worth potentially ruining these young people's futures? Anyway, I'm afraid that we still can't do more unless your son changes his statement.'

Isobel had stared at the sergeant, his words circling around her. She knew the police were overworked and underfunded, but to say it might be best to forget about it because it might ruin kids' lives? Because Isaac might somehow be involved in wrongdoing? No. No *way*.

Had her mother got to him? she wondered. Had she convinced him that whatever had happened, it wasn't worth investigating? Fresh anger flooded through her at the thought of her mum downplaying her own grandson's attack. How could she ever have thought her mother cared for anything but the school?

She'd slammed out of the station and fumed all the way to East London.

'You're back.' Alex grinned at her from his spot at the hob as she came through the door. The homey scent of garlic and onions curled through the air, and despite everything, she couldn't help returning his smile. 'Where did you hurry off to anyway?'

Isobel sank onto the sofa, curling her legs up on the cushions and drinking in the calm atmosphere. 'I found a photo on Isaac's camera – your camera, actually. The one you lent him.' She winced. 'I'm sorry, but the lens is cracked. It must have happened when he was attacked.'

'It's no problem.' Alex waved a hand, but she could see his shoulders stiffen, and guilt swept through her. It must have cost a load of money. 'What was in the photo?'

'It doesn't show much – a person with dark hair wearing dark clothes, and unfortunately, you can't see the face. It was taken the day Isaac was attacked, and the timestamp shows it was around the same time too. The camera must have taken it at some point during the assault. I understand it's not much help identifying who might have been with him, but it proves Isaac wasn't at school alone that afternoon. The police hardly *looked* at it, though.'

Her hands started shaking as the frustration built. 'I feel so helpless. I mean, this wasn't only a black eye. This wasn't just something that "got out of hand".' The officer's words rang in her mind. 'Isaac could have died. He could have died, and right now... Right now, it's like he's barely alive. He's disappeared.' She balled a cushion in her hands, thinking she knew that feeling only too well. 'He might want to be alone, but he shouldn't be. He needs to talk.' A tear streaked down her cheek, and she swiped it away.

'I understand,' Alex said, and Isobel forced a nod. He couldn't understand. No one could unless they'd been through something similar themselves. 'I know, I know,' he said, as if he'd heard her thoughts. 'Everyone says that, but I do know what it's like to want to help someone and to have every door closed.' His face tightened, and Isobel wondered what had happened in his life. 'It tears you apart. It tears everything apart.'

He met her gaze. 'Do you want me to try to speak to Isaac? Sometimes, it's easier to speak to someone besides a parent.'

Isobel turned the idea over in the head, her heart aching. She'd never thought that Isaac would find it difficult to talk to her in the first place, but she'd been wrong: not just about the attack, but also about the past few years. Maybe Alex was right – maybe talking to someone new would help. Isaac had barely looked at Alex since they'd come here, but she knew he liked him; respected him. It was worth a shot anyway. 'That would be great. Thank you.'

'I'll try tonight,' Alex said. 'Why don't you get some rest before dinner? You look exhausted.'

'Maybe I will.' She touched his arm. 'Thank you. For everything.' He'd been here for both her and Isaac when they'd needed him most, and she'd never forget his kindness.

She went up the stairs and into her bedroom, but as soon as she was inside, she knew she couldn't relax. She'd been banking first on Isaac talking, then on the police actually taking the photo seriously, and she'd struck out. Alex *might* be able to get something out of her son, but she wasn't going to count on it. She thought of Isaac's face – of how he'd told her he'd deal with it alone – and pain swept through her. She had to show him she was here; that she wasn't going to let anyone get away with hurting her son. If the police wouldn't act, then she would.

But how?

Isobel wandered into Isaac's room, thinking that if he was awake, she'd try to talk to him yet again. What else *could* she do? She sighed as she spotted his eyes were closed and his breathing heavy. His mobile phone screen was dark, the handset on the bedside table and not in his hand like it usually was. She stared at the mobile, an idea filtering into her head. If he wouldn't talk, then maybe his friends would. She could find their numbers on the phone and get in touch. Or maybe... maybe there was something on there that would give her a clue about what had happened.

She picked up the mobile. One of her rules was that she knew Isaac's password, and he'd never seemed to have minded. She'd said she'd never use it without talking to him first, and she'd never needed to. But now...

She typed in the password, holding her breath it was the same and that he hadn't hidden that from her too. But the phone stayed locked. Trying to stay calm, she typed it in again, praying she'd entered it wrong, but no. Her heart sank: it was one more sign of how he'd shut her out of his life. She sighed, her brain spinning. What would Isaac use? His date of birth? No, that was too obvious. Maybe... taking a punt, she entered '8888'. It had always been his favourite number, and... yes! She was in. Thank goodness that hadn't changed.

Her hope faded, though, as she flicked through the message folder. The inbox was empty, and there were no recent calls coming in or going out. She was sure she'd seen him on the phone in the past few days, but the log was empty. She went through all the other apps on his phone, but there was nothing – not even the silly photos he used to take of them together. He must have erased everything.

Frustration flooded into her, and she went back across the hall to her own bedroom. What was she going to do now? In order to find out anything, she'd need access to the school and the students, and her mother would never let that happen. Maybe... she bit her lip as an idea came into her head. Maybe... Cecily? Would she help?

Hope grew again as she thought of her sister's worry and concern: how she'd wanted to visit Isaac, and how she'd said they could stay with her. Isobel didn't want to put her sister in an awkward position, but she needed her now, like never before. Cecily knew the school community. She was inside the school and had access to the students. Maybe Isobel could ask her sister the names of any kids Isaac hung out with and get their phone numbers? Have Cecily canvass students about the afternoon of the attack; maybe show them the photo; see if she could find out something. *Anything.*

Isobel slid the mobile from her pocket and dialled Cecily's number. She paused, thinking that she'd never actually rung her sister. The feeling that Cecily did care – that after all these years, she was there for her – made Isobel feel warm inside, and she realised that she'd never stopped looking up to her.

'Cecily?' she said when her sister's voice came on the line. 'I need to see you.'

TWENTY-SIX

RUTH

The rain hammers down and the wind rattles the windows. I turn up my radio, trying to drown out nature's wrath... trying to fill the silence in the house. I squint across the square, praying the school's roof holds and that the floor won't be slick with water in the morning. As I break eggs for my omelette, I can't help remembering the night I first met Isaac and cooked him this dish. He was so shy, but within a minute of chatting, I could see he felt comfortable with me. We didn't need time to make a connection. We were family.

We *are* family, I tell myself, trying to breathe through the panic creeping in... the panic that they're still not back. I was so confident Alex would help Isobel see clearly, but it's coming up to a week since the accident and the house – my heart – is still empty, aching for company. I can almost hear its plea for life and laughter echoing through the quiet rooms. How many more days will I have to wait?

Maybe I'll call Alex and see how the documents are coming along. This investment won't just offer Isobel and Isaac a future, it'll also show Isobel the school is solid. If a private equity firm is giving us millions, it must be safe. And even better, it's Alex who's making the decision... someone Isobel trusts.

My mobile rings, and I smile as I spot Alex's name. It's like he's heard my thoughts. 'Hello there,' I say, turning down the radio. 'I was just thinking of you. Of the investment,' I clarify quickly, then roll my eyes at myself. There's no need to clarify, and doing so makes me look... weak, maybe. He doesn't need to know how desperately I want my family back. 'Are the documents ready?' I try to ignore how my voice echoes around the room. I never noticed it until Isobel and Isaac left.

'Almost,' Alex says. 'I've been leaning on the lawyers, and I'm hoping to courier them to you in the next couple of days. You should have them by the end of the week.'

'Wonderful. And... and Isobel and Isaac?' I stir the omelette vigorously, as if the faster I stir, the better the response.

He sighs. 'Actually, that's why I'm calling. Isobel found a photo on Isaac's camera, taken on the same date and around the time of his attack.'

I suck in my breath. A *photo*? Questions swirl through my mind, and my heart beats fast as I wait for him to continue, but he doesn't say more. 'What does it show?' I ask, when I can't wait any longer.

'Just a person in dark clothing. The face is too blurry to make out. She brought it to the police, but there's not enough for them to take any action. But she thinks it's proof that there was someone there, and she's more determined than ever to investigate.' He pauses, and my heart sinks. I need her to calm down, not to become more inflamed. How long will it take for her to get over this? 'I'm trying my best, but if she starts digging around, I need to be certain that there isn't anything else out there that could come back on us; something more she could find. No CCTV images, no teachers who haven't been checked out properly, anything like that?'

I swallow, struggling to take in his words and find the right ones to reassure him. I can't let anything shake this investment; not when we're so close. 'There's nothing. I promise you. Our CCTV wasn't recording at that time' – he doesn't need to know it hasn't been recording for months – 'and all the teachers have been checked out thoroughly, of course, like always. We take safe-guarding very seriously.'

'Yes, I'm sure,' Alex says, and I can tell from his tone that he believes me. 'But as you're aware, we are preparing to invest a huge sum of money in the school. If there is something we need to know, it would be better to tell me now. When we do sign the documents, we'll put out a press release with our plans. We'll be in the lime-light, and the last thing we want is for any skeletons to come out of the closet.'

For just an instant, an image of that boy I spotted in the year-book and his sister comes into my mind, but I push it away. Nothing came of that, and nothing ever will. 'No, there's nothing. The school has an impeccable past and present.' Despite every-thing, a small thrill goes through me at the thought of the Square being in the limelight once more, and I can't help picturing the envious expressions of all those headteachers who would kill for something like this.

'All right. You understand I had to check,' Alex says in his smooth voice. 'I'll keep an eye on Isobel, and I'll update you if anything changes. I'll let you go now. Enjoy your evening.'

'I will. You too.' I hang up and sit down at the kitchen table, leaving the omelette mixture on the counter. I'm too full of emotion to think of eating right now. I'm relieved the police won't be taking things further and that the investment is proceeding, but I'm also uneasy. If the photo was taken around the time of the attack, then someone else *was* inside the school that day. The thought unnerves me, opening up the door to admit the doubt and uncertainty I thought I'd put to rest.

Who was this person?

Could they have done something to my grandson?

Could Isaac have been assaulted?

Is he staying quiet out of fear, like Isobel claims?

The thought jars a memory, and my mind turns back to a time many years ago in this very square. My mum had died about six months earlier, and I'd been so lonely, drifting around the place, trying to find a way to survive without her. I was a sensitive, anxious child, and the all-girls' school I went to was no place for someone like me: slow to grasp concepts, slow to make friends. I think the other girls could sense my pain and despair, and it drew them to me, like the strong feel compelled to pick off the weak.

They'd corner me in the toilets and shove me around like a pinball. They'd trip me up in the hallway so I tumbled to the floor. They'd pinch my arm, twisting the skin so hard that tears would streak down my cheeks. If there was a way to hurt me, they would do it. Of course, I could never talk to my father about it. We never talked about anything, really. He'd always left the talking to my mother, and when she was gone, we had no idea how to communicate.

Then one day I was shrugging on a cardigan when my father caught sight of a massive bruise on my arm. I'd got it the day before when one of the girls had pushed me down the stairs, and I'd fallen into the railing. I tried to make something up, but he could see I was lying, and before I knew it, the whole sorry tale had spilled out. I was part fearful, part relieved: now something could actually be done. And within ten minutes, all five girls who'd been my constant tormentors were excluded. My father had power like that.

I woke up the next morning eager to go to school. I got dressed and practically skipped the short journey. And that was when they pounced. I could feel the anger in their punches and kicks, feel the *hatred*, and when they'd finished and left me lying there, I only just managed to drag myself back home and into bed. I hid under the covers and told my father that it was a bad period – he never questioned 'women's things' – and I'd be fine.

But I wasn't fine. I lay there trembling, wishing I'd never said anything. Why on earth had I? I was more scared than ever. I could deal with the bullying before. I knew it was confined to the school, and once I left, it would stop. But now I had to look over my shoulder at all times.

That was the day I learned that it's best to keep quiet, because while things might not get better, they definitely won't get worse.

And usually, things *do* become better. Those girls would have left me alone eventually, I'm sure. Instead, I spent the next few months afraid to leave the house except for school, taking refuge inside the Square at the end of my day since I was too nervous to be alone. I can still remember the relief that gushed into me when the door locked behind me. It felt like the building had gathered me in its arms, providing a protective shield.

I get up now and give the eggs another stir, slamming the door on doubt. The school is safe. This photo on Isaac's camera... like the police have said, it proves nothing. Maybe someone was in the building with Isaac that afternoon – I can't believe I didn't spot them – but that doesn't mean they were there when the incident happened. That doesn't mean Isaac was attacked. And even if I *did* think my grandson had been beaten, based on my own experience, I would still question whether stirring things up is the best for him.

Stay silent and life can go on. It's better than tearing it wide open, then falling through the hole.

It's a lesson I've remembered my whole life.

It's a lesson that Isobel needs to learn... fast.

TWENTY-SEVEN

ISOBEL

Isobel hurried towards Spitalfields Market, eager to meet Cecily. Cecily had asked a million questions about why Isobel needed to see her so urgently, but Isobel hadn't responded. This was something she wanted to ask her sister in person, and she prayed that she'd help. Anything – any titbit of information Cecily might be able to pass on – would be better than what Isobel knew right now: nothing. She sighed, thinking of her son's angry face. Hopefully, Alex could get through to him tonight.

Shivering, she tugged her threadbare coat around her body. At least London didn't have the bitter sea winds of Brighton, she thought, remembering how she'd longed for a thick, downy winter parka to ward off the cold. London's damp chill could reach down to your bones, but it was nothing compared to the salty wind that ripped right through you. She pushed through punters buying the world's most expensive scented candles, thinking that despite living there for years, she really didn't miss Brighton.

She glanced around the market, smiling at the mix of stalls. Stuck inside her little bubble growing up, she hadn't realised this city could be so... alive. In East London, she'd discovered a whole different side: chaotic, unsanitised, *wonderful*. Maybe she and Isaac would stay here, in this neighbourhood. Maybe this could be the life they were seeking. It might not be miles from the square, but it was definitely a world away.

She lifted a hand as she spotted Cecily, standing ramrod straight in the middle of the covered courtyard in the entrance to the market. People swirled around her and a group of secondary-school kids were playing Christmas carols on steel drums, but she was staring ahead, her eyes fixed on the street in front of her. Isobel paused for a minute, thinking how odd it was to see Cecily outside of their tiny bubble... in a place other than the school. Somehow, she didn't seem to fit.

'Hello!' Isobel smiled as she came towards her sister, pulling her coat tighter. As always, Cecily was immaculately dressed, looking every inch the professional in her dark blue suit and cream coat. Now that she wasn't in the school office, Isobel had reverted to her usual at-home wardrobe of oversized T-shirts and leggings, although she had made an effort tonight by throwing on a jumper and a pair of jeans. Still, as they hugged, she thought that they couldn't look more different.

'Thank you for coming all of this way,' Isobel said, as she led her sister into a nearby café. 'I know it's quite a journey.'

'It's all right.' Cecily unwound an expensive-looking scarf and straightened her navy blazer before she sat down. 'Actually, it's rather nice to get out of the square. Sometimes, I feel like I never leave!'

Isobel nodded, surprised to hear Cecily echo her thoughts.

'Does Alex live nearby? How's everything going with Isaac?'

'Alex is just around the corner on Folgate Street, not far from here,' Isobel said. 'And Isaac, well...' She sighed, thinking of her withdrawn, angry son. 'His bruising is getting better, but he's hardly talking – to me, to Alex, to anyone.' She bit her lip, remembering how Cecily had wanted to visit. 'I'd take you to see him, but he's definitely not in the mood for visitors.'

'That's all right. I understand. So...' Cecily tilted her head. 'Why did you want to meet?'

'Right.' Isobel drew in a breath. 'As you know, the police have said they can't do anything unless Isaac says it was an assault. Until now, there's been no evidence – apart from his injuries – that it wasn't just an accident.'

'Until now?' Cecily leaned forward.

Isobel took the camera from her bag and flicked through to the photo. 'Isaac's camera took this the afternoon of the incident. It's timestamped around the time we think the attack took place. His camera must have taken it by mistake, maybe when he was being beaten or when he fell.'

Cecily peered at it, silent for a minute. Isobel's pulse raced as she watched her sister study it intently, as if she might have recognised something. Could she identify the figure in the photo? Could she shed some light on all of this? *Please God.* Isobel would do anything for this nightmare to be over.

Cecily looked up. 'It's a shame you can't see the face,' she said finally, and Isobel's heart dropped. 'And that there's nothing to identify this person. Have you taken it to the police?'

Isobel nodded. 'Yes, but they say it's not enough to investigate further – unless Isaac talks. I showed him the photo, but of course he denies knowing who it is.' She shook her head, frustration pouring through her once more.

Cecily shifted in the chair, a look Isobel couldn't identify sliding over her face.

'Anyway, since the police won't do anything, and it's now pretty bloody obvious Isaac wasn't alone, I was hoping that maybe you could give me the phone numbers of the kids he was friends with? Show the photo around to some students at school, and see if any of them can identify who this is? Ask if any of them noticed anything unusual, or if they know of anyone who might have had it out for Isaac?' Isobel shrugged. 'Perhaps just being the head's grandson put a mark on him.' She couldn't imagine anyone being brave enough to cross her mother, but stranger – and more horrific – things had happened... happened to *her*.

Cecily was silent, and Isobel tried hard to make out what her sister might be thinking, but she still couldn't decipher her expression.

'Isobel...' Cecily sighed. 'Look, I agree with you that it might not have been an accident. You know that. Mum might think differently, but... are you sure you really want to investigate? It's just...' She leaned back, her face serious. 'I need to tell you something. Maybe I should have told you before, but I promised Isaac I'd keep it between us, and I really didn't want to betray his trust. But I think you need to know now – why Isaac might not want to talk about whatever happened.'

'What is it?' Isobel's heart started beating fast. What else had Isaac not told her? Was the sergeant right when he'd suggested Isaac might be involved in something?

'A few days before the incident, I was over at Mum's getting some files from her office. Isaac was there, too, working on his photos. His phone started buzzing, but he had his headphones on, and he didn't hear it. I picked it up to give it to him, and...' She cringed.

'What?' Isobel's voice rose. What on earth had her sister seen?

'There were several pictures coming through, one after another. Pictures that... well, that were very explicit.'

Isobel's mouth dropped open. '*Explicit?*'

'Dick pics, I think the kids call them.' The word sounded so funny in Cecily's mouth that for a split second, Isobel was tempted to laugh.

'Someone was sending Isaac dick pics? Maybe it was a joke? Or...' Isobel thought of how he'd been bullied back in Brighton. Maybe this had been part of it. Maybe it was still happening.

But Cecily shook her head. 'No, it wasn't a joke. I dropped the phone in surprise, and Isaac turned around. When he saw me with his mobile and the photos that were open, well... you can imagine. He was absolutely beside himself. I told him that he shouldn't be sending or receiving those kinds of photos, of course, and I asked who'd sent them – it's a huge safeguarding issue. Technically, he's still a child.'

Isobel could only stare, trying to take it in. She thought of her son, and the absolute embarrassment he must have felt at having his aunt see the pictures.

'He wouldn't tell me, but he did say it wasn't a stranger – that it was a friend, someone he knew well.' Cecily paused. 'He didn't come right out and say it, but it sounded like maybe it was a boyfriend, which did make me feel a bit easier about it. I asked him if it *was* a boyfriend – I wanted to be sure it wasn't someone trying to take advantage – but he got so worked up again that I stopped asking. Has he ever talked about his sexuality?'

Isobel shook her head slowly. She'd suspected Isaac might be gay, but they hadn't discussed it outright – not yet anyway. She'd always thought he'd come to her when he was ready.

'He begged me not to say anything – not to tell you or anyone else. I tried to say it was all right: that no one at the school would judge him, and that we have clubs and societies to help, but he wouldn't calm down until I promised to keep quiet.'

Isobel gazed at her sister, her heart going out to her son as dismay and hurt flooded into her. He hadn't just been hiding the bullying in Brighton, or the attack in the Square. He'd been hiding his very *identity*. She could understand why – he'd had names flung at him and been tormented for years – but she was his mother. She'd told him over and over that she'd never stop loving him. She'd prided herself that he knew he could come to her for anything... that he'd never feel as alone as she had.

She couldn't have been more wrong.

A sense of failure washed over her, and she tried to keep breathing through the pain in her heart.

'Thank you for being there for him,' she said finally. 'I wish you'd told me, but I'm glad he had someone to talk to. But...' Her brow furrowed as she attempted to piece everything together. 'What does this have to do with talking to kids at school about the attack?'

Cecily glanced at the photo on the camera. 'Maybe this person is his boyfriend, and that's why Isaac didn't want you to show it to others: not because it's anything to do with the assault, but because he doesn't want you or anyone else to know about his relationship. And if I start asking kids questions about who it might be, or who they've seen Isaac with... Honestly, if you'd seen how distraught he was. It took me ages to calm him down. And hasn't he been through enough already?'

Isobel looked at the picture. Maybe Cecily was right. Maybe this person *was* Isaac's boyfriend, and that's why Isaac had reacted so strongly to the photo. But Isaac's boyfriend could also be the attacker. Maybe they'd had an argument, or...

She shook her head. Whatever the reason, someone had hurt her son. She could understand fear and shame. She'd lived with that too. She could understand secrets, but secrets could ruin your life. And while she didn't want to force Isaac to reveal anything before he was ready, she couldn't let someone get away with this. She couldn't walk away. Not this time.

'I understand that you want to find out what happened to Isaac,' Cecily continued. 'I really do. Maybe I'm not a mother, but I get it. I just think it's best not to push this.'

Isobel let out her breath. Why did everyone say they understood, then not want her to do anything about it? 'You don't understand. Not really.' Cecily's face tightened. 'Not because you're not a mother,' Isobel added hastily, hoping her comment hadn't hurt her sister. Maybe she *had* wanted to be a mother. 'But because, well...'

She hesitated, wondering if she should finally say what she'd suffered – why she had left, and how the trauma of the attack had followed her, no matter how far she travelled and how much she'd cut herself off from the world where it happened. But she couldn't. And anyway, this wasn't about her. This was about her son.

'Don't worry about Isaac,' Isobel said at last. 'He doesn't need to know that you're asking around. Just see what you can find out. Please.' She hated her begging tone, but she needed Cecily to realise how important this was – and that there was no one else she could turn to.

But her heart sank as Cecily slowly shook her head. 'You really don't know what you're asking me, do you?'

'Isaac will be fine,' Isobel said once more. 'Just—'

'Isaac might be fine,' Cecily interrupted. 'But...' Her eyes bored through Isobel, and Isobel raised her eyebrows. What now? Was Cecily worried that this might put her in a difficult place with their mother?

'Mum doesn't need to know,' Isobel said quickly. 'I'm sure you can ask around without her finding out.'

'You're living on another planet if you think I can ask those kinds of questions and keep everything quiet,' Cecily said. 'It's not just Ruth finding out – it's everyone. Kids will talk, parents will talk and then... well, once there's a hint it's not an accident and we have no idea who's done this – that our CCTV system was down, and their kids aren't safe – parents will pull their children out so fast we won't know what hit us. Schools like ours survive – thrive, in our case – on reputation. You know that. Once that sours, it's over.' Her hand came down on the table with a thud. 'And then you'll leave. Again. You'll make a new life, doing whatever you want. I'll be left to pick up the pieces. Just like last time.'

Isobel drew back. 'What do you mean, like last time?' Cecily had been at university when she'd run away. There'd been nothing to pick up. Her mother had tried a few times to get her to come home, and that had been that. Cecily hadn't even rung, not that Isobel would have expected her to. They'd barely talked before she'd left anyway.

Cecily sighed. 'I was never supposed to work at the school, you know that. I never wanted anything to do with it. I wanted to travel – to live and work in other countries, just like Dad.' Her eyes took on a faraway look. 'When I finished at Cambridge, I got a great job at the British Consulate in Hong Kong. It was perfect – the start of a life in the diplomatic corps, and everything I'd ever wanted. I'd decided to spend a few months travelling in Asia before I had to begin. I'd pored over all the guide books, made my bookings, and got on the plane.' She looked down at the table, and Isobel waited for her to continue.

'And it was wonderful. It was everything I wanted: everything I'd thought the world away from our little cloister could be. It was hot, crazy, dirty, smelly... *life*.' Isobel nodded, feeling a connection between them. That was exactly what she'd just been thinking. 'I stood there in the heart of Bangkok, right smack dab in the middle of the pavement, and just let the crowd flow around me, and I'd never felt more alive. I told myself I would never go back to the square. That this was where I belonged: out here, in the real world. This was where I'd make my life.'

'What happened?' Isobel asked softly, shaking her head as a waiter approached them. She didn't want her sister to stop now. She had to hear the rest of the story.

'I was about halfway through my trip when I got a message at the hotel. Ruth had collapsed at home, and she was in surgery. It was serious – a stroke, they thought, and she might not make it. I should come home.'

Isobel jerked in surprise. Her mum had almost died, and she hadn't known? Her heart lurched and she steeled herself against any rogue emotion, reminding herself that her mother hadn't been who she'd thought.

'I got on the plane straight away and came back. We were never that close, but Ruth was always there – even if she wasn't around much. I knew she'd never leave, not like Dad. Or you.' She looked up to meet Isobel's eyes. 'I couldn't imagine life without her. She was in hospital for a long time, but she was recovering slowly. She was happy to see me, but what she really cared about was the school.' Cecily's face twisted. 'She wanted to make sure someone was there to keep things running smoothly while she was out – someone in the family; someone she could trust – and to let everyone know she'd be back, stronger than ever. Control the narrative, so to speak.'

Isobel nodded. None of this surprised her.

'Of course, I agreed. I had a couple of months before I needed to be back in Hong Kong for my job. But then her recovery didn't happen as quickly as she'd thought. Days turned to weeks and then months, and soon it was almost time for me to go.' She swallowed, and Isobel could see this was still so painful. 'She called me into her room, about a week before my departure date. She said that she knew she was asking a lot, but that she wouldn't unless she didn't have to. I knew that was true. She never asked me for anything.' Cecily paused. 'She wondered if I could delay my start in Hong Kong, just until she could get back to the school. Maybe another month, at most. I'd been doing a great job, she said, and she needed me to keep going.'

Cecily shifted in her chair. 'I didn't want to stay, but I have to admit that part of me was flattered. Ruth had always said growing up that I wasn't ideal for the Square – that I was better suited elsewhere. And now... now she needed me. Now the school needed me. And so, I said yes, and thankfully my job agreed to wait a month. But the month stretched to two, and by the time she was ready to go back to school, they'd found someone else. With apologies, of course. They understood the situation and were very sorry, but they couldn't wait any longer and had to fill the vacancy.'

Isobel nodded, her heart going out to Cecily. All of this had happened and she'd had no idea. She'd thought she'd been the only one struggling – the only one paying a price for their mother's dedication to the school – but her sister had too. It made her feel closer than ever to Cecily.

'I was disappointed, but I thought I'd find another job. But the weeks dragged on, and Mum still needed help, and by the time she was finally up on her feet and able to run everything like she used to, more months had passed. I applied to a few jobs and got turned down, and I suppose I started to lose my confidence. I was a 22-year-old living at home and working with her mother, for goodness' sake. I told myself to stop applying for a bit, but the reality was that I was scared – of rejection, of never getting back into that world where I'd felt so alive. It might seem strange, but it was easier not to try, to put it off, than confronting that possibility.' She brushed a speck of lint from her blazer.

'And the years went on. The school, well, it sucked me in. The square I'd tried to escape from – the square I *had* escaped from and told myself I would never return to – became a kind of safety zone where I didn't have to face all that I might have become.' She looked up into Isobel's eyes. 'I never went to Hong Kong. I never got married, never had a family. I barely know how to talk to men any more. I mean, look at Alex. He couldn't have been less interested in me if he tried.' She sighed. 'I have the school, and that's it. And then you ask me to do this. To risk threatening the one thing I have.' She shook her head. 'I can't, Isobel. And I beg you... please. Just let it go.'

Isobel held her sister's gaze, thoughts racing through her head. She understood what her sister was saying, and she didn't want to hurt her – she'd suffered more than Isobel had realised. They were more alike than she'd ever thought. They were both shaped by the square, the school, their mother... both stunted and twisted in their own ways.

But Isaac was her son, and what had happened to him was a crime. She wasn't going to let the square affect him the way it had them. She *couldn't*.

'I can't,' she said, pushing back her chair and standing. 'I'm sorry if that hurts you, but I can't let it go.'

'Please.' Cecily clutched her hand, and Isobel glanced down at it. She couldn't remember Cecily ever asking her for anything, and her heart twisted.

'I'm sorry.' She yanked her hand away and turned to go, unable to bear the desperation in her sister's eyes. As she strode from the courtyard, she swivelled to look at Cecily, hoping she was okay. But instead of the pleading expression, her sister's face had hardened now... hardened into the serious, solemn mask she usually wore. Her face was set, but her eyes burned with an intensity that made Isobel shiver.

Isobel quickened her pace away from Cecily's stare, the steel drums beating like a call to arms.

TWENTY-EIGHT

RUTH

It's raining again as I hurry across the square to the school. It's seven in the morning, and it's not yet light. Even with the street lights on, the darkness hovers heavy in the air. An image of a figure with a blurry face floats into my mind – that figure Alex described in the photo – and I shiver, then shake it off. There's nothing sinister about that picture. Sooner or later, Isobel will have to accept that. The equity documents should arrive tomorrow, I'll review them and light a fire under my lawyers, and then... then I'll be able to breathe. Then I'll know that when my daughter and grandson come back to me, the Square will be waiting, welcoming them to their future with open arms.

Then our legacy will carry on, uninterrupted, just like my father would have wanted.

I unlock the school doors and go inside, turning on the lights. The patter of rain is heavy on the windows, and I send up my now-daily prayer that the roof has held. I do my usual checks, and I'm just about to head back down to my office when I see light under the door of Cecily's office. What's she doing here so early?

I walk down the hallway to say hello, my mind flashing back to when my father bought this building that now houses the secondary school and sixth form, then oversaw knocking it through

and connecting it to the main school. He was so pleased; so *proud*.
I never saw him as happy as when he was doing something for the
Square. I think for him, the school was a way to be closer to my
mother. They were a team, living and breathing this place together.
Once she was gone, he clung to that.

I sigh, thinking how much I'd wanted that with Alan too –
maybe a bit too much. If I hadn't pushed the school so hard at him,
would we still be together today? Would he have needed to escape
so desperately? I'll never know now. We haven't talked for years,
and I think it's best that way. It's too difficult to block out the pain
of him leaving if he's still in my life.

I pause outside Cecily's door, a thought hitting me. Have I
done the same with Cecily – pushed the school at her? After all,
she gave up so much to stay here with me. I never would have
asked, but I needed someone I could trust... someone who was
family, who wouldn't try to exploit any weakness. But no, I tell
myself. She didn't need to stay after that first year, and I told her as
much. I said I'd buy her a ticket to wherever she wanted, but she
shook her head and declared she was staying put for now.

She's here because she wants to be. It's nothing like what
happened with her father. And when I sign the contract, she'll
have the chance to combine travel and teaching. Maybe she can be
the headmistress at our New York school! The best of both worlds.

'Good morning!' I say, opening her office door. 'What are you
doing here so early?'

Cecily glances up from her computer screen. 'Just wanted to
get a jump on things. Actually... I'm glad you're here. I really need
to talk to you.' She gets up and closes her door, not that she needs
to. The whole place is empty but for us.

I raise my eyebrows as she settles back into her chair,
wondering what she's going to say.

'Isobel asked me to meet up with her last night,' she says finally,
and my heart lifts that Isobel has reached out to us. Maybe it wasn't
to me, but to ask for her sister... that's a good first step.

'What did she say?' I pray that she's coming round.

'She showed me a photo that Isaac's camera took around the time of the attack,' Cecily continues, and my heart drops. Oh, God. *The photo*. But why would she show Cecily? I catch my breath as a thought hits. Is Isobel trying to convince her it wasn't an accident? I hold my daughter's gaze, realising that I don't actually know what Cecily believes happened. I've been so focused on Isobel that I never asked. I assumed she'd be on the same page as me, but...

'What's in the photo?' I ask, remembering that as far as she's aware, I don't know anything about it. It's getting harder and harder to keep track of everything – I can't wait until all of this is behind us.

'Nothing useful,' Cecily answers. 'A dark figure with a blurry face. She's taken it to the police, but they're not going to do anything. But Isobel believes it proves Isaac wasn't alone.'

I shift in the chair, still staring at my daughter. Has Isobel managed to convince her? And if so, then what will she do?

'She's more determined than ever to find out what happened,' Cecily says, and the unease I tried to shake off earlier balloons inside. Why can't Isobel just leave things alone? Why *can't* she learn the lesson that it's better to stay quiet? My heart aches at the pain she must be going through. Believing her own mother is trying to cover up an attack on her grandson must be unbearable. I'd give anything to help her – to help her see what's real – but I'm not there. And now she's trying to influence Cecily...

'She wants me to ask around school and try to talk to the kids – to see if I can find out anything,' Cecily continues. I hold her gaze, my chest tight with tension. Has Cecily *agreed*? I can't imagine she would: she knows what this could do to us. But staring at my daughter, I realise once more I have no idea what she thinks.

My mind races. If Cecily wants to pursue this, then I'll tell her what's at stake. I'll tell her all about the investment and the future waiting – for her, for me, for all of us. The deal is almost done. We're close; so close. If I need to, I'll tell her.

'I said I couldn't, of course.' Relief shoots through me, and I slump in my chair. *Thank goodness*. 'I tried to convince her to let it go, but she won't. I think it's possible that she might start trying to question students herself.'

I suck in my breath, imagining the gossip that would ensue: not just that there was an attack at school – an attack involving my grandson – but also that my own daughter is crusading against me. Despite everything, I have to admire her determination... her fierce love for her son. She has no idea what she's threatening though. And as much as I'd love to let her know, I can't take that risk – not like with Cecily, who has years behind her at the Square. Isobel ran from here before she could start her life, and I can't let her ruin this too before the contract has even been signed.

'She doesn't know any parents or kids at school, does she?' My heart is beating fast. 'I can ask Gary to keep a watch out front for her, in case she tries to get kids on their way to and from school.' Gary's our caretaker and about as scary as Santa Claus, but he's built like a tank. No one can get past him.

'I don't think she has any connections to the school,' Cecily says. 'Having Gary out front is a good idea, but we can't control everywhere outside the Square.' She takes a breath. 'That's why we need a plan.'

I tilt my head. 'A plan?'

'Something that will discredit her; make her seem unreliable – that what she says can't be trusted.'

'Like what?' I ask, a knot of fear inside. I'm not sure I want to hear this. I love how much Cecily wants to help the school, but...

'Well, the kids know there was an accident here, right? And most know now that Isaac was involved since he's been absent. So, I was thinking that perhaps you can say he had some sort of mental-health crisis. Something a mother would find difficult to accept – something she'd rather believe was caused by someone else than her own son self-harming... or something along those lines. If it's down to believing her or believing you, there's really no choice. Parents wouldn't risk alienating you.'

I draw in my breath, imagining the look on Isobel's face when confronted with that story, because it doesn't just damage her, it damages Isaac too. Not only that, but it proves exactly what she's claiming: that I'm willing to sacrifice Isaac for the school. And that's not true. It couldn't be further from the truth. The Square belongs to Isaac, and vice versa. Everything I'm doing is not just for the school, but also for my grandson.

I shake my head, wondering at the apparent ease with which Cecily is suggesting this. She and Isobel are *sisters*, and Isaac is her nephew. I'd thought our family was finally coming together, but... We will, I tell myself. We're under a lot of stress right now. Cecily cares about Isobel and Isaac – I've seen it first-hand. She's just trying to help.

She doesn't have to, though. I have my secret weapon: Alex. Maybe he hasn't been able to work his magic yet, but I have every confidence that he will. He's put so much effort into this investment that I'm sure he wants it as much as me. He cares about Isobel, and he understands it's in her best interest not to mess things up. I'll talk to him; make sure he knows what Isobel might be planning, and get him to step it up – fast.

'I'll take care of it,' I say.

'Sure?' Cecily looks sceptical, and the urge to tell her about Alex grows. I want her to know that things will be okay... no, better than okay. We may not have a 100 per cent family-owned business any longer, but we'll have a spectacular future... with plenty of opportunities for her, if she wants them. 'Cecily, I—' I stop myself. The deal's not done, and although it's almost as good as final, I don't want to set her up for disappointment.

'Nothing,' I say, waving a hand. 'Do you think you can lead the staff meeting tomorrow morning?' It'll be good practice if she decides to take the job in New York.

Cecily's eyebrows shoot up, and happiness diffuses through her face. 'Really?' For a second, she looks like the child I remember.

I nod. 'Yes, really. I don't know what I'd do without you. You've been invaluable.' I reach out and squeeze her arm, and it hits me that as much time as we spend together, we rarely touch. 'Now, can you photocopy this for me?' I ask her, smiling cheekily as I hold out a stack of papers. 'I'm too old for those stairs.'

'You're in better shape than I am,' she says, rolling her eyes, but she takes the papers and leaves the room.

I wait until she's gone, close the door, and pick up the phone to call Alex.

TWENTY-NINE

ISOBEL

Isobel drained her thousandth cup of tea that day, rinsed it, then stood in the middle of the lounge. It was only morning, but already the day felt endless. She wasn't used to having so many hours to fill. Ever since she'd left the square, almost every spare minute had been taken up with survival.

Of course, she did have something to keep her occupied: finding out the truth of what had happened to Isaac. She just hadn't figured out exactly *how* yet. Cecily would have told her mother about the photo by now, and the two of them would likely be patrolling the square, defending their turf against any intrusion. Isobel wouldn't put it past them to have hired security. God, she wished she'd stayed quiet and told her sister she'd simply give up rather than let her emotions get the better of her.

A mix of hurt, anger and pity flooded in as she thought of her sister's pleading face last night. Cecily knew it wasn't an accident. She knew whoever had done this was still out there. Did she really care about Isaac, or had she only been using that to stop Isobel from investigating further? Isobel could understand how the Square had become the only thing in her life. But if the school closed, she *could* move on. She could find somewhere else. People who'd been traumatised didn't always have that luxury, and Isobel was going to do everything she could to help her son recover.

Isobel sighed and flicked on the kettle. Cecily's voice had followed her home last night, echoing in her brain with every step. *He was so distraught... hasn't he been through enough already?* Doubt had flashed through her, and she'd wondered once more if she was letting her past control her – propelling her down a certain road, despite what it might do to Isaac. *Would* it be better for him if she backed off; to leave him alone, like he'd asked? She'd thought of his angry face and how he was refusing to even look at her now. If she pushed too hard, would they ever be able to come together again?

But then she'd gone inside Alex's house only to hear shouts and a crashing sound coming from Isaac's room. Her heart had pounded and fear poured through her, and for a split second, she'd wondered if whoever had harmed Isaac had found out they were here. She'd forced her legs faster and when she'd rounded the corner to his bedroom, she'd seen Isaac curled on the bed with Alex standing beside him. Relief had swept over her, making her muscles sag. Thank God Alex was here.

'What happened?' She'd glanced down at Isaac, but he wouldn't turn to face her. 'Isaac, are you all right?'

'I was coming up to talk to him, and I heard him calling out and thrashing around,' Alex had explained, when it became obvious Isaac wasn't talking. 'He was still asleep. I tried to wake him up, and he started lashing out. Must have been a nightmare.'

Isobel had sunk down on the bed, closing her eyes as anger and pain replaced the relief. *A nightmare.* Oh, God. She'd been right: the person who'd done this to Isaac had come back again... in his dreams, just like he had with her. She put a hand on her son's back, feeling the tension in his body. 'Thanks, Alex. I'll stay with him.'

Alex had nodded and left the room, and Isobel had stared down at Isaac, certainty returning. The only way to end the nightmares was to face what had happened. It might be difficult for a myriad of reasons – not least of which could be Isaac's fear of his relationship being discovered – but no matter what other secrets her questions unearthed, finding out the truth would be more than worth it.

It would save her son.

She wandered up the stairs now to the next level, peering into the office across from Alex's bedroom. Sun streamed in and Isobel squinted as light reflected off the thick silver frame of a photo on the desk. Unable to stop herself, she moved closer, angling the frame away from the sun so she could see who was in it. It was a woman, maybe early thirties, petite with dark hair and blue eyes. She was laughing up at whoever was taking the picture, one arm slung around a narrow tree trunk while the other was outstretched into the air, as if she was embracing the void. Isobel could feel the life and vitality streaming from her.

'She's beautiful in that photo, isn't she?' Alex's voice rang out from behind her, and Isobel jumped. She hadn't heard him come home. 'Sorry, I didn't mean to startle you.'

'That's okay.' Isobel breathed in, trying to slow her racing pulse. 'I'm sorry, I shouldn't be snooping. I was just enjoying the sun, and then the photo caught my eye. She looks so happy.' Isobel turned towards him, wondering who it was. A girlfriend, maybe? Isobel hadn't seen any sign of one so far, but that didn't mean there wasn't one. Perhaps this was why she'd never felt that romantic connection with him... because he was with someone else?

'That's my sister.' His face dropped. '*Was* my sister. She died last year.'

Isobel touched his arm. 'I'm so sorry,' she said, gazing at the photo again. It was hard to believe the woman was no longer with them. 'Were you close?'

'As kids, yes. She was only a couple of years older, but she always watched out for me; took care of me when my parents weren't around. But then...' Alex cleared his throat, and Isobel put the picture back on the desk. 'Anyway. How's Isaac doing today? Come down, I've made some tea.' He gestured her down the stairs, and she followed. It was clear he didn't want to speak about the past. However his sister had died, it must still be too painful.

'He's the same.' Isobel sighed. 'Not eating, not talking.' She paused for a second, wondering if she should tell Alex what she'd found out about Isaac's boyfriend, and if he might be connected to the assault. But no, she decided. That was Isaac's secret to share, not hers. The last thing she wanted was to make things more difficult for him. 'Thanks again for helping last night with the nightmare. Maybe you can try talking to him again tonight.'

'Of course. Anything to help.' He cocked his head at the sound of the kettle switching off. 'Until then... there's always tea.' He handed her a mug, and she breathed in the comforting scent of Earl Grey.

Her phone buzzed and she drew it out of her pocket, scanning the words. It was a reminder of Isaac's form's Christmas breakfast tomorrow morning. Students and parents were welcome to come along Friday, 4 December, at 8 a.m. to the Hill Brasserie, just around the corner from the school, for croissants and coffee.

Isobel's eyes widened as a thought hit. This was the perfect solution to her problem of how to talk to kids. Her mother never went to these things, saying parents needed to let off steam away from her. Besides, if she attended one, she'd have to attend them all, and she'd barely enough time to get through the work of the day. Isobel could chat face to face with some students, hopefully away from their parents, and try to find out *something*. They might be able to tell her who'd hung around with Isaac – who had been his best friend... his boyfriend. Hell, it might be one of them!

'What is it?' Alex asked.

'I've just found a perfect way to find out more about what might have happened to Isaac.' Excitement and hope surged through her.

'What?'

'There's a form breakfast tomorrow, for kids and parents. Mum won't be there, and it'll be a great opportunity to talk first-hand to some students who might know Isaac. It's a starting point anyway.'

Alex held her gaze, silence falling between them. Isobel wondered what he was thinking. That she was crazy to push so hard? That she *should* let it go and move on?

'You know, I really admire you – your strength,' he said finally.

Isobel sat back in surprise. Was she strong? She'd never felt it.

'You'd do anything for your son,' he continued. 'You're not going to let anyone shunt you away or put you off. I just wish...' He shook his head. 'I wish I'd been as strong as you. I'm trying now. I'm doing everything I can, but it's still too late.'

His face tightened as if he was in pain, and she wondered if he was thinking of his sister again. Whatever happened must have been awful. 'I'm so sorry,' she said, reaching out for his hand.

'I'm sorry too,' he said, squeezing her fingers. 'Good luck tomorrow. I hope you find what you need.'

Isobel nodded. She hoped so too.

THIRTY

ISOBEL

Isobel smoothed down her hair and tucked in the white blouse she'd bought on a mad dash to Primark one day when she couldn't bear wearing Cecily's clothes any longer. Thankfully, despite its thin fabric, the blouse still looked crisp and fresh... exactly how she didn't feel after spending all evening trying to rouse Isaac enough to eat supper and maybe have some kind of human interaction. He'd shouted at Alex when he'd tried to talk to him again, telling him to go away. Isobel had spent ages apologising, though Alex told her not to worry. But she *was* worried. This anger wasn't like her son, and it made her more determined to find the truth so he could start recovering... start making a new life.

She stared at the mirror, gearing herself up for the next couple of hours at the form breakfast. As far as she knew, the whole school community thought what had happened to Isaac was an accident. How would they react when she started questioning their children about who Isaac was hanging around with, if anyone was angry at him, and what they might have seen that day, insinuating that it hadn't been so accidental, after all? How would they feel when she showed them the dark figure in the photo?

It was bound to reach her mother's ears eventually, but Isobel hoped she'd at least be able to get some helpful information before her mum tried to clamp down on everything. If she could, of course. Because once the genie was out of the bottle... well, wasn't that what her mother and Cecily were so scared of? The flying rumours, the gossip? Isobel bit her lip as she thought once again of her sister's pleas; of the desperate look in her eyes. She didn't want to hurt her, but...

One hour later, Isobel was striding down the wide pavement towards the Hill Brasserie. Coming from the depths of East London, the swirling silence and the huge stately houses seemed surreal. Even the streets gleamed, with a cleaner fastidiously removing every last errant leaf from the pavements. She paused outside a red wooden door garnished with holly and fir boughs, gazing at the gold nameplate that gave the only clue this was a restaurant. Taking a deep breath, she pushed the door open.

The noise of women, men, boys and girls stuffed into the small space hit her like a wall, and for a moment, the crowd felt impenetrable... as if they were one solid mass, guarding against any secret escaping. She pressed forward, scanning the room for someone she might recognise. She didn't see anyone, but then, she hadn't expected to – besides Alex, she hadn't spoken to anyone but her mother and Cecily. She hadn't been here to make friends.

She took off her coat, glancing around for a place to hang it.

'Oh, would you mind?' A blonde woman with leather trousers and a cashmere jumper passed her long camel-coloured coat to Isobel. 'Thank you so much.' Isobel stood there, dumbfounded, as the woman shot her a cursory smile, then disappeared into the crowd. Why the hell had she given Isobel her coat? Then it hit her, and her cheeks flamed. With her cheap white shirt and black trousers, she didn't look like one of them. She looked like a waitress. Anger and embarrassment mingled inside, and she plonked the coats down unceremoniously on a banquette, then pushed into the crowd, determined now to talk to the kids. She *wasn't* one of them – how could she ever have thought she could be? She didn't need to worry about who she offended or what the fallout was. All she needed to think of was her son.

The room was cleared of tables and chairs, with only a Christmas tree in one corner and a long table laden with pastries on the other side. The kids – mainly boys – were gathered around it, picking up pastry after pastry and shoving them into their mouths, barely pausing to chew before grabbing another. Isobel thought of Isaac, lying in bed and hardly eating, and anger flared once more. Her son had been fit and healthy before they'd come here. Someone had turned him into this, and she was going to find out who.

She leaned in to take a pastry, turning to smile at the boy beside her. 'Which one is the best?' she asked, thinking food was always a safe place to start.

'Oh, the *pain au chocolat*, without a doubt,' he said, his mouth full. She nodded and took one, impressed with his perfect French accent. He probably spent most of the holidays at his family's holiday home in France. When she'd been attending the Square, she'd been the only one who hadn't gone away on breaks. Her mother had never taken holidays.

'Thanks.' Isobel bit into it, nodding although it was way too rich for her stomach right now. 'Delicious,' she said, once she'd swallowed. She held out a hand. 'I'm Isaac's mother.'

'Oh! How's he doing?' A girl beside them butted in. 'I heard he had an accident or something at the school? That he fainted and hit his head in the art room? Is he okay?'

Isobel set down her pastry, her heart pounding. This was it. This was the moment she burst her mother's neat little bubble; the moment she started to let in the truth. 'No, actually.' She swallowed, attempting to get rid of the sticky sweet taste in her mouth. 'No, he's not okay. And it wasn't an accident. Someone hurt him, and I'm trying to find out who.'

'Wait, someone *hurt* him?' The girl drew back. 'Like, beat him up?'

Isobel nodded. 'Quite badly. He was unconscious when I found him, and he's still recovering.'

'Oh my God.' The girl covered her mouth, and the boy looked shocked.

'Did you know him well?' Isobel swivelled from one to the other. 'Did—'

'What's going on?' A tall, leggy brunette with long glossy hair swooped in, putting an arm around the girl. 'I'm Octavia's mother, Hania.' She held out a hand. 'And you are?'

'I'm Isaac's mother, Isobel,' Isobel said, cursing that this woman had interrupted just as she was getting started.

'Isaac?' The woman tilted her head.

'He started just after half-term,' Isobel said with a tight smile.

'Mrs Cosslett's grandson, Mum. I told you about him.' Octavia rolled her eyes.

'Oh! Mrs Cosslett's grandson!' The woman's eyes lit up, and she put a hand on Isobel's arm. Isobel couldn't help noticing her perfectly shaped nails with immaculate deep-mauve polish that matched her lipstick. 'I told Octavia to be extra nice to him, help him settle.'

'And I was, Mum.' Octavia sighed, then looked back to Isobel. 'Wait, do you think that's why he was attacked? Because he was the head's grandson? I mean, everyone loves Mrs Cosslett, and I can't think why someone—'

'Hold on.' Hania held up a hand. 'What are you talking about, Octavia? Isaac was attacked?'

Isobel groaned internally. She had to get away from this woman and talk to as many kids as she could, but Hania was still holding her arm with a firm grip.

'He was attacked in the art room at school, yes,' Isobel said quickly. 'His injuries were very serious, and I'm trying to find out what happened.'

'He was attacked at *school*?' Hania's voice went up an octave. 'Why haven't we heard anything about this? If there's been a serious incident on school premises, the parents should have been informed.'

'You would think,' Isobel muttered, finally managing to wrench herself away. She looked at Octavia and the boy. 'Do you know who he hung around with? Did either of you see Isaac arguing with anyone?' Her frustration grew at the girl's blank face – not that she blamed her. Isobel was asking a teen about something that had happened a week ago; something that required her to be aware of those around her. And teens weren't exactly known for their talents in that area, were they? Still, she had to try. 'Anything you can tell me – anything at all – would be helpful. Are any of his friends here? Maybe you can point them out to me.'

'I don't think Isaac had many friends in the form,' the boy said, reaching for another *pain au chocolat*. 'We all liked him, but he was a little shy. All I know is that he used to spend a lot of time in the art room. Some kids from the upper years hang out there – they call themselves the Group of Six or something. I'd seen him with them.'

'The Group of Six. Thank you.' Isobel smiled, relieved to have got something, but disappointed none of them would be here. 'Do you know their names?' She scrambled in her bag for her mobile, so she could show them the picture she'd taken of the photo on Isaac's camera. 'And do you—' A cheer and clapping cut off her question, and she turned to see what was happening.

Her heart dropped when she spotted her mother, waving to the kids and greeting parents with her customary warmth for anything connected with the school. What the *hell* was she doing here? Had she discovered Isobel was coming? But how?

Isobel swallowed, staring at her mum's face. She was immaculately groomed as always, but the lines around her eyes were deeper and her back was slightly bent, like she was carrying something heavy. As if she sensed Isobel's gaze, her mother turned towards her. Their eyes met, and although every bit of her wanted to look away, Isobel couldn't. Her mother's stare burned through her with such intensity that Isobel could almost *feel* the emotion radiating from it. Was it anger at what Isobel was trying to do? Determination to protect the school? Or... Her mum's face softened, and something flickered inside Isobel, just like it had that night Silas had thrown the brick. Isobel tore her gaze away. That emotion hadn't been real then, and it wasn't real now. Isobel wouldn't be sucked in this time. Her mother loved only one thing, and that was the school.

'Hello, everyone!' her mum said, her clear voice ringing out. Instantly, the room went silent. 'I hope you don't mind me crashing your breakfast, but I had a craving for a croissant.' Immediately she was ushered over to the table, handed a plate, and served a croissant. Isobel watched, amazed at the power she wielded. Meanwhile, people had thought she was a waitress.

'Mrs Cosslett!' Isobel's stomach tightened as Hania pushed her way over. 'I've just heard about Isaac. It's terrible. An *attack*.' Her voice was breathless. 'If there's anything we can do to help – anything at all – please let me and Octavia know. What do the police say? Are they doing anything? I can have my husband make a call, if you like. You know he's friends with the head of the Met?' She stepped closer. 'You *can* assure me our children are safe, yes? I mean, with an attacker still on the loose. Who would do such a thing? It's just shocking.'

Parents swivelled towards Hania, and a low murmur rose from the crowd. Isobel wanted to scream in frustration. She'd managed to get a little information, but she'd been hoping to talk to more kids and show them the photo. With her mother here now reassuring everyone it was nothing, it was going to be impossible. No one would want to get involved. Maybe Isobel could corner the boy she'd been talking to and at least get the names of that Group of Six? She glanced around the room for him when a sharp clap made her stop. The space fell silent once more and every eye turned towards her mum. Isobel shrank back against a wall, wondering how she was going to respond. She must have planned for this, despite her attempts to pretend it never happened.

'First of all, I need to extend my apologies.'

Isobel's eyebrows shot up. Apologies? Was her mother... was she finally going to concede what had really happened to her grandson? No. Isobel dismissed the thought, telling herself not to be ridiculous. Her mother wouldn't do anything to damage the Square. She'd made that very clear. So, what was she going to say?

'I always strive to maintain the height of professionalism in everything I do at the school,' her mum continued. 'I'm very aware this is what you expect from Burlington Square School, and I hope you feel that's what we deliver.'

The crowd murmured and nodded. Isobel leaned forward, every bit of her straining to hear her mother's next words.

'But right now, I need to address something as a mother and a grandmother. Something I didn't want to divulge, for the sake of my own family. But I need to in order to clear up any misunderstandings. The last thing I want is for you to think that your children might not be safe. Because they are, I promise you that.'

Isobel drew back. What? How could her mother promise that? The children weren't safe – not at all. Not when the attacker still hadn't been found.

But maybe he had, she thought suddenly, excitement darting through her. Maybe that's why her mother was here, when she'd usually steer clear. Maybe a student had talked, or maybe Cecily... Isobel swallowed. Maybe Cecily had done the right thing, after all. Maybe she had recognised the person in that photo. Isobel didn't know why her mother wouldn't tell her about it first, but maybe she wanted to take action before apologising. She knew how upset Isobel had been.

Isobel held her breath, trying to guard against the hope pressing in on her... trying not to think of the look on her mother's face earlier.

'Many of you are aware that one of your form, my grandson Isaac, sustained some serious injuries at the school recently. He's still recovering and receiving the very best care. You may have heard today that those injuries *weren't* accidental,' her mum said. 'And that's correct too.'

Isobel let out her breath in a whoosh, almost unable to believe her ears. Her mother was going to tell the truth. Finally, she was going to admit that something had gone wrong in her precious school. Finally, she was standing up for Isaac. It had taken the threat of a photo to get her to act, but she *was* acting. Isobel stared at her, willing their eyes to meet so she could feel her strength again... the strength she was putting behind her family once more.

Her mum pushed through the crowd, parting it like the Red Sea, until she was standing right by Isobel. She threaded an arm through Isobel's, and Isobel breathed in the familiar scent of home; of the life full of love that she remembered.

The life – the love – that just may have existed, after all.

'Today's youth face a great many challenges when it comes to mental health,' her mum continued, and Isobel stiffened. Mental health? *What?*

'Sometimes, our teenagers become overwhelmed, and they don't know who to turn to,' her mother said. 'They act rashly, without thinking of the consequences. It's so hard to accept that we weren't there for our child when they needed us most. Often, it's easier to latch onto external reasons – to look for blame elsewhere; to believe someone else caused harm rather than accepting our loved one did this to himself. As parents, I'm sure we can all understand that.'

Isobel started to shake. What the hell was her mother saying? She couldn't be implying that Isaac had tried to harm himself... could she? And that Isobel couldn't accept it? No. She *couldn't*.

'So no, there wasn't an attack,' her mother went on. 'And I'm sorry to have told your children it was an accident, but I hope you can understand that I was protecting my family. Everything is being done to get my grandson back to full health, and I know the school community will rally around to support him. And may I ask for your understanding of my daughter, please, as she comes to terms with all of this. It's a lot for any parent to deal with, and so hard to accept.'

The crowd's gaze swung to Isobel now, still locked in her mother's grip. She couldn't move. She couldn't *breathe*. Her mother's scent swirled around her, more poisonous now than homely. One lungful more of it, and she'd collapse. Hania's eyes were wide with horror, while the rest of the crowd wore an expression of both pity and fascination.

'I'm in the process of organising a counsellor to come in to speak with any child who may feel affected by this,' her mother said. 'As always, please don't hesitate to reach out to me if you have any concerns. Now let's get back to enjoying our morning.' And with that, parents gathered around her, everyone vying to offer their condolences and support.

Finally, Isobel managed to rip her arm away. She shrank back as the crowd swallowed her mother, nausea swirling inside. The bile in the back of her throat mixed with the sweet taste lingering in her mouth, and for a second, she thought she might be sick right there. How could she be so stupid to believe her mother would put anything but the Square first? That cosy life full of love hadn't existed: not then, not now. Isobel scooped up her coat and pushed outside, the bright sun blinding her as it reflected off the white facades. Even though she couldn't see it, she could feel the Square looming in the background, lording its victory over her. She forced her legs towards the Tube as fast as she could, desperate to get away.

Only when she was sitting on the train, being whisked from the square, did it finally sink in what had happened. For the sake of the school, her mother had not only refused to help Isaac, but now she had actively damaged him, telling a roomful of parents and peers that mental-health issues had caused his 'accident'. Her *grandson*, and she'd sacrificed him. And, of course, the parents had swallowed it hook, line and sinker. They'd never go against what her mother said.

Isobel breathed in. She didn't care what her mother claimed about her: that she had problems accepting what had happened;

that it was easier to blame others. She didn't care that her mother had now throw away any hint of a relationship, or reconciliation. But she wasn't going to let *anyone* hurt her son.

She'd just never thought that 'anyone' would be his own grandmother.

THIRTY-ONE

RUTH

Parents gather around me, each offering their condolences and pouring out sorry tales of their own child's mental health... seemingly oblivious to the gross invasion of their child's privacy. From the corner of my eye, I see Isobel grab her coat and head for the door, and my stomach churns with so many emotions I'm not sure I can unpick them. Relief that no one will believe Isobel now? Anger that she would actually come here, knowing what her actions could do to the school?

Guilt for my earlier words? Earlier *lies*?

She turns and our eyes meet once more, and one emotion echoes inside so strongly that it blocks out all the others. *Pain.* I've lost her... lost her again, for good, because I know there's no coming back from what I've done. How could there be? I only pray that she doesn't tell Isaac what I've said about him – what I've told his *class* about him. But even if she keeps quiet, I know I've lost him too. She'll never let me see him again. My heart aches so much it's difficult to breathe. It's all I can do to keep a sad smile nailed onto my face for the benefit of those around me.

How could I do that? How could I lie about Isaac that way? I didn't want to say those words. I really didn't. I'd rushed inside the restaurant, praying I wasn't too late... that I could get Isobel out of there before anything happened. But Isobel had already said something to Hania Dugas, of all people. That woman is like a dog with a bone – I've never met a parent quite so persistent (maybe *insistent* would be a better word), and given the number of parents I've dealt with over the years, that's saying a lot.

I needed something plausible to nip this thing in the bud before it got out of control, and goodness knows nothing takes long in this community. And in my panic, all I could think of was Cecily's suggestion to discredit Isobel. I was horrified that she could be so cold-blooded as to think up such a scheme. Well, now I'm worse because I've gone through with it.

I've protected the school, yes. I've saved the investment. But the very people I was doing all of this for – my daughter, my grandson – won't be a part of that now. *Daughter. Grandson.* The words ring in my mind, and my gut clenches as loss swirls through me. They've only just become part of the fabric of the family; of the school and its future. And now I've ripped them from it, and there's a gaping hole inside of me again... a hole that will never be filled. Because no matter where they are, and no matter what I've done, I *will* always be a mother and a grandmother.

A mother and grandmother who's driven away the people she loves the most.

'Cup of tea?' Hania appears at my elbow, and I force a smile and nod my thanks. I need to get back to the school, but I can hardly make an announcement like that and cut and run. No, I have to stay and accept the pitying and sympathetic looks, the people who are staring at me now like I'm actually human.

And I don't want that. I don't want to be human; to feel anything any more. I'll do what I always do and keep moving forward, keep playing the headmistress and waiting for that hole inside to become bandaged over, even if it never fully heals. I have the school, and – I swallow, remembering the contract should be arriving later today – I'll have the future.

I can almost see the Square smiling in triumph, but right now I feel anything but victorious. For the first time, the school feels less like something lifting me up and more like a weight I have to carry.

THIRTY-TWO

ISOBEL

Isobel collapsed in a heap on the sofa back at Alex's house. Upstairs, Isaac was still sleeping. She'd tried to tempt him out for some fresh air by promising him lunch at the market, but he'd barely responded through the closed door. Fury rose inside at the thought of her mother *daring* to suggest he'd done this to himself. It was like saying Isobel had brought the pregnancy and attack on herself too – although given what she'd seen from her mother today, she didn't doubt any longer her mum might have said exactly that. Anything to keep the school safe.

'How did it go?' Alex came down the stairs. He'd offered to stay at home this morning until she got back, which she'd gratefully accepted. She hadn't wanted to leave Isaac alone. 'Did you manage to find out anything?' He sat down on the sofa beside her, a concerned look on his face. Isobel moved closer, thinking how ironic it was that she'd met one of the most supportive men she'd ever known at the same place that had torn her apart. Thankfully, there was no more overlap between their worlds than that.

'It was dreadful,' she said. 'But actually, I did manage to find out *something*. A boy in Isaac's form said that he used to hang around with some kids called the Group of Six.'

A smile played around Alex's mouth. 'I like it. Very artistic. Did you get their names?'

'No. My mum...' She shook her head, still unable to believe what her mother had done.

'What happened?' Alex's sympathetic expression made her eyes fill with tears.

'I was about to show some students the photo and try to find out more when one of the parents butted in, and then Mum came through the door.' She breathed in, trying to stay calm. 'She must have known I was there – I don't know how, though. She never goes to those things.'

Alex nodded.

'Anyway...' The rage exploded and she started to shake.

'Hey.' Alex gently put an arm around her, drawing her close. She leaned against him, feeling the strength of his support. Finally, she felt calmer and she pulled back.

'This parent confronted Mum, asking if the kids were safe at the school and why they hadn't been told about the assault.' Alex winced, and Isobel nodded. 'I know. And then my mum...' She gritted her teeth, pushing down the emotion that threatened to clog her throat. 'She told them that Isaac had done this to himself... that he was self-harming or trying to kill himself – that was the implication. She said he had mental-health issues, and that I couldn't accept it so was looking for someone else to blame.'

'Wow.' Alex looked stunned.

'I know.' Isobel lowered her head. 'I knew my mum would do almost anything to protect the Square... like covering up the assault; trying to pretend it never happened. But I never thought she'd go as far as hurting her own grandson – of making up harmful lies about him.' She let out her breath. 'I should have known better. The reputation of the school is everything. *Nobody* attacks the Square, or they become collateral damage. Including members of her own family.'

'I don't... I don't know what to say.' Alex touched her arm. 'What happened next?'

'I left. It felt like I was running away, but I really didn't know what else to do. I don't know what else to do now.' She sighed, thinking of her angry and withdrawn son upstairs, refusing to talk to his mother and now damaged by his grandmother, the subject of gossip and pity... and all because she wouldn't stop. *Was* she doing more harm than good?

Alex looked at her, his eyes soft. 'I think you should take some time to de-stress. This weekend, next week, next month – you can stay here as long as you like, don't worry. What happened this morning... that's enough to throw anyone for a loop, even someone as strong as you. Chill out now, watch a film, have a glass or three of wine.' He smiled. 'And when I'm back tonight, we can talk more then, if you want.' He patted her hand, then got up. 'I'm so sorry, but I've got to get into the office now.'

'Go, go.' She forced a smile and made shooing motions with her hands. 'God knows we've taken up enough of your time.'

He shrugged on his coat. 'I have a late meeting, so don't wait for me to get back to have supper. Give me a call if you need anything, okay?'

She lifted a hand as he went out the door, then wandered upstairs to check on Isaac. He was sleeping on his side, his body facing away from her, his dark hair the only splotch of colour on the pillow. She stared down at him, her mind tumbling. *Could* she let this go? Would she be letting him down, or would she prevent more distress and hurt? She was doing all of this to protect him – to stop him from suffering future pain and fear like she had. But what if the damage she caused in the present was irreparable?

Sighing, she tucked the duvet closer and turned away. Even if she did decide to keep going, right now, she didn't know what to do. Perhaps Alex was right and she just needed to chill for a bit. She went into her room, lay down on the bed, and closed her eyes.

The sharp ring of the mobile jerked her awake. She wiped her mouth, glancing at the clock with surprise. It was almost four! How on earth had that happened?

She grabbed the phone, squinting at the unknown number on the screen. 'Hello?'

'Hi, Isobel? I don't think we've met, but my name's Julia and I'm the mother of a boy at the Square. I hope you don't mind me calling – I got your number from your form rep. I heard what happened today at the breakfast. I'm sorry.'

Isobel swallowed, trying to contain the anger inside.

'My son Henry is friends with Isaac,' the woman continued before she could respond. 'They have an informal art club that Isaac's joined.'

'The Group of Six.' Isobel sat up, now fully awake.

'Yes, that's it,' Julia said. 'Apparently, they perform this small initiation ritual to any new boy who wants to be a part of it.'

Isobel sucked in her breath. Initiation ritual?

'Henry came to me just now, after hearing at school how Isaac hurt himself. He was worried that Isaac might have been upset by the initiation that afternoon, and that it contributed to... what happened. He promised me it was nothing major; very innocent by the sounds of things. They blindfold the boy, then have him try to find art supplies and paint one of the group by memory. Quite tame compared to what we used to get up to at my school.' Julia paused. 'Anyway, apparently Isaac passed with flying colours, but of course he made a mess and had to stay late tidying up.'

Isobel was quiet, trying to take in her words. This explained why he'd been in the art room so late after school. But he hadn't done this to himself, so clearly the initiation hadn't upset him. Anyway, it sounded pretty tame to her too.

'Henry would like to come by and see Isaac, if you're all right with that? He feels just dreadful. He's been in pieces since he came home from school today.'

Isobel stayed silent, turning things over in her mind as excitement filtered in. Maybe she'd considered taking a break from all this, but now, well... this boy might actually be able to tell her something. He'd been there that afternoon, part of Isaac's group of friends. He might be the one who'd texted Isaac the photos, the person who'd attacked him, or both. But whoever he was, if she could just talk to him, then maybe she could finally find out something useful.

'That would be wonderful,' Isobel said, jumping at the chance. 'I'm sure Isaac would appreciate it.' She wasn't sure if he would or not, but it didn't matter because Henry wouldn't be meeting Isaac tonight. He'd be meeting her.

'I'm doing everything I can to get Isaac out and about, to help his recovery,' Isobel said. 'But he's still quite tired from everything. Would Henry be able to come here, over to East London? The boys could have a meal out in Spitalfields Market, if you're okay with that.'

'Oh, that's brilliant. Henry would love it,' Julia said. 'I realise this may be short notice for you, but is tonight all right? The sooner Henry talks to Isaac, the better.'

For me, too, Isobel thought. 'That's perfect. Six o'clock? I'll text you the name of a restaurant they can meet at.'

'Great. Henry will be so happy. I'll go tell him now.' Julia paused. 'Take care of yourself, all right? Our kids need us most when things are hardest.'

Isobel nodded, thinking that was more than true.

THIRTY-THREE

ISOBEL

The air was cool and fog curled around the street lights as Isobel made her way towards the buzz of the market. This part of the city was Jack the Ripper territory – she'd passed by guided walks with groups of wide-eyed tourists many times – and tonight, it was easy to believe. She drew her coat tighter around her neck and quickened her pace, her breath making the air in front of her cloudier, as if she was seeing through haze. Actually, it felt like she'd been seeing that way ever since she'd returned to London. Only one thing shone clearly: her love for Isaac, and her desire to do what was best for him.

She hadn't wanted to leave him alone, but at least the massive bowl of pasta she'd served up had tempted him from the bedroom. With his bruises now yellow and his long hair a greasy mess, he'd looked awful – and he hadn't smelled much better either. She prayed he'd shower before crawling back into bed.

She wandered through the busy market, breathing in the life around her. Tonight, she might find out something that could help her son. God, she hoped so. She couldn't wait to focus on what was really important: getting back on their feet again and building a life together, some place safe. Maybe Alex could help them find somewhere... somewhere nearby? He was such a good friend.

She'd never really had one; never let someone in like she had with him.

'There's going to be two of us,' she said to the host at a busy restaurant where she'd arranged to meet Henry. Better to have him for a meal, she'd thought, rather than a quick drink where he could duck out if he wanted. If Henry was anything like Isaac, he'd do almost anything if there was food involved. Well, at least that was how Isaac used to be. Anger surged through her.

The restaurant was heaving, and the host seated her by the window. She tapped her fingers on the table, realising too late that she'd no idea what Henry looked like and that he'd be searching for Isaac, not an older woman. She craned her neck towards the entrance, keeping an eye out for any teen around Isaac's age.

Finally, she spotted a boy hurrying into the restaurant. She stood and raised her hand, waving it in the air to catch his attention. God, she hoped it was Henry. The boy turned towards her and met her eyes, and everything stopped. She couldn't move; couldn't breathe. All she could do was stare at his face, her heart pounding as he came closer and closer.

A hand in her hair. A body on hers. The whistle as he walked away from her, leaving her silent on the floor.

The dark green eyes, the thick black hair, the strong jaw and thin nose... the boy approaching her now was the image of the man who'd haunted her for years – haunted her still. She blinked, hoping her vision would clear, but when she opened her eyes, the same face was coming towards her.

'I'm looking for Isaac?' the boy was saying, giving her an uncertain look. 'Is he here?' Isobel kept staring, feeling like she was trapped in a nightmare. Was she dreaming now? No, she told herself, gripping onto the table to anchor her. She wasn't in the past. She was just tired, that was all, and this whole thing had really shaken her up. She drew in a breath and forced herself to look closely at him. Actually, now that he was right in front of her, she wasn't sure there was much resemblance, after all.

'I'm sorry – you just reminded me of someone I knew years

ago,' she said finally. 'Isaac's not able to make it, I'm afraid. He's not feeling well.' She indicated the chair across from her. 'I'm Isobel, his mother. Please, sit down. Order whatever you like and we can have a chat. I'm happy to pass on anything you'd like to say to Isaac.'

'Okay. Thanks.' Henry shrugged off his coat and slid into his seat, meeting her eyes nervously. 'I'm really sorry about what happened. We didn't mean to upset him, not at all. It was just a bit of fun. I guess... we never thought...' His face twisted, and Isobel could feel his distress. She wanted to reach out and comfort him, but she couldn't do anything until she knew what role, if any, he'd played in all of this. For a split second, his face morphed once more into the man who'd damaged her, and she pushed it away again.

'Why don't we start from the beginning,' Isobel said, sliding a menu across the table. 'You're part of the Group of Six, right? Isaac used to hang around with you?'

'Mrs Nowak lets us stay after school sometimes to do our coursework. We noticed Isaac there one day Photoshopping some of his pictures. He's really good. We got talking, and soon he was part of the group. We all like him.'

'And this initiation?'

Henry stared down at the table. 'It's stupid, I know. Mum had a huge go at me for it. It was just a bit of fun, and Isaac didn't seem to mind. He wanted to do it.'

'And you all left afterwards? Except for Isaac, I mean.'

Henry nodded. 'Jez had to grab something from his locker before he went home, but the rest of us went straight to the door.'

'And Isaac was okay when you left him?'

'He seemed to be.' Henry's face dropped. 'I wish I'd known he was struggling. We'd never have done the initiation. He's a few years younger than me, and he was kind of like a kid brother, you know?' He glanced up at her. 'I'm adopted. I never had a sibling. Mum always says that's why I like taking people under my wing – to make up for it.'

The server swooped down with a cheery grin, and they gave

him their orders. Isobel tried to hide her surprise as Henry ordered a sea bass and a liver pate starter after her burger and chips. Clearly, he was more cultured than she was.

'This Jez...' Isobel tilted her head, trying to find the words to frame the questions she wanted to ask. 'He wouldn't do anything to hurt Isaac, would he? I mean, they hadn't argued or anything?'

Henry raised his eyebrows. 'Jez? Hurt Isaac? No. No way. I don't think he's ever thrown a punch in his life, and he really likes Isaac. They get on really well, always having a laugh and mucking about.' Isobel wondered for a second if Jez could be the boy who'd sent Isaac those photos. 'Anyway, he came out after a minute or two, and then we walked home together.' He leaned back in his chair. 'Why are you asking if Jez hurt Isaac? Do you think Isaac might have been bullied, and that's why he did what he did?'

Isobel shook her head. 'Isaac didn't do this to himself.' She watched his face closely to see his expression.

Henry's mouth fell open. 'Really? You don't think he self-harmed, or tried to...'

'No, I don't. Someone did this to him – someone viciously attacked him, then left him unconscious on the floor.' Isobel paused, taking in Henry's shocked expression. It *seemed* real enough, but... 'What I don't understand is who would do this – or why. Isaac, well... he won't say a word about it. Not yet anyway.' If Henry was involved somehow, she didn't want him to think he was off scot-free. 'But I'm going to find out. Whoever it was has to be punished.'

Henry was silent for a minute as their drinks were placed in front of them.

'Can you think of anything unusual you might have seen that afternoon?' Isobel asked as he sipped his Coke. 'Anything different? Did you see anyone hanging around the art room when you left?'

He shook his head, and Isobel's heart sank. 'I'm sorry. I didn't notice anything.'

'And Isaac... Did he hang around with any one person in

particular?' She wanted to ask more about Jez, but she didn't want to give away too much.

'Not that I noticed, but then I only really saw him in the art room. I'm not in his form, so...' Henry paused. 'I think he met up with someone outside of school, though. An older man, who was showing him how to take photos. The same one who gave him the camera? He'd get a message and then go off to meet him. We ribbed him about it, calling him Isaac's sugar daddy. It was just a bit of fun,' Henry added quickly. 'Isaac would blush and get all embarrassed, but he thought it was funny.'

Isobel nodded. She'd known Isaac met up with Alex. That was nothing new. Silence fell between them as she tried to think of what else to ask. Could she believe Henry? Was he telling the truth, or was he trying to hide something? She sighed, frustration swirling inside. Every time she thought she might be closer to finding out what happened, it seemed to go nowhere. At least she could ask Henry for Jez's phone number and talk to him too. If he and Isaac had got on so well, hopefully he could – hopefully he *would* – tell Isobel more.

'You know how you said I reminded you of someone...' Henry ran a hand through his hair in a gesture so much like Isaac that for a second, it almost felt like she was sitting here with her son. 'Well... can you tell me who?'

Isobel froze, staring into his eyes.

'It's just... like I said, I'm adopted. I've been trying to find out more about my father.'

'Your father.' An icy shard of dread lodged in her stomach. She swallowed, attempting to hold it at bay.

'This person I reminded you of... did he live around West London?' Henry didn't seem to notice her unease. 'I know my birth mum was from there. My parents adopted me from a council adoption agency in Kensington. I have my mum's name, Leana, from the birth certificate, but my father wasn't listed. She got pregnant really young, still at school. She was younger than me, my mum said.' Henry sighed. 'She's dead now. When I told my mum a few months ago that I wanted to start looking for my birth parents – I mean, my parents are great, but I was just curious, you know? – we came across her death certificate, but there was nothing on my father.'

Isobel held his gaze, feeling the ice spread, the chill seeping into her bones with every breath she took. *Kensington. Pregnant. Still at school. Younger than me.*

Could it be possible... possible that the man who'd abused her was Henry's father too? That maybe she wasn't the only girl he'd done this to? That Henry's mother had also stayed silent, but instead of running, she'd given up her baby?

'Can you tell me his name?' Henry's voice jolted her back to the present. So much emotion was swirling inside she could hardly breathe. How could she begin to tell this young boy that the man he resembled had abused her – and could have abused his mother too? She couldn't. She could never do that.

But it was more than that. She didn't want to say the name. She didn't want to even think of the name. She hadn't for years. She *couldn't*.

Her stomach heaved, and she pushed back from the table.

'I have to go,' she said, staggering to her feet. 'I'm very sorry, but I'm not feeling well, not at all. I'll pay for everything on the way out – you stay and enjoy your food. I'll tell Isaac that you'd like to see him soon.' She spoke as fast as she could, desperate to get away.

She grabbed her handbag and coat, then pushed towards the exit, knocking over an empty chair in her wake. She barely heard the bang as she hurried up to the till. There was too much going on inside of her; too many horrific images clamouring to breach the dam that kept them at bay during the day. As she raced down the street, the dark water was rising. No matter how hard she forced her legs forward, the sand of the past pulled at her every step, slowing her escape until she couldn't move any longer. She sank down against a wall and put her hands to her head to try to shield herself, but it was too late. The black waves were washing through her consciousness, dragging her back to the afternoon when she'd found out she was pregnant. When she'd lingered outside the French club to let him know, hoping he'd tell her what to do; that he'd take her in his arms and make everything better.

When her life had ended.

Hands on her throat. Bruises blossoming on her arms. The whistle echoing down the corridor as she slumped to the floor, trying to breathe...

Pain ricocheted through her now, as if her body had also kept the memory of how he'd grabbed her arms, pressing his thumbs into her flesh, shaking her hard while hissing that this had nothing to do with him. He'd only given her what she wanted, he'd said, and she wasn't going to fuck up his life for a few rubbish shags. She wouldn't tell her mother – or anyone else. No one would believe her anyway, he'd sneered, as he squeezed harder.

She'd tried to say she wasn't going to tell, but he put his hand over her mouth and nose, pressing more and more until she couldn't breathe, and then, just as the world began to go dark, he let go. She'd sunk to the floor as he walked away, whistling that same song... as if he hadn't just about killed her – and his baby too.

Finally, she'd managed to get to her feet. Her arms throbbed where he'd grabbed her, and her whole face felt bruised and tender. Her head pounded and her vision was blurry, but she had to get out of there. Although his hands were no longer on her face, she could still feel them suffocating her. She could feel the fear and shame pressing down on her, squeezing any remaining breath from her lungs. And she'd realised then that the only way to survive was to lock all of this away, as tightly as she could, and run. From him, from her mother, from *herself*. It had worked too – at least during her waking hours.

But now... now she could feel those hands again; the fear and the shame. Now it wasn't just confined to the night. It had finally burst free, swallowing her down into its darkness. She bent over, gasping, struggling to breathe as his words echoed in her head, his voice blocking out everything else.

I'm only giving you what you wanted. I'm only giving you—

'No.' She forced the word out with the air that remained, then managed to draw in another breath. 'No,' she said louder, her chest heaving up and down. With each lungful, she felt stronger, as if the air was cleansing her, washing away the soot from her soul. What had happened to her... that hadn't been what she'd wanted; none of it had. She hadn't had the words to tell him that then. She hadn't the words to tell anyone. She hadn't the strength to face it all alone... or so she'd feared.

'*No!*' The word bounced up and down the pavement, and people turned to stare.

'All right, love?'

'Yes,' she said, her voice loud and steady. 'Yes. I am.' She pushed back from the wall, almost unable to believe that she actually *was* all right. She didn't need to live with fear and shame. What had happened wasn't her fault. She felt that even more after learning that he might have done this to other girls too. She hadn't been the only one.

And she didn't need to live in fear of the terrible images that had haunted her. She didn't have to run any more, or rely on anyone else's strength. She *was* strong enough to withstand them on her own. She didn't have to let the past have power over her.

She didn't have to let *him* have power over her.

Isobel strode towards Alex's house, her footsteps ringing out like gunshots in the empty street. Maybe tonight she hadn't unlocked what had happened to Isaac, but somehow, she'd managed to unlock herself.

THIRTY-FOUR

ISOBEL

'Everything okay?' Alex flicked off the television as she came in the door. 'I managed to get home earlier than I thought, and Isaac told me you had to go out. He's fast asleep now, by the way. Where did you go?'

'I'm so happy you're back.' Isobel stepped out of her shoes and shrugged off her coat, then sat down on the sofa beside him. After everything that had happened, she should feel exhausted, but every bit of her buzzed with energy. For the first time in years, she felt free... free from the school and the horrors there. Free to start finding a way back to herself, to a person who wasn't consumed by trying to hold back the past.

She took the glass of wine Alex gave her and sipped it, turning to face him. 'I went to meet with one of Isaac's friends. I thought he might be able to give me some clue about what happened to Isaac.'

'And?' Alex leaned closer.

'And...' She met his eyes, realising she was finally ready to talk about her past. She *wanted* to. After all of these years, she did have the words now. And she wasn't a victim any longer – she didn't have to keep it a secret. 'You'll never believe what happened.' Alex's face tightened, and Isobel could see how much he was invested in all of this. He stayed quiet, waiting for her to speak, obviously sensing there was so much more she needed to say. She loved how he got her, without the need for explanation. She was glad he was the first person she was opening up to.

'Isaac's friend... seeing him gave me such a shock,' she began. 'He looked so much like the man... the man who abused me. The man who *attacked* me.' She took a big breath in. 'Philippe Gauvin.'

Finally, she'd said his name out loud. She'd been so afraid that somehow it would rear up larger than life, embodying all the emotions she'd feared. But now... now, it didn't. It was just a name. The name of a man who'd done horrible things to her – who had changed her life forever – but couldn't harm her any longer, emotionally now as well as physically.

'What?' Alex's voice was quiet, despite his shocked expression.

Isobel nodded. 'It's how I got pregnant with Isaac so young. Philippe was a teacher at the school. My mum's school.' The words tumbled out. Now that she'd started talking, she didn't want to stop. She couldn't stop. 'He taught French, and I thought he was so cool. We began talking; flirting. I liked the attention. And then one day, he kissed me.' She swallowed. 'It progressed from there. These days we'd call it grooming, I guess. I was naïve enough to think it was a real relationship – that he really liked me. I couldn't have been more wrong.'

She shifted on the sofa, so grateful Alex was letting her talk without asking any questions. 'When I told him I was pregnant, he attacked me. He grabbed me, putting his hands over my nose and mouth so I couldn't breathe. He told me I should never tell anyone what had happened. That if I did, they wouldn't listen to me anyway.'

She met Alex's eyes, stunned to see the anger there. His normally open face was so clouded and dark that he almost looked like a different person. 'I never told anyone – not even my mother. Not because I didn't think she wouldn't believe me, but because I couldn't bear her disappointment and how what I'd done might affect the Square, if it ever came out.' She let out a laugh. 'Ironic, isn't it? That I ran away to protect the school and my mother? And now...' She shook her head, holding Alex's steady gaze. 'I've never talked about what happened – until now.'

'I'm so sorry,' he said, getting to his feet and pacing back and forth. 'So sorry this happened. It shouldn't have. It never should have.' He paused, turning towards her. 'I'm glad you told me, though – glad you can finally talk. Because you know this isn't your fault, right? None of it is.'

She nodded, loving how he was echoing her thoughts. 'I know. I know that now. And I think hearing that it might have happened to someone else – to another girl – well, it made me see that it wasn't just me. It took away the last bit of shame. It made me strong enough to face the memories.'

Alex sat down beside her. 'Another girl?' His voice was shaking, and she could see how much what she'd said had affected him.

Isobel nodded again, Henry's face filling her mind. 'I can't say for sure, but it's very likely. It's awful to think Philippe could have done this to someone else. I can only hope it was just the two of us.'

'How do you know it happened to another girl?' Alex's eyes were boring through her.

'Isaac's friend Henry – the boy I met tonight – is adopted. He doesn't know who his father is, but he said that his birth mother was from Kensington and that she got pregnant when she was very young... at school.' She swallowed. 'I could be wrong, and I hope I am. But he looks so much like Philippe that I think he must have been his father.'

Alex leaned forward, looking at her intently. 'Did Henry know... did he know his birth mother's name?'

'He did. He told me, but I'm not sure I remember. Sorry. Maybe... Leanne?' It wasn't quite right, but it was something close. 'Why?'

But Alex didn't answer. His face stayed the same, but something in it changed – something she couldn't read.

'Alex?' she said, putting a hand on his back. He was so hot it felt like a furnace. 'Alex, what is it?'

He shook his head, his face returning to normal. 'I'm just

shocked by what you told me. That it could have happened to other girls too. Just... just give me a minute. I'll get some tea.'

'Okay.' She sat back on the sofa, savouring the feeling of lightness and quiet inside. If only she could somehow explain this to Isaac, she thought, closing her eyes. If only she could make him understand that he, too, was strong enough to face the truth. That if he did, he'd feel so much better. He—

Alex's mobile bleeped on the sofa beside her, and she glanced down as a message flashed onto the screen. She squinted, eyebrows rising in surprise as her mother's name appeared. Why was her mother contacting Alex? Were they working together again? He hadn't said anything. Unable to stop herself, she picked up the phone.

Documents perfect. Ready to sign. Let's get this investment rolling! Exciting times ahead for Burlington Square School – world, here we come. I'll be at school in the morning. Come by around ten?

She stared at the message, trying to take it in. Documents? Investment? Exciting times ahead? What the *hell* was going on?

'I brought you some whisky,' Alex said. 'I thought you might need something stronger. I...' His voice trailed off when he saw her face and the phone in her hand. Slowly, she turned the message towards him.

'What is my mother talking about?' Isobel asked in a low voice, trying to keep a lid on the emotions clamouring inside. There must be a logical explanation. There had to be. 'Are you investing? In the school?'

Alex sat down beside her. 'Isobel, I...' His voice trailed off, and her heart dropped.

'You're not an educational consultant. Are you?' He shook his head, and pain ripped through her. 'And you're investing in the school.' She prayed he'd deny it, but instead he just stayed silent. 'All of this time, I thought I could trust you. I thought you could be there for me... for Isaac. For God's sake, you're the first person I ever told what happened to me!' She laughed incredulously. 'But this whole time you've been talking to my mother. You're bloody *investing* in the school! Guess you'll keep what I told you under wraps, won't you? Is that why you were so upset when you heard? Because if it ever got out, it might hurt your investment?' She waited an instant for him to deny it, but his face told her it was true.

'Why did you agree to have us stay with you?' Horror filled her as a thought hit. 'Was it so you could keep an eye on us? See what I might find out about Isaac's attack and report back to my mum?' She shook her head, her mind connecting all the dots. 'Is that how she knew I was going to be at the form breakfast? Oh my *God*.' She got to her feet, staring into his stricken face. He wasn't who she'd thought he was. He wasn't a friend, someone miles away from the world she'd escaped – someone she could trust, who'd sat beside her and listened to her speak, who was there for her the moment she'd finally sloughed off the past. Instead, he was a part of that world, in a way she could never have imagined.

She thought of his carefully timed questions and cautions: if maybe what had happened could have been an accident, of how she should get some rest and relax... words that she'd thought were because he cared. Nausea swirled in her stomach as she realised it was just the opposite. He didn't care about her or Isaac. He only cared about his investment.

He was no better than her mother.

'Isaac and I... we'll be out of your hair as soon as we find somewhere else to stay.' She couldn't bear to look at Alex any longer, so she turned and rushed up the stairs, sinking onto her bed as her stomach churned.

She sat for a minute, trying to breathe; trying to contain everything. She'd faced down the darkness. She'd even talked about what had happened, and at last she'd been at peace. But now... now her anger had resurfaced, ripping through her with a vengeance. No matter how much she tried to get away from it – no matter how far she went and how strong she was – she could never outrun the school's reach; never escape its influence. It had forced her from home, ripped her family apart, and now it had tainted the one moment she'd finally felt free, reminding her that she was anything but.

She crossed the hall into Isaac's room, staring down at the peaceful face of her sleeping son. Until now, her determination to find the truth about what had happened and punish the person responsible had been solely for him, so he didn't have to endure the trauma she had. Whatever effect it had on her mother and Cecily and the school was only collateral damage.

But this wasn't just about her son and his attack. Not any more. This was about her and Henry's mother. This was about the place where everything had happened – the centre of it all. The place that *did* consume people, sucking the life and potential from them with glee.

This was about the school. And the only way to really rid herself of this anger and pain was to destroy it – to take away its power. To damage it, just like she had been.

She'd get Isaac away from here first. And then... then she'd get started.

THIRTY-FIVE

RUTH

It might be a Saturday, but I'm dressing with particular care this morning, slipping into my cornflower blue silk shirt and taking out the suit that I usually reserve for end-of-year graduation ceremonies. Today is the day I'll sign the documents to finalise Alex's investment, and I figured if I'm going to be ushering in a new era, then I should mark the occasion. I stare in the mirror, taking in my rounded waist and lined face, such a contrast to the young woman who took over so unexpectedly decades ago. The years have passed and much has changed. People have come and gone – my father, my husband, Isobel and Isaac – but I'm still here, and so is the school.

I put a hand to my face, thinking that I can't really say that I'm still here. Because ever since Isobel and Isaac left – ever since I said those horrible things – I've floated around this house like a ghost. Even inside the school, I don't feel solid; real. Being headmistress used to fill me up, but now... I swallow, turning away from the mirror and forcing my thoughts to the meeting ahead. I just need to sign the contract – to do something *right* – and then maybe I'll feel a bit better. I can take comfort in knowing the school will live on. I need to take comfort in that.

I'm not glossing over the fact that this is the first time anyone else will have a stake in the school, of course. It won't be 100 per cent family run, not any more. But when I think of the future and the global recognition the Square will have, the warm glow casts a little light on the darker places inside me.

The morning passes slowly in the empty school. Finally, it's five to ten and time to meet with Alex. I smooth down my suit and tuck in my shirt – this silk shirt refuses to stay neatly tucked; I knew there was a reason I rarely wear it – and pace back and forth, unable to remain seated. After what feels like forever, I hear the buzzer ring. I try to take my time, but excitement hurries my legs forward.

'Alex,' I say warmly as I open the door. 'So good to see you again.'

'And you.' He smiles back, but there's something... something I can't quite read in his face. I eye him closely, noticing the bags under his eyes. He looks exhausted, as if he hasn't slept all night. I hope things are okay with Isobel and Isaac. Every inch of me strains to ask, but I can't right now. I can't risk anything throwing this off.

I usher him into the meeting room. He sits down, then draws out a huge stack of papers from his black leather satchel. 'There have been some last-minute changes, I'm afraid,' he begins, and my heart starts to sink. What kind of changes? Surely, they can't be too big at this stage; my lawyers and his have already picked over everything ad nauseum. And I'm ready to sign now. I don't want to wait any longer.

'All right,' I say slowly, still trying to read his expression. But his normally warm and open face is closed, and apprehension stirs within me. What exactly are these changes?

He puts a thick file on the desk. 'As you know, we agreed on what we initially thought was a fair percentage of the business in exchange for our investment. That's the number you saw in the documents: 40 per cent.'

I nod slowly, my apprehension growing. *Initially thought?*

'But with the recent economic downturn, our analysts wanted

to run some new projections, just to be certain the numbers stack up. Unfortunately, those projections showed that the educational sector isn't as stable as it could be right now – the return isn't as lucrative. I still think you're a solid investment, of course. I never would have put you forward otherwise. But given these new figures, the investors felt we should secure a greater share of the business in order to move ahead.'

My chest squeezes. I can't lose this investment. After everything, I *can't*. 'A greater share?' I say carefully, trying not to give away what I'm feeling. 'Forty per cent is already considerable, given that this school was founded by my grandfather and relies on my family's reputation.' I pause. 'On *me*.'

Alex nods. 'Yes, I know, and my investors realise that too. But as you're aware, the school isn't in a great place financially. It *does* rest mainly on your reputation right now, and what if something were to happen to you? Cecily may be invaluable, but she doesn't have your charisma or standing in the community. You're such an asset, and if we could keep you on forever, we would.'

I nod, feeling absurdly flattered.

'But you'll have to retire sometime, I'm afraid. And if we can't have you, then we want the school to rest on its own merits. Just getting the building back up to where it should be will take a considerable amount, never mind improving facilities and hiring more specialised teachers. And we'll need to ensure everything is perfect before moving on to our future plans.'

'What exactly are you proposing?' I'm almost afraid to ask. I try to keep my voice steady, to keep holding his gaze despite the pounding of my heart. The school needs this deal. I need this deal.

Alex taps the document on the desk. 'Everything is outlined here in detail, but the new deal proposes the same amount of investment – £24 million – for an extra 15 per cent share of the business.'

An extra 15 per cent? I blink as the number hits me. That would bring Alex's share to 55 per cent.

That would mean I no longer own the school.

No. Every inch of me violently rejects the notion.

'I understand the significance of this.' Alex looks at me now with that gentle, understanding smile that drew me to him in the first place. 'I know the school has been in your family for years, and I know what it means to you. But this isn't giving it up. This is giving it a future, Ruth. This is a chance for the school to be so much more than it is now.'

I hold his gaze, trying to comprehend his words, but all I can see is that number floating in the air. The number that effectively takes away everything my family has been building. *Fifty-five per cent.*

'I'm sorry to spring this on you, but I wanted to explain everything in person,' Alex says. 'Have a read through the amended documents. The lawyer has highlighted any revisions made since the last version. But I would recommend signing this sooner rather than later. Our investors are keen to secure the deal.' There's something in his tone I can't identify, and my chest tightens. Does he know something I don't? He mentioned they'd been looking at other schools before coming to us. Are they starting to reconsider? Or... I take a breath to quell the anxiety inside. Is Isobel causing problems again? What's she going to do next?

I look down at the document, then back up towards him. With 55 per cent of the business, he won't be able to force any major decisions without my consent; he'd need 75 per cent for that. He *will* be able to control more minor things, though... like removing me as director. I trust him, of course, but business is business. If I'm going to think of agreeing, then I can't rely on instinct. As much as I want to sign this today, I need some guarantees that will protect the school... and me. 'I want to make some changes to the shareholders' agreement,' I say, tapping the paper. 'As a minority shareholder, I'll need to add a few clauses to protect my rights.'

Alex flips open the document. 'I thought you might – I wouldn't expect anything less. I've already had our lawyers make some additions, and I'm happy to add more, if you like.' He pauses. 'We're on the same page here, Ruth. We both want to give this school the future it deserves. To give you and your family what you deserve.'

I take the documents from my desk and scan the pages. The numbers leap out at me, exactly the figures Alex has just told me. I read through the shareholders' agreement, noting with relief and approval the long list of things that all shareholders must consent to before any action can be taken, from appointing or removing company directors to how shares will be transferred. The fact that he's added this in without me asking shows he really does understand how much this school means to me.

I meet his eyes. He's right: we can't hold out much longer, relying solely on our family's standing. That was clear even before Isobel showed up. I don't want to sign away our family business, but if I don't, we may not have much of one left in a few years' time. While Cecily won't have the legacy that I've been harping on about to placate my guilt at her staying, she'll still own a substantial chunk of the school once I'm gone. Forty-five per cent of any business isn't anything to sneeze at, and the school looks set to be a very successful one at that. With all the precautions in place, she'll have significant input into its future. And with Isobel and Isaac out of the picture now and Cecily unlikely to marry, we wouldn't have a long legacy anyway.

It's really not much of a choice, is it?

I pick up my pen – the pen my father gave me when I first started teaching here. It's heavy in my hand and I feel the weight of what I'm about to do. He entrusted me with this place. It was up to me to keep it going, like it was for him and his father. And while the school has retained its top reputation, and while I know that times have changed and the private-school market has shifted, we've reached the end of the road – and it's while I was in the driver's seat.

I almost put the pen down again and choose another, but then I take a breath. No. It feels right somehow that my father witnesses this; that he's here for this step. Because while I may not have been able to keep the past alive, I am securing a future. I can feel the school urging me on, telling me to do what's right for it... to give it everything it deserves, like Alex said.

I scrawl my signature on page after page where it's required, then set down the pen and meet Alex's eyes. 'There,' I say, handing the documents back to him.

He reaches across the table and holds out his hand. I put mine in his, noticing how his engulfs mine. As we shake, it feels like I've built a bridge to something bigger. The Burlington Square School will be better than ever before, and I'll be headmistress, right at the helm.

I smile at Alex, waiting for the relief, the happiness, the *excitement* to rush through me. But inside, I still feel numb... hollow. Let it sink in, I tell myself. It's such a huge step that I need time to absorb it.

I'll feel better soon, I'm sure.

THIRTY-SIX

ISOBEL

Isobel yawned and sat up, rubbing her eyes as she stared at the clock: almost noon. It made sense, she guessed, given that she'd barely slept at all last night. She'd tossed and turned, Alex's face drifting in and out of her mind, hurt mixing with anger. How could he *lie* to her like that, as if he had nothing to do with the school when in reality, he was investing in it? How could he pretend he cared when he'd been watching her every move for her mother? How could the first person she'd trusted with her past betray her like that... betray her by choosing the school over her, the very same way her mother had chosen it over Isaac?

Would she ever be able to damage the Square the same way it had damaged her?

Isobel shook her head and slid from the bed. Maybe not, but she wasn't going to fade away into the woodwork like they probably hoped. First things first, she had to get out of here and find a place where Isaac could continue to rest and recover. Then she'd talk to Henry and get Jez's number; hopefully find out more. And then... then, she'd hit the school where it hurt.

Her eyes widened as an idea flew into her mind. Perhaps she could go to the media? With Isaac's graphic injuries and the photo as proof he hadn't been alone, there was enough to make a good story – whether she found out more from Jez or not. And the media loved to rip apart a world of privilege and wealth, didn't they? Especially when family members were at war. She could almost imagine the headlines now. But... she bit her lip, thinking of Isaac's horrified reaction. If he wasn't talking to her now, he definitely wouldn't if he found out she'd gone to the press.

Maybe she could share her own story? The thought curled into her mind and she held it there for an instant before shoving it away. If the people learned what had happened to both her and Henry's birth mum, the scandal would be more than enough to close the school. But she could never risk Isaac finding out he'd been born as the result of an abusive relationship – that she'd left her life because of him; that she'd been terrified of his father. She hadn't wanted him to deal with that horrific information before, and he certainly wasn't strong enough now.

So what could she do?

I'll think of something, Isobel told herself. In the meantime, the most important thing was getting out of here. She threw on jeans and a sweatshirt, ran a brush through her hair, then went into the corridor. Thankfully, the rest of the house was quiet – Alex must still be out with her mother. The very thought made her feel sick.

She heard a noise across the hall, and she knocked on Isaac's door. He'd started barricading it, making it impossible for her to get in to check on him. She understood, though. Blocking the door had made her feel better in those first few months, too, though she'd quickly come to realise that nothing was strong enough to hold back her subconscious.

'Isaac?' She smiled at her son as he opened the door, happy to see him up out of bed – even if it was just to let her in. At least he *was* letting her in. His fringe stuck up at an odd angle, and her mind flashed back to the little boy he once was and how he always woke up with what they called 'rooster hair'. She'd try to wet it down before school, but it always sprang up again.

'How are you feeling?' she asked, sitting on his bed. God, she missed him. It was as if he'd gone somewhere else these past few weeks, not that she blamed him. But even before the accident, she'd felt like she was losing him, piece by piece, to the Square. Anger tore through her again, and she swallowed it back.

He nodded. 'I'm okay.' He twisted his torso, wincing. 'Ribs still hurt, but not as much as before. I just wish my eye would go back to normal. It's disgusting.'

Isobel took his chin, tilting his head back and forth. The white of his right eye was still blood-red. The thought of how close he might have come to permanently damaging it made her shudder. 'At least the swelling has gone down and the bruises are fading. Soon you'll be my handsome boy again.' *Please God*, she thought, happy to see him rolling his eyes.

'So, look,' she began. 'We're going to be leaving Alex's. It was nice of him to let us stay, but we don't want to overdo it.' She didn't want to tell him the real reason they were going. Isaac had looked up to Alex. They'd become good friends before this whole thing happened and Isaac had pulled away. She'd hoped they could remain friends, but... she shook her head. Just one more thing the school had taken away.

'Oh, good.' Isaac's face lit up. 'You believe me now? We're going back to Gran's?'

'No, Isaac. I'm sorry,' she said softly. 'We'll get a hotel room or something.' She swallowed, thinking that her money wouldn't go very far. 'And then, well, then we'll get a place of our own.'

'I want to go back to Gran's. I want to go back to school.' Isobel could see the determination in his eyes, shining through the fear: determination to move forward, to shove aside what had happened and pretend everything was fine.

But she was just as determined. And there was no way he was going anywhere near that school – or anyone connected to it – ever again.

'Isaac, I'm sorry, but you can't go back to Gran's. Staying away from the square and the school... that's the best thing for you.' Her voice came out much louder than intended, and she cursed silently when she saw Isaac's face harden.

'You don't know what's best for me, Mum.' Isaac slid from the bed and gazed down at her, and it hit her once again how tall he was now. 'You don't know me at all.' He dug out his carryall from under the bed and unzipped it, then started shovelling clothes into it. Isobel watched, frozen. What was he doing? 'I'm going to Gran's,' he said. 'And I'm going back to the school. You can't stop me.'

Isobel felt panic rise inside. 'We'll find another good school, maybe one that specialises in art. And if this is about leaving someone special, you can keep in touch. He can come visit you, wherever you are.' The words tumbled from her mouth before she could think about it, and too late she saw the horror on Isaac's face. Oh, God. What had she said?

She tried to grab onto him as he slung the bag over his shoulder, but he jerked away from her and went down the stairs. She ran after him, her breath coming fast as he jammed his feet into his trainers, then grabbed his coat from the hook on the door.

'You can't leave.' She made another swipe for his arm, but he spun away. 'You can't do this. You—'

But her words were cut off as the front door slammed behind him.

Isobel sagged against the wall, her mind spinning. Why the *hell* had she mentioned someone special? She didn't know for sure if he had a boyfriend, for God's sake. He'd know now that Cecily had told her about the photos. He'd be mortified. She'd been so desperate to have him stay that she'd grasped at anything. Instead, she'd only succeeded in driving him further away.

No matter how he felt, though, she couldn't let him go back to the woman who had sacrificed both her and him to save the school. He had no idea what his grandmother was really like; what she was capable of. And there was no way he could return to the Square, especially when they still hadn't found who had done this to him. There was every chance something equally horrifying could happen again, and Isaac had barely recovered in the first place.

The school may have failed to devour him the first time, but she wasn't about to give it a second chance.

She couldn't exactly drag him away, though. He wasn't a little boy any longer. Isobel straightened her spine and shook her head. Maybe he couldn't be reasoned with, but her mother could. She'd go see her mother now and tell her not to let Isaac stay, or Isobel would tell him the truth about what she'd done – how she'd told the whole form he had mental-health problems to save her own skin. Isobel only hoped her mother had an ounce of humanity left.

She went up the stairs to pack her things. The sooner they were both out of here, the better.

THIRTY-SEVEN

RUTH

I lean back in my chair at home and close my eyes, trying to let the tension of the day – of the past few weeks – drain away... still waiting for that happiness and excitement to fill me up. The documents are finally signed, and the school will maintain its rightful place as the best in London, and perhaps even become the best in the world. As much as I keep telling myself this, though, I can't help feeling that the only thing I really want is to see my daughter and grandson again. I steel myself against the longing, trying once more to swing my thoughts back to the Square. Like always, it will be my saviour. It has to be.

'Gran?'

My eyes fly open, and I turn to see my grandson in the entrance. 'Isaac!' For a second, I wonder if the strength of my desire has conjured him up, and happiness blooms inside at the sight of him. 'What are you doing here? Shouldn't you be in bed?' He certainly looks as if he should: sweat plasters his dark hair to his forehead, his face is glistening and the yellowing bruises make him look jaundiced. His eye is still dreadful, and he's lost weight – he didn't have any to spare in the first place.

'I'm okay. I'm bored of bed.' He grimaces. 'Anyway, my ribs don't hurt as much any more.'

'Well, it's good to see you,' I say tentatively, wondering how much he knows. He seems glad to see me, so I doubt Isobel's told him what happened yesterday morning. Was it only yesterday? It feels like an eternity. I stand, wanting to hug him, but unsure how it would be received... unsure if I can bear to feel my grandson in my arms again when I know I've already lost him. I hold out my arms awkwardly in a rather ambiguous gesture, unable to stop the warmth flooding through me when he steps into them. I put my arms around him gently. I don't want to hurt him. But he squeezes me tightly, and tears spring to my eyes.

'Gran, is it okay if I stay with you?' he asks, pulling back, and my eyebrows fly up. 'I want to go back to school too.'

Surprise spurts inside as I meet his hopeful look, and the longing I've tried to hold back grows in intensity. I've missed him so much, and I'd love to have him here again. But if he returns to the school, someone is sure to ask how he is – to tell him they know about his self-harming and what really happened in the darkroom that day. And when he discovers his own grandmother spread those rumours... I suck in a breath at the thought of him hearing what I've done, guilt gripping me like a vice.

I've got to tell him he can't come back. I don't want to push him away. I really don't. But...

When will this all end? something inside me screams.

'Isaac...' I turn towards him. 'Have you asked your mother yet?' There's no way, not in a million years, Isobel would ever agree to this. Maybe I can use her as a reason to reject his plea.

He drops his head. 'She told me no. She doesn't want me to.' He lifts his eyes. 'But Gran, she doesn't listen to me. She doesn't get me. Not like you do.'

I can't help smiling, remembering our many conversations and the bond I felt with him... the same one I felt with his mother, before she left. 'I'd love to have you stay and come back to the school. But...' My heart aches as his hopeful expression starts to fade. 'I think it's best if you go back to your mother. I—'

'Forget it.' His voice is tight with hurt and anger. I stretch out a hand, but he moves away from it. 'Just forget it.' And before I can say any more, he grabs his carryall and slams out of the house.

I want to go after him, to tell him to come back, but I can't. Instead, I sink into a chair and lower my head into my hands, trying to breathe through the sorrow. I'm not sure how long I've been sitting like that when I hear the door open again. Could that be Isaac? I was hoping he'd return so I could at least try to explain... to come up with something about why I can't let him stay. I can't bear to leave things like this.

My heart drops when I spot Cecily, and I remember that I invited her out for a rare weekend lunch to finally tell her about the investment – as something to celebrate, over a glass of champagne. But now, after seeing Isaac and having to turn him away, I'm even less in the mood for celebrating. I need to, though. I need to pull myself together and conjure up something besides pain. Because if I can't celebrate now, then...

'You okay? What happened?' Cecily's worried voice interrupts my thoughts.

'I'm fine. Just a little tired, that's all.' I force a smile and grab my coat. A glass of champagne will help, I'm sure. 'Ready? I made reservations for half past one.'

'Reservations?' She lifts an eyebrow. Usually, our lunches out consist of a quick sandwich at the nearest café.

'I thought this warranted something special.' I can see by the way Cecily's staring at me that she's wondering why, and a tiny bit of uncertainty stirs inside. I hope she'll be happy. I have secured the school's future, after all... and though she'll never have as much control of it as I did, she will still have a considerable stake.

Outside, the air is fresh and cold. It's only noon, but it feels more like late afternoon. The heavy grey sky presses down, but the elegant Christmas decorations on the houses around the square make the atmosphere festive. As we near the restaurant, it sounds like celebrations have started early. Noise and laughter spill out towards us and warmth engulfs us. We peel off our coats and follow the host to a table in the corner, overlooking a garden with a Christmas tree standing proudly in the middle.

'This is nice,' Cecily says, settling into her chair. She gazes at the laughing, happy crowd around her, and I spot sadness in her eyes. It hits me that she doesn't really have friends. She has me and the school, and that's it.

I *have* done the right thing, I reassure myself. She can stay if she wants, or she can shrug off the responsibility and finally strike out on her own. She has a choice now.

The waiter comes and I order a bottle of champagne to start us off, trying to hide my amusement at Cecily's enquiring looks. I know she's dying to find out why I'm making such a big deal of this. Who's going to speak first?

We chit-chat about the students and teachers, watching as the waiter pours the champagne into glasses that glisten under the light. Finally, when the waiter is gone, Cecily leans forward, shaking her head and smiling.

'I know you think you're leaving me in suspense,' she says, 'but I have a pretty good idea why we're having this special lunch. It's been coming for years.'

I tilt my head, surprise running through me. There's no way she could know... is there? I've always taken great care to hide the investment details from her. Is it possible Alex said something to her? He wouldn't though, I'm sure. He promised, and I trust him.

'It'll be a big change, of course,' Cecily's saying, 'for both of us. But I really think it's time, don't you?'

I meet her excited gaze. Somehow, she *does* know, but at least she's happy. Relief flutters through me, but before I can say anything, she pours some bubbly into my glass, fills her own, then lifts it up. 'Here's to you, Ruth! Happy retirement!'

My heart drops. *Oh no.*

'I've been waiting for this moment for ages,' she says, taking a sip, not noticing in her excitement that I haven't joined the toast. 'I mean, not that I don't want you around, of course. But it's always been you, you know? You've always been the figurehead, the leader, the one everyone looked up to – the one who really embodied what the school was.' She takes another gulp from her glass. 'And that was fine because I knew my turn would come – although I did wonder when Isobel came back!' She lets out a little laugh and shakes her head. 'What a palaver that turned out to be! Anyway, thank you.' She touches my hand, continuing to speak before I can respond. 'I know this can't have been an easy decision for you. But I promise you, I won't let you down. I won't let the school down. I'm just so proud to be leading the family business now. Finally, it's me. I'm the one in charge.'

I stare at my daughter, her words washing over me in a cold wave. She thinks I'm retiring. She thinks her time has come... her time to run everything; to take over the family tradition; to have control, like I told her she would. I draw in a deep breath, trying to figure out what to say: to tell her that not only am I not retiring – I couldn't now anyway, with so much to organise after Alex's investment – but that the school she's been looking forward to taking on is no longer ours. Yes, we'll still have considerable input in whatever happens, but we *have* lost control.

'What?' Cecily asks, finally clocking my reaction. She squeezes my hand. 'I know. It's a lot to take in, after so many years.'

I shake my head, marshalling every bit of strength. 'Cecily... I'm not retiring. Not yet anyway.'

Her face drops, and she sets her glass down with a thump. 'What? I thought... the champagne, the lunch out...'

'I'm sorry.' I curse myself as the words slip out. I need to frame all of this in a positive light, not as something to apologise for. I need to make my daughter feel like I've given her an opportunity, not taken it away. 'I *did* invite you here to celebrate something.' I grasp onto my glass like a lifeline. 'You must have noticed our enrolment dropping – how parents are choosing other schools now. Our building is old and in dire need of a massive overhaul.'

I wait for her to respond, but she says nothing.

'We probably could have carried on being okay for a little while. But when have we ever been happy with "okay"?' I pause.

'Cecily, I had a chance for the school to be something we'd never imagined. To be able to make the repairs we desperately need, get new computers and equipment, hire specialist teachers, open a new London campus and maybe even go global.' I smile. 'How does New York strike you?'

'New York?' Cecily looks at me like I've grown two heads. 'But... but... What do you mean, "you had a chance"? How?'

'Well, I have to admit that I haven't exactly been truthful,' I say. 'But I thought it best to keep everything quiet until it was confirmed.' I sip my drink, finally able to relax a bit. Cecily likes Alex. She'll be happy to hear that although she may not have complete control once I retire, he's the one she'll be working with. And maybe my vision of the two of them getting together will one day come to fruition. Stranger things have happened. 'Alex Lovell isn't an educational consultant. He runs a private equity firm and approached me about a potential investment. We've been working on the terms for the past few weeks.'

Cecily sits back, her mouth falling open. '*Alex?* Alex is an investor? And...' She shifts in her chair. 'What exactly *are* the terms?'

I swallow. Here's where it gets a little tricky. 'Well, they're giving us a huge investment. Our outgoings have increased the past few years, and we need to undertake substantial repairs and become as well-equipped as befits a school of our reputation. And you can imagine the costs involved in opening up new campuses around the world.'

Cecily nods. 'Yes. And?'

'To that end, the firm will own 55 per cent of the shares of the school.' I meet her eyes, holding her stare. It's important to show her this was the right thing. That this was the only thing. And that I've fully agreed to it. It's important she sees that I stand behind it.

'Fifty-five per cent,' she repeats dully. '*Fifty-five per cent.*' Her voice rises. 'So the school doesn't belong to us any longer. You've given it away. You've given away my legacy.'

My heart starts to beat faster, and despite my prepared responses, I'm struggling to speak.

'Do you remember what you said to me after your stroke, when I had to leave to start my job in Hong Kong? When you weren't ready to return to the school, and you still needed my help?'

I purse my lips, my brain working. That time was filled with frustration, anger and panic because I wasn't ready to return, no matter how much I wanted to be. I would have said anything to get her to stay; to help. I was desperate to keep my weakness under wraps, and desperate to have someone I could trust to do whatever I said, for as long as I needed them.

'You told me that this school was mine,' she says. 'That no matter what I did in life, and no matter how successful I was in any other career for any company, I would never have that... never have complete ownership, the way I would for the school. You said that when you retired, I would have something of my own – something I could be proud of. Something I could steer with autonomy.'

My gut clenches. It sounds like something I'd say, though I don't remember the exact words. Clearly, she does. I'd no idea it meant so much to her. Once again, it strikes me that I don't really know my daughter at all.

'Nothing will change,' I say, trying to calm her down. 'Not really. We can still block any major decisions we don't agree with. The only difference is we'll have a partner to help us – to give us what we need to really move forward. Everything will carry on as usual. Better, even.'

'As usual. *Better*.' Cecily shakes her head. 'How stupid do you think I am? Nothing is the same.' Anger twists her face. 'It's not ours any longer. You sold off the one thing you promised me this life would give me.' She narrows her eyes. 'But you were seduced by the future, weren't you? By how the school could be shiny and new, and expand globally! All on your watch, too, because you're going to stay on, right? You'll get the credit, the glory, as usual. And what will I get? Nothing, because you traded it all in for yourself.'

She pushes back her chair, stands and grabs her coat. 'I wish I'd never stayed,' she says, her face full of something like hatred as she stares down at me. 'No, scratch that, I wish to God I'd never come *back*. You didn't deserve it. You don't deserve anyone. And that's why you're still alone. Enjoy the school because that's all you have left.' She pauses. 'Actually, you don't really have that any more, do you?'

She pushes between the tables and out of the restaurant, leaving me alone with the festive cheer that rings in my ears like mocking laughter. I want to shout that I've done this for her, not me... so that she still has *something* in her life; something that won't go bankrupt in just a few years' time, but that will grow and thrive. Something that will bring her the same fulfilment through the years that it brought me.

But the words stick in my throat, and as I sit stone-still watching the happy faces around me, I can't help feeling emptier than ever.

THIRTY-EIGHT
ISOBEL

Isobel shoved the last of her things into her carryall and slung it onto the bed, sitting down to take a quick breather before the journey to her mum's house. She'd gathered her belongings as fast as she could, eager to talk to her mother before Isaac settled in. Downstairs, she could hear Alex making his super-strong coffee just the way she liked it, and anger juddered through her. She'd been hoping to leave before he came home. She didn't want to speak to him. She could barely stand to think of him.

She was just about to zip up the bag when she heard the front door open, and then... she cocked her head. Was that *Cecily*? What was her sister doing here? Unable to hold her curiosity at bay, she tiptoed into the hallway.

'How could you do this? How the bloody hell could you do this?' Cecily's voice rang loud and clear through the house, and Isobel jerked in surprise. Do what? What was Cecily talking about?

'You can't take the school,' Cecily continued, and Isobel breathed in. Ah. She must have found out about the investment. But what did she mean, 'take the school'? 'I don't know what you said to my mother, but you can't just take it away. It's ours.' Cecily's voice shook, and it struck Isobel that somehow it didn't sound like her sister.

She crept closer so she could see down the stairs. Cecily was standing there, tightly coiled with tension, facing off against Alex. But Alex looked remarkably calm, holding a cup of coffee and staring down at her with a perfectly pleasant smile. It was the smile of someone who could afford to be casual; someone who knew he'd won a fight. Isobel wondered what exactly that fight was.

'You seduced Ruth into thinking this investment was the best thing for us, blinding her with all your talk of new campuses and franchises, taking over the world,' Cecily said. 'Did she have a lawyer look at that contract before she signed over the majority of our shares? She's not well, you know. She had a stroke a while back and it's affected her thinking. She didn't want anyone to know, of course, but—'

'Ruth was perfectly aware of what she was doing,' Alex cut in coldly, and Isobel stepped back in shock. Her mother had signed over the majority of their shares? As long as Isobel could remember, her mum was banging on about the family legacy and how important it was.

But actually, it wasn't really surprising, was it? It was more than obvious now that, despite her words, family was nowhere as important to her mother as the school... nowhere as important as *herself*. And by the sounds of things, Alex had promised her the moon. The personal glory of it all had overwritten everything else. Isobel thought of what Cecily had told her – how she'd traded in the life she'd wanted for the future her mother had pledged – and sympathy went through her.

'But look, if your mother *is* ill, then you don't need to worry about the future,' Alex said in that same calm voice. 'There's been a change of plan anyway.'

'You're going to give us back our shares?' Hope lit Cecily's face, and Isobel inched closer. What was the change of plan? Was he going to back out of the investment after what she'd told him last night? Did he actually have a conscience?

Alex was silent for a minute, then his words fell like knives in the heavy air. 'After this year, Burlington Square School will be no more.'

Isobel's mouth dropped open. *What?*

Cecily stared, her body still as a statue. 'But... why? Is this some kind of sick joke? It makes no sense. Why would you go through the hassle of investing in something, of making grand plans for the future... only to shut it down?'

'Oh, there will still be a school,' Alex said. 'But I'm going to change its name – and its management.'

Two circles of red burned on Cecily's cheeks. 'You can't do that,' she said. 'Ruth would never agree to it. She told me we can still block anything we don't want.'

'And that's true,' Alex said. 'But given what I know, I'm quite certain she *will* agree.' He paused, staring hard at Cecily. 'Agree that it's in the business's best interest not to have *anyone* in the family near the school.'

Isobel brought her hand to her chest. Was he going to use what she'd told him about Philippe to force her mother to step down? Tell her to quit or he'd say what had happened? Downstairs, her sister was turning as white as a ghost.

'In fact, I think she'll agree to resign from the company too. I'm more than happy to buy out her remaining shares – it'll be much easier for all of us. The school I'm opening will be nothing like Burlington Square School. And that's a good thing. A very good thing.'

Cecily was shaking now. 'You're bluffing. You don't know anything. We'll take this contract to lawyers. We'll do everything to make sure this doesn't happen. It *won't* happen.'

'Let's wait and see, shall we?' Alex smiled, his eyes hard. 'I can tell you, though, that I'm very much looking forward to the future.'

Silence swirled in the air as Isobel waited for her sister's response. But without saying anything more, Cecily strode to the door and slammed it behind her so hard the house shook.

Isobel crept down the stairs, and Alex turned towards her.

'Isobel...'

She met his eyes, trying to take everything in – trying to figure out the man before her. She'd thought he wanted to boost the school; extend its future. Why had he told her mother all of those plans, only to turn around and say the world was a better place without the Square? Was it just to get her mother to sign over her shares? If what he planned came true, then the school Isobel had so desperately wanted to destroy would be no more. She waited for a sense of relief, of happiness, of *something*, but all she felt was the same anger reverberating inside.

'Who are you?' she said finally. 'Why are you doing this?'

'I wanted to tell you my plan,' Alex said, taking a step towards her. 'But I couldn't. I couldn't risk anything spoiling it.'

She stood her ground, staring at his face.

'I went to Burlington Square School,' he began slowly. 'I was a student there until I was thirteen.'

'You went to the Square?' Isobel shook her head. Just one more thing he'd never said. Could she ever have seen him there? She didn't know his exact age, but she thought he was slightly older than her. She hadn't started at the school until she was fourteen, though, despite begging her mother to let her transfer from her all-girls' school. He must have been gone by then.

'I did.' He paused. 'Until your mother kicked me out. Well, maybe not so much kicked me out. But "suggested" to my parents that both me and my sister leave.'

'Why?' The word floated between them.

'My sister was abused when she was a student. By a French teacher. The same teacher who abused you: Philippe Gauvin.' Her mouth dropped open and surprise swirled through her. 'I'll never forget that name. *Ever.*'

Isobel nodded mutely, her chest squeezing. She wouldn't forget that name either. How many girls had Philippe abused? Henry's mum, Alex's sister, her... were there more?

'My sister was fifteen when it happened,' Alex said, and Isobel froze. It was the same age she'd been when it started.

'I... I saw them together one day. I was two years below her, and I'd just finished an after-school club. She'd told me she was going to be in the library and to come get her when I was done. Then we'd walk home together.' He sighed. 'Thinking about it now, I realise it's amazing that she actually wanted to spend time with her annoying little brother, rather than the group of friends she had – and she had loads. Everyone wanted to be with her.'

Isobel held his gaze, waiting for him to continue.

'Anyway, she wasn't in the library like she'd said she would be. I tried ringing her mobile, but she didn't answer. I figured she'd forgotten we'd walk home together, and I went to my locker to get my things. And then I thought I heard her voice, so I walked down the corridor and looked into one of the classrooms.' His face twisted. 'And that teacher – Philippe Gauvin – was...'

Isobel had to look away. She couldn't bear the anguish on his face, a reflection of everything she'd shut away inside for so long.

'I rushed home. I didn't know what to do. I knew it was wrong, of course, but I didn't want to get her in trouble. I mean, she didn't seem upset by it. I thought that maybe I'd just keep quiet and everything would be fine.'

Isobel met his eyes again, anger tumbling through her as she remembered her own muddled emotions. After all, she'd liked Philippe. She'd flirted with him, and she'd willingly slept with him – time and again.

'But it wasn't fine.' He shook his head. 'It *wasn't*. She stopped talking to me, stopped laughing. She stopped eating. I'd watch them together, and I could see this expression in her eyes – like she was dead. Somehow, the light had gone out. I knew I had to do something, and so I sent an anonymous email to your mother.'

Isobel jerked. To her *mother*? She'd known about Philippe?

'I told her what I'd seen. And I waited... I waited for something to happen.' He exhaled, rage burning out from him. 'But nothing did. My sister continued to sink deeper into herself. I'd still hear them; catch them together. It made me sick. I couldn't believe no one else had noticed.' He sank onto the sofa. 'But finally, after a couple of months, something *did* happen. Although it wasn't quite what I expected.' He got up again and started pacing, back and forth, back and forth, lighting the floor with his fury.

'I only found out when I got home from school one day. My parents were sitting in the lounge, waiting for me. Straight away I knew it was something terrible. I thought it was about my sister.' He swallowed. 'I thought that maybe... maybe she'd run away, or something like that. I almost wish she had.'

Isobel nodded, thinking that's exactly what she had done herself.

'My parents told me that we were going to change schools. They'd had a think and decided boarding school would be best for us both since we needed more attention than what a nanny could give. With the help of your mother, they'd got us into two of the best in the country. My sister would go to a girls' school, and I'd be off to Winchester.' He paused. 'They told me it would be better for us both and that I should go and start packing my things. They'd be taking me there tomorrow.'

He turned to face her. 'I went up the stairs, and I could hear my sister crying. I tried to get her to talk, but all she said was that she'd messed up and she was sorry. She was sorry that it was affecting *me*. Oh, God, I can't bear it, even now.' He swiped a hand over his face, as if he could rid himself of the memory. 'Imagine, a teacher abusing a young girl, and she comes away from it thinking she's done something bad. How fucked up is that?'

Isobel nodded. She knew exactly how wrong it was.

'*She* was the one being punished, and not the monster who'd done this to her. Your mother... my own parents... they just wanted to sweep it all under the rug and forget it ever happened. But she never would. And neither would I.'

He started pacing again. 'I went off to boarding school the very next day. I hated it. I was so angry. At my parents, for not doing anything – at my sister, even. But most of all, I was angry at your mother. Because she'd known what had been going on... for weeks.

I *told* her. And nothing happened to Philippe... nothing. We were the ones who had to leave.'

Isobel's gut clenched. Nothing *had* happened, and he'd carried on. Carried on, and done the same thing to Henry's mother. Done the same thing to *her*. She started to shake as the pit of anger inside her overflowed, rushing through her body like molten lava. She drew in a hot breath as a thought hit. Was this why Philippe had been so sure that he could get away with it? Because he had before, and nothing had happened? Was this why he'd sneered so cruelly as he told her that no one would believe her anyway?

'I didn't know anyone at my new school,' Alex was continuing. 'I missed Leana like crazy. I tried to call her; to text her. But she never responded.'

Leana. The name swirled around her. She'd heard it somewhere before. But where? She sucked in air as it hit her. Henry, Isaac's friend. He'd said it that night at the restaurant.

Leana was his mother's name.

Henry was Leana's son.

'When you told me about Henry, it all made sense. Terrible, horrifying sense. She was having a baby. A baby she was forced to give up.' He turned to look at Isobel, and she could see the anger in his eyes. 'She never told me. My parents never told me. When I asked to come home and they said they wouldn't be here, I thought they just didn't want me around. I was so angry, so bitter. I never realised they didn't want me around because they didn't want me to see Leana.'

He let out his breath. 'Leana went up north when she finished school. She was supposed to be in uni, but my parents discovered she'd dropped out. She never came home, though. She stayed in Liverpool, and I thought everything was fine. I went to visit her a few years ago – that was the photo you saw – and I was happy to see her so well. I had no idea she was struggling. None at all.' He paused, as if the weight of his words was too much to continue. 'And then my parents called. They told me Leana had died... that she'd taken her own life. That she hadn't been well in years, and that they'd tried to help, but...' He shook his head. 'They'd done something, all right, but it hadn't helped. Forcing her to stay quiet; to give away her baby... It only made everything worse.'

His face tightened, and Isobel wanted to turn away from his naked pain, but she couldn't. In Leana's story, she could see herself... see what might have happened if she had stayed, given up Isaac and kept quiet. Isaac had been the one thing that had kept her going through the nights of fear and panic, when she'd jerk awake covered in sweat, feeling Philippe's hand over her mouth. Without her son, well... she might have had a similar fate to Leana.

Their lives might have taken different paths, but both of them had been irreparably damaged by one evil man.

One evil man that her mother had enabled.

The lava churned inside, seeping into her soul and searing it with a stinging pain. If her mother had listened to Alex, Leana might still be here. If her mother had listened to Alex, then none of this would have happened. Isobel wouldn't have fallen pregnant. She wouldn't have been attacked. And she wouldn't have spent years hiding away, fearful of the past. She would have had a life – the life she deserved.

'I knew I had to do something,' Alex was saying. 'I couldn't let the school – your mother – continue. I had to stand up for Leana, finally. Even if it was too late. I had to get some justice for her. With my father so unwell, he'd signed over his business to me. It was my chance to do something right.'

His face contorted, and for an instant he looked like a stranger. He *was* a stranger, she realised once again, and there was still so much she didn't understand. 'But why would you help my mother keep what happened to Isaac a secret?' she asked, confusion swirling inside. 'If you hated the school – and her – so much, wouldn't you want it to get out?'

'I wasn't helping her, not really,' he said. 'The only thing I couldn't resist telling her about was the photo you found on my camera. I wanted to make her fearful and afraid, for once.'

Isobel shook her head. 'That's not all. You told her I was going to the form breakfast too. Didn't you?'

'No. She must have heard about the breakfast and worried you'd be there. I didn't say a word. And I hated what she did to you and Isaac. Although I can't say I'm surprised.' He paused. 'And I *did* hope Isaac's attack would get out because I knew that would only work in my favour. I couldn't use Philippe against her without giving myself away, and I needed something extra... more leverage to ensure she signed the contract. If the school was damaged, it would be that much easier to convince her she needed this invest-ment... and to convince her to give me the majority of shares. I didn't need a majority for my plan – I'd always have what I knew about my sister over her, once I got her to sign – but I *wanted* it. I wanted to have power over the place that changed my life forever. To own it, then destroy it.'

He tilted his head, his voice going low and dark as his stare burned into her. 'And I wanted to hurt your mother, the same way she hurt Leana. I wanted to hurt her family. I wanted her to feel the same pain that comes when a brilliant future is snatched away; when a loved one is damaged.' He stepped closer. 'I'm sorry, Isobel. If I'd known what had happened to you, then maybe...'

'Maybe what?' Maybe he would have told her about his plan? Maybe he would have helped her more? Silence stretched between them.

'Maybe things could have been different,' he said finally. 'But you'll be fine. Isaac will be too. He's a great kid and he didn't deserve... any of this. Neither of you do.' He sighed. 'I never meant to hurt him... or you. I never wanted to cause you pain. It was all for your mother, and I'm sorry you both got caught up in it.'

She held his gaze, her mind spinning. Who was this man? First, she'd thought he was kind and trustworthy, taking her son under his wing. Then she'd believed he'd betrayed her. And now... now, she'd discovered he hated the school as much as she did, for the very same reason. That he'd been planning to close it all along. That he'd wanted to hurt her *family*.

She sucked in air as Alex's words echoed in her head. *I wanted her to feel the same pain and fear that comes when a loved one is damaged... I never meant to hurt him. If I'd known... I'm sorry.*

Had Alex... could he... she swallowed. Could *he* have been the one who'd assaulted Isaac? Could he have lured him in, like he'd lured their mother, and then turned on him? *I needed something extra...*

Isobel stared, images pouring through her mind. Alex, befriending Isaac at the school drinks night. Offering to give him his very expensive camera. Inviting him on countless photo shoots. How Isaac had really looked up to Alex and hung on his every word, gazing at him with something like a schoolboy crush.

She moved back, remembering Henry saying how Isaac had blushed when they called Alex his 'sugar daddy'. Bile burned her throat, horror sweeping through her. Those pictures Cecily had seen... could Alex have sent them? Could he have been trying to hurt Isaac the very same way his sister had been hurt? The same way *she* had been? An older man, an inexperienced naïve young person... for a second, she thought she might be sick right there.

No. He couldn't have. He *couldn't.*

Could he?

She didn't think so, but... Isobel shook her head, unable to start processing the horror if he'd abused her son. But even if he hadn't gone that far, there was still a chance he'd attacked Isaac. It would have been so easy for Alex to get Isaac into the darkroom. Alex did have access to the school, after all. He could have met her mother that afternoon, then waited around. He could have assaulted Isaac, then left him there, all alone. He'd hurt someone from the family and damaged the school, all in one blow.

Isobel's heart pounded as she remembered how, after the attack, things had changed between Alex and Isaac. Isaac hadn't wanted to be here. He'd barely looked at Alex and couldn't wait to get away from him. His nightmares had started, and he'd barricaded his *door*, for God's sake – right after she'd asked Alex to talk to him. She winced at the memory of the shouts and crashes she'd heard the night she'd returned to find Alex standing over Isaac's bed, and how for an instant, she'd thought the attacker had come back for more.

What if he had? Isobel had put Isaac's behaviour down to shock and trauma, but what if it was more? What if the attacker wasn't only in Isaac's dreams, but in his *reality*... and his own mother had delivered him straight to the lair? Isobel's legs weakened and she struggled to stay standing.

'Isobel...' Alex reached out a hand, but she jerked away. 'I want you to know that the school I'm going to open... I'm naming it after my sister. It will be a place that supports children who have been through trauma, either physical or emotional. It will be the kind of place I wish had existed for Leana... and for you.'

Isobel met his eyes, thinking that right now, he looked like the man she'd thought she'd known: open, friendly and kind. His idea for the school seemed exactly the right thing to replace an institution where so many bad things had happened. Could the same man who was opening that school be the one who'd brutally attacked her son? He hated her mother, yes, but to unleash such physical force on a young boy... It was almost unfathomable, but she knew better than anyone that some people were capable of anything; that they could hide their darkness under a myriad of disguises.

Was Alex one of them?

She shook her head. Maybe he was. She didn't know. So many thoughts were running through her head that she couldn't grasp onto any clear answer right now. She needed time to take things in; time to talk to Isaac. If it had been Alex, perhaps Isaac would open up once they were away from him. But in midst of all the confusion and uncertainty, one thing was certain. One person she knew she *could* blame for all of this... for everything. One person at the heart of it all, connecting the dots in a line of horror.

Her mother.

It wasn't the school she wanted to damage, Isobel realised now. Alex was going to close it, but it made no difference to her heartache and rage. It *was* just bricks and mortar, nothing more. It didn't have any power on its own. It was the people who made it what it was. People like her mother, who'd turned it into a place of darkness and pain. People like her mother, who could have saved her daughter's life... who'd chosen not to.

Owning her story had given Isobel a minute of peace, but she would never be free until she finally told her mother the truth about everything, past and present – until her mum heard the consequences of all that had happened; of everything she'd caused. Until she felt the same pain and anger that Isobel had all of these years.

Until she tore apart whatever was left of her mother's life, the same way hers had been.

THIRTY-NINE

RUTH

It's been a hell of a day. Every inch of me throbs with fatigue and my chest is so tight that breathing feels like an effort. This should have been a day to celebrate, but instead all I feel is guilt and sadness. Cecily's angry face flashes into my head, followed by Isobel's and Isaac's, and I sink onto my sofa. I haven't lost Cecily too, have I? How was I to know that having something of her own meant so much?

She'll come around. She'll realise what an amazing opportunity this is and how stupid I'd be to turn it down. But even as I think that, I can't help recalling her furious words at the restaurant. *Was* I seduced by the size of the investment and how that would raise the school's stature? Could I have done something else... something that wouldn't have meant relinquishing control?

Have I traded in my family for *status*?

It's too late now, I tell myself, sliding off my specs and rubbing my eyes. It's over. I've signed the papers, and whatever happens I'll just have to deal with it... like always.

There's a banging at the door, and my eyes fly open. Is that Cecily? Maybe now that she's had a chance to think...

My jaw drops when I open the door. It's not Cecily: it's Isobel, and her face is angrier than I've ever seen. Given recent events, that's saying something. What's happened now? Has she found out that Isaac came here? 'Come in,' I say, stepping aside to let her pass.

She strides into the lounge, and a memory of when she first arrived, just weeks ago, comes into my mind. She crept inside with her son trailing after her, like a mouse entering a lion's den. Now, it's as if she is the lion. Am I the mouse? The thought sends a shiver through me, and I tug my blazer tighter around me.

'Is Isaac here?' she asks. Ah, so she did find out.

'Yes, he was, but—'

'Did you tell him he could stay?' Her eyes bore through me, and I shake my head.

'No,' I say. 'He asked, but I didn't think that was a good idea.'

'Right.' She's practically vibrating with rage, and I gesture towards the kitchen. 'Why don't you sit and have a cup of tea?'

'No.' The word bursts from her. 'I'm not staying. I'm going to tell you what I should have said years ago – why I left. And then I need to find my son.'

'Okay,' I say slowly, dread pricking me. I've wanted to know for so long. I've questioned why endless times. But now that she's about to tell me, I'm not sure I'm ready to hear.

'I got pregnant,' she begins, and my eyebrows rise. 'But that wasn't the reason I left.' I nod, trying to take it all in. Why did she go then?

'It was how I got pregnant,' she says, as if she's heard my thoughts. 'How I got pregnant… and by whom. And what happened next.' Her voice drops to a whisper, her face twisting in pain.

My chest tightens with each of her words, that feeling of dread sitting heavy upon me. What on earth happened?

'Philippe Gauvin,' she spits out, and my eyes widen. Philippe Gauvin. The *teacher*. 'You remember him, don't you?'

My mouth works. I want to talk. I want to say something. But I can't. Too many memories are running through my mind – memories of another student, a few years before Isobel, who…

'He abused me for months,' Isobel continues. 'I was too young to know that's what it was. I thought he liked me. I really did. But when I told him I was pregnant, he attacked me and told me never to tell you – not that you'd believe me anyway, he said.' She shudders, and nausea roils through me because I know exactly why he said that. I swallow, the details slowly coming into focus.

Someone had sent me an anonymous email about Philippe being inappropriate with a student. I have to admit, I didn't put much stock in it. It could have easily been a prank or a disgruntled student. I did talk to Philippe, though, just to keep everything above board. He was shocked, strenuously denying it, and I believed him. He'd come highly recommended with stellar references. Everyone loved him; he'd even received a teaching award the year before. Things were fine, but then, a couple of months later, a girl went to her parents and repeated this same horrible accusation, and I had to act.

It didn't take much pressure for her to back down. Her parents didn't want a big scandal, and we came to a mutually beneficial arrangement: I'd get their kids into the country's best boarding schools, and they'd never say another word about this. Thankfully, they never did.

'I... I...' I stutter, so many emotions battering me that I can barely keep my head up. How can I respond? How can I tell Isobel that I was wrong? That I'd believed the wrong person. That actually... I swallow. That if I had listened, if I'd *done* something to remove Philippe, I could have saved my daughter. Guilt grips onto me so hard that I can barely take in air.

'You thought you'd got away with it,' Isobel continues. 'And you never stopped to think about how other people's lives could be ruined. Your very own daughter's life. You never stopped to think about anything other than yourself.'

Her words echo what Cecily said to me earlier, and I flinch at the pain in my daughter's eyes. I didn't mean to hurt Isobel or Cecily... or Isaac. I didn't mean to hurt my family. It wasn't a deliberate choice. If I'd known...

I jerk as the realisation hits. I didn't want to know. I didn't want to find out anything that could hurt the school, so I turned away from it. It *was* a deliberate choice: a choice to put the school above everything. I told myself it was for everyone else... my grandfather, my father, my family, even the building itself. But the reality is that it was for me because I *am* the school. Yes, I'm also a mother and a grandmother – and a wife once too. But none of those roles could eclipse the school's place in my life. I wouldn't let them. The Square is at my very core, baked into me since I was young. I need it... need the power it gives me, the protection. I guess that's why I staked everything on its survival. But staring into my daughter's eyes now, I desperately wish things had been different.

I wish *I* had been different.

'Well, you didn't get away with it,' Isobel says, her voice like ice. 'Alex is the brother of the girl Philippe abused before me. Alex is the one who sent you that anonymous email. The email you ignored,' she says, and my blood runs cold. *Alex?* A memory flashes through my mind of that photo in the yearbook, the one I thought I'd recognised. Perhaps that was him, after all. But... I shake my head to try to clear my blurry vision; to attempt to clear my confusion.

'And do you know what happened to that girl? To Leana?' Isobel asks, crossing the room towards me. 'She was pregnant, like me. That's probably why she told her parents. She gave away the baby, but she never got over it. She killed herself last year.'

Oh, God. My heart starts to pound and my breath comes in little gasps. Isobel waves in front of me, as if she's a vision from the past here to haunt me. It takes everything I have to stay upright in the chair; to hold her gaze. Because as much as I want to collapse, to prevent more words from coming, I need to hear this.

'And you could have stopped all of this. *You.*' She thrusts her finger at me. 'If only you'd acted like a responsible professional. If only you cared. You could have stopped Leana getting pregnant. You could have stopped *me* being abused, getting pregnant. You could have stopped me living a life of survival, every day hand to mouth, alone. I could have had a life – a real one, not plagued by years of fear and trauma.'

I want to speak. I need to speak; to tell her I'm sorry... sorry for Leana, for her. But how do you find the words to apologise for failing your daughter? For subjecting her to trauma that forced her from her home, from her life? There will never be enough words. I can never make up for that.

She tilts her head, as if mocking my silence. 'You don't care, do you? Not about me, not about Isaac, not about Cecily... not the family legacy. The only thing you do care about is yourself. Your reputation. Your success.' Isobel lets out a bitter laugh, and I close my eyes to try to block out the pain. She's wrong. I may have made some terrible mistakes, but I do care. Because no matter how much I let the school overpower me, it couldn't take away *love*. It was there, running underneath everything, flooding into me when Isaac and Isobel returned. It's there now, coursing through me with such power and strength I can barely catch my breath.

'Well, guess what?' Isobel's voice rings in the empty house. 'Alex is going to close the school.'

What? My eyes fly open. Alex wants to close the school? All that talk of the future, the international campuses, the building renovations, the franchises... none of that was real? The investment, the documents, ensuring minority rights protections... why would he do all of that if he really wanted to shut us down?

No. Isobel must be wrong. None of it makes sense. Only someone who was very disturbed would go through all that effort: meeting me, reeling me in with extravagant plans, flattering me with talk of reputation and stature, investing *millions*... I blink, taking in my daughter's irate face. She must be making all of this up to hurt me. After everything, I can hardly blame her. Even if Alex wanted to close the Square, though, he couldn't. Not without my consent.

But Isobel's next words cut straight through me.

'And you'll need to agree, or he'll tell everyone what you've done – or, rather what you haven't. That you didn't protect your students. That you *enabled* an abuser.' Her eyes flash. 'No more Burlington Square. No more Headmistress Cosslett. You'll have nothing. *Enjoy.*'

I stare at my daughter. Her face morphs into Alex's sister's, and I recall the bleak look in her eyes when I said she'd have to leave... the way she shrank as if my words had snuffed something out. And I think of Alex as a boy, of how he tried to save his sister and of his tear-stained cheeks when he came to clear out his locker that final time. I remember his steady gaze when I signed the contract this morning – his words that he wants to give the school 'the future it deserves' – and I shudder.

Isobel is telling the truth. Alex does want to close the school, and of course I'll have to agree. Because if I don't, and he says what happened... I shake my head. Does it matter? Does it matter what my life becomes? Once the school closes, I'll have nothing. I will be nothing, and perhaps... perhaps I deserve it.

No, not perhaps. I *do* deserve it.

There's a rustle behind us, and Isobel and I both turn. Isaac's standing on the steps, staring at us. And from his expression of shock and disbelief, it's clear he's heard every word.

FORTY

ISOBEL

Isobel froze in fear when she saw her son at the door. How long had he been standing there? Panic clutched at her when she thought of everything she'd said: the horrific way she'd fallen pregnant, what her mother had done, how she'd spoken about her life with Isaac.

His face was pale as he stared from her to her mum and back again, his eyes wide with hurt and pain.

'Isaac...' She bit her lip, struggling to find something – anything – to say. Words darted in and out of her mind, but she couldn't grasp onto any of them. She hurried towards him and held out her arms, desperate to comfort her son – to do something to cushion the multiple blows he'd just received. But instead of stepping forward, Isaac moved away. His mouth worked as if he wanted to say something, but nothing came out. Then he turned and ran across the square.

'Isaac!' Isobel shouted, her voice ricocheting off the houses' white facades. 'Come back! Please!' He didn't stop, though. She squinted in the gathering darkness, trying to keep him in sight as he picked up pace.

Her mother appeared beside her on the pavement, her face white. 'Go back inside,' Isobel said. 'This is between me and my son. I want him as far away from you as possible. We both want to be as far away from you as possible.'

'Isobel, I'm sorry.' The words left her mum's mouth as if they were being dragged from the depths of her, and Isobel could hear the pain and guilt lodged within them. *Good*, she thought. She deserved it. She deserved an ounce of what Isobel had felt all these years.

'I'm so sorry for what happened to you,' her mother continued, stepping closer. 'I wish it hadn't. I wish to God I'd done things differently. That I'd listened.' She paused. 'I can't change the past and all of the mistakes I made. But I *do* care. I love you – please believe me. I just...' She sighed. 'You were right. I was only thinking of myself.'

'That's not really love then, is it?' Isobel shook her head, remembering how much she'd believed in the strength of her mother's love – so much that she'd run to protect her mum from its consequences. 'If you love someone, you do what's best for *them*. Nothing should stop that.' But even as the words left her mouth, she remembered Isaac saying that she had no idea what was best for him. Was it true? Had she let her own anger and pain blind her to the point where her son had to run from her – the same way she'd run from her mother?

The sound of glass breaking filtered across the square, and Isobel and her mother turned towards it.

'What was that?' her mum asked.

'Sounded like it came from the school.' Was that Isaac? He'd be angry. He'd be hurt. He'd want to do anything to let it out – to damage something in return, just like she had. Isobel ran across the square and stood in front of the building, her heart sinking at she took in the smashed glass of the front door. It swung wide open in the wind, admitting the world into its darkness.

'Do you think he's inside?' Her mother's voice came from behind her, and Isobel turned, surprised to see her.

'I think so.' She went in and her mum flicked on the lights.

'Let's split up, shall we? See if we can find him? I'll take the junior school wing if you take secondary, all right?'

Isobel paused, uncertain if she wanted her mother's help. She wasn't sure she could ever forgive her mother; ever have a relationship with her again. So much had happened, both past and present. Maybe she could understand how emotions led you astray from what was really important, but her mother hadn't just had a momentary lapse of judgement. She'd allowed her ambition and desire to destroy her *family*. It was hard to believe that the future with her would – could – be different.

But Isobel needed her now. They had to track down Isaac before he did something he might regret. The building was a labyrinth, and the more people searching, the better. She just hoped that he didn't run again when they found him.

'Okay.' Isobel nodded, then hurried down the corridor towards the secondary wing, shuddering as she entered the darkness. Where the hell were the lights in here? She felt around on the wall but couldn't find them, so she switched on her phone torch and made her way up the stairs. She'd start from the top and work her way down.

Her footsteps echoed in the empty stairwell, her breath loud as she forced herself to take the stairs faster and faster. Finally, she was on the top floor. She tried the door, but it didn't budge and she remembered that this floor was closed because of the damage to the roof above it. She shivered as a blast of cold air hit. Where had that come from?

She took a few steps forward, her heart dropping as she realised the door to the roof must be open. Oh, God. Was Isaac up *there*? It wasn't safe! Fear shot through her, and she took the steps two at a time, racing through the open door and up onto the flat roof.

A dark shape was only just visible in the gloomy night, huddled in the opposite far corner of the roof.

Her son.

She drew in a breath, not wanting to scare him so he didn't make any sudden movements – he was already so near to the edge.

'Isaac?' she called softly, slowly closing the space between them. 'Isaac, it's me. It's Mum.'

'Go away.' The dark shape stood and Isobel could make out the pale face and his gleaming eyes.

'Look, I understand. You're angry and upset.' She drew in a breath. 'And sometimes when we feel that way, it's easier to cut ourselves off from everything – even from the people we love. You might think that by running, you can put it all behind you, but that's not true. The only way to cope is by talking about it... by facing it. I know that now.'

'I don't want to talk about it.' Isaac shook his head and stepped closer to the edge, and panic curled inside her. She may have faced her past, but had she destroyed the person she loved most in the process?

'Isaac...' Isobel moved closer, stretching out her arm. 'Come on. Come away from there and let's get off this roof. We don't need to talk if you don't want to. Let's just...' She closed the gap between them, praying to touch him; to yank him back towards her and into the safety of her arms. Finally, after what felt like forever, her fingers grazed his and she managed to grasp onto him, moving him away from the crumbling stonework of the edge.

'We'll be okay,' she said into his ear as she tightened her grip around him, feeling his body shake with sobs as he let go. 'I promise, we'll be all right.'

But just as she said that, the roof beneath them began to give way.

FORTY-ONE

RUTH

I hurry through the corridors of the junior school, pausing only to gaze through each classroom window to see if Isaac's inside. Memories pour through my mind: when I started here as a teacher, with Alan by my side, and how happy we were. My first day as headmistress after my father died, and how I'd been shaking with nerves, but somehow managed to make it through. And those terrible months after Alan left me, then losing Isobel... then Isaac and Cecily.

And now... I stop for a second, reaching out to touch a wall. Now this very school will no longer be mine. It won't even exist. Grief pours through me and tears come to my eyes, but they're not about the school. They're about my family, the people I've damaged... for nothing. Because no matter what I told myself, this place *is* just a building. It's an empty shell that I poured myself into, using its walls as protection. Walls I was so desperate to defend that I destroyed anything that could give me real happiness.

I rub my fingers along the hard plaster, coldness seeping into me. After hearing the reason my daughter left, one thing is clear: I need to let the Square go. Not because I have to protect myself from Alex's accusations, but because I *want* to. I may never get my family back, but maybe with it gone, I'll finally have the courage to step out from behind it.

First, though, I need to find Isaac.

I finish checking the first floor, then the second and third, then head back down to the ground floor to cross to the secondary wing where Isobel is. There's no sign of her on the first floor, so I climb to the second and peer down the corridor, my heart lifting when I spot a light on. Has Isobel found him? I tilt my head. That's Cecily's office. Is she here too?

Has Isobel told her about Alex's plan? I wonder. Does she know the school will be no longer? I wince, thinking that if Cecily was so upset over losing control of the family legacy, what will she be like when she finds out she won't have any part of it?

I hurry towards the light and push open the door, praying that Isobel and Isaac are inside. My heart sinks when I spot only Cecily.

'What are you doing here?' she asks.

I meet her surprised gaze. 'What are *you* doing?'

'I'm trying to find a way to stop Alex,' she says, her eyes wild as she turns to rifle through the papers on her desk that I recognise as the equity documents. She must have searched my office to find them. 'Do you know what he's planning? He wants to close the school! He's going to try to force you to agree with it.'

I take in a breath, my heart sinking at her distress.

'But there's no way he can. You don't have to. He doesn't know anything – nothing can be proved. He's just trying to scare us. There has to be a way to stop him. We can talk to lawyers, and—'

I put a hand on her arm, trying to calm her down. 'He *does* know, Cecily. He does. He can prove it too.'

The colour drains from her face. 'But how? How does he know? Did Isaac say something?'

'Isaac?' What on earth is she talking about? 'Cecily, I—'

She shakes off my hand and moves back. 'I'm sorry. I'm sorry, but I had to.'

'You had to.' I repeat the words, trying to understand what she's on about. Had to *what*?

'You really have no idea, do you?' Her gaze burns through me. 'You have no *clue* how much I want this – how much I was looking forward to finally having something that was mine.' She pauses. 'That brick through the window. That wasn't Isobel's ex. That was me – I arranged for that to happen. I wanted to scare her. I wanted her to go, but you convinced her to stay. I wasn't enough, was I? After everything, I wasn't enough. You kept trying to give her more. To give her my future.'

My mouth drops open. That brick was *Cecily*?

'So I had to do more, didn't I? If Isobel wouldn't leave for her own safety, then I had to threaten someone close to her.'

Her words swirl around me. I can't take them in. I don't want to. I shake my head, trying to dislodge the horrific thought attempting to gain access. She couldn't have. '*Isaac*.' The word barely emerges through the fog of disbelief.

Cecily nods. 'It was a solid plan, if only it had worked.' She swivels in the chair to face me. 'I saw some photos on Isaac's phone – explicit photos another boy had sent him. I don't know if it was his boyfriend, but whoever it was, Isaac was desperate to keep it a secret. He was beyond distraught that anyone had seen them.'

My eyebrows rise. Another boy? I'd suspected Isaac had been seeing someone, but I hadn't realised it was a boy. That explains why he didn't want to talk about it, I guess.

'I knew if I could have a kid get hold of that mobile, then Isaac would be worried about whatever else was on there being found; coming out. Messages, more photos... I knew how frantic he'd be to keep all of that hidden. I'd hoped just the phone going missing might be enough to burst his perfect little world at the school – enough for him to ask Isobel to leave. And if it wasn't, I'd give him a nudge.'

'A *nudge*?' Horror washes over me at the thought of the measures she'd taken next. 'You call attacking him a nudge?'

Cecily drops her head. 'That's not what I meant. That wasn't supposed to happen,' she says. 'If he didn't leave, then I was just going to send him an email from a fake account, threatening to release content recovered from his phone... or something like that. He was never meant to get hurt.' She meets my eyes. 'Don't look at me like that. You were willing to say Isaac tried to kill himself to save your own skin.'

Shame shoots through me. She's right. 'So what happened?'

'You know Simon Barnes?'

I nod, a picture of him coming into my head. Eighteen years old, burly... barely passing, despite all the extra tutoring at home and here. He caused a bit of a stir in September when he lost his cool and punched a hole in the chem lab. It's still there, actually.

'I told him I'd write a solid reference letter for uni if he managed to get Isaac's phone for me. Told him how, as Isaac's aunt, I was worried about some content on there. That much was true anyway.' She pauses. 'Trouble was, Isaac always had the bloody phone in his hand – he barely let go of it. I was getting impatient and might have pushed Simon a little too hard.'

'So...' I breathe in. 'What *happened*?' It's one thing to take a phone and another to beat someone so severely.

Cecily shifts in her chair. 'That day of the attack... Simon called me in a panic. He'd seen Isaac go into the darkroom and thought it was the perfect opportunity to grab the phone and get back out. It'd be dark, he'd said, and Isaac wouldn't see him.'

I shake my head. What a stupid, *stupid* boy.

'But Isaac wasn't alone. There was someone else there with him – an older boy, one of the art-room group – and they were kissing. Simon said that Isaac went a little crazy, screaming at him to get out; pushing at him. The boy Isaac was with tried to calm him down, but Isaac yelled at him to go and kept pushing at Simon. And then Simon... well, he said it was self-defence and he was just protecting himself. He might have lost his temper, and I don't think he realised how hard he was hitting Isaac. He told me that Isaac was fine.'

'So that's why Isaac didn't want to talk,' I say slowly, trying to piece it all together. 'If he accused Simon, then the whole story might come out... how he'd been with another boy. Or maybe Isaac was scared because he'd been aggressive as well. Maybe he thought it was his fault.'

'Maybe.' Cecily shrugs. 'Anyway, if Alex does somehow know I was behind it, then we can just deny it all, right? Simon will never say anything, and there's nothing besides Isaac's word to prove it was him – if there was, then the police would have talked to him by now. You don't need to agree to anything.' She turns back to the documents on the desk. 'I'm prepared to do anything to keep this school open. I deserve it, don't I? I've proved that to you. We need to find a way to get out of this agreement. To make the school ours again.'

'Cecily...' I step forward and put a hand on her arm. I'm horrified, but I also know that she's not the only one to blame. I am, for taking her away from the life she wanted. For not seeing how important this school really was to her. For not noticing my own daughter and what she was becoming. She *would* do anything to protect the school, even turning against her own sister and nephew. But then, just as she said, haven't I done the same?

She *is* like me.

'I understand what it's like to want something so badly that you'll damage anything and anyone. You made the Square your life, but once you wanted so much more than this. You *are* so much more than this.' I stare into her eyes, hoping that I am too; that I can be. 'The school will be closing. I'm not going to fight Alex on this. I don't want to. It's over, Cecily. I'll help you however I can, but... you need to find your own way now.'

'Find my own way?' She laughs, her mouth twisting. 'There's nothing for me now. Nothing.' She takes in a breath. 'I never meant for Isaac to get hurt. That wasn't my intention – not at all. And I wouldn't have done anything with the phone, of course. Isaac never would have known I was behind it all. I just wanted him and Isobel to leave.'

'I know. I didn't mean for anyone to get hurt either.' And I didn't, but I didn't allow myself to think about it. I didn't want to. As long as I had the safety of the school, everything would be okay.

But it wasn't. And underneath, *I* wasn't. I might have seemed content – I might have seemed strong. I might have thought I was content and strong, but I wasn't. Inside, I was cowering, fearful and scared.

'But we can't just let the school go, not like this,' Cecily says, desperation tinging her voice. 'What would your father say?'

Her words go through me, straight to the core. What *would* Dad say? I always knew he'd be proud of the school. But would he be proud of me? I shake my head. I know the answer. Maybe there's still time, though. Time to do the right thing. Time to force change... for us all.

'I'm sorry, Cecily,' I say. 'But the school is finished.'

She stares at me, her body slumping as she finally accepts what I'm saying. Then, through the open window, voices float down from above us. I catch my breath. Is that Isobel and Isaac? Where the hell are they? I pause, listening. Are they on the *roof*? My pulse picks up pace and my chest tightens. They can't be up there! It's not safe – not safe at all.

'Why are they here?' Cecily asks, getting to her feet.

I shake my head. It's too much to explain, and I don't have the time. I have to get up there and tell them to come off before something happens.

'Wait here,' I say to Cecily as she follows me into the hallway, but she puts on her coat, then swivels to face me. For a moment, we stand there, in the dark silent corridor, and without speaking, I know what she's saying: goodbye. It's what she should have said all those years ago – it's what I should have *let* her say. I pray that she's able to make a life somewhere, far from everything that's taken place here.

Finally, she blinks and turns to go. Her footsteps echo in the hallway, the stairwell door slams shut behind her, and she's gone. My heart aches, but what I said earlier is true: she does have to make her own way now. We both do.

I hurry down the corridor and up the dark stairs. Cold air pours in from the open door at the top, and I wonder how on earth Isaac managed to get past the locked door and onto the roof. I shake my head as I eye the smashed door in front of me, the rotten wood split. That's how.

I walk onto the roof, my heart pounding so hard I can barely hear anything else. It's so dark that it takes my eyes a while to adjust, but when they do, panic swells inside. Isobel's on the far side of the roof, gingerly approaching Isaac who – oh my God – is standing right at the edge.

I almost yell, but I don't want to scare them, so I wait... I wait until finally, finally, Isaac takes a step away from the edge and into his mother's arms. But they're still not safe, and just as I'm about to shout to them that they need to get out of there, I hear a strange sound: a kind of creaking, tearing noise, coming from where Isobel and Isaac are standing.

And I know in an instant what that is.

The roof starts to sag around them, and I don't even think. I just fly towards them, pushing them as far and as hard as I can manage – as far from the danger as I can. Just as they tumble forward onto what I hope – what I *pray* – is solid ground, the roof beneath me gives way. And before I can move, I feel myself falling... falling into the darkness of the school below.

Then everything goes black.

FORTY-TWO
ISOBEL

Isobel covered her mouth in horror, staring at the huge hole her mother had disappeared into. Fingers shaking, she dialled 999 and relayed what had happened, her lips forming the words though her brain could barely take it in. Isaac wrapped his arms around her, and she held him tightly for a second, trying to impart as much love and comfort as she could.

She looked down into the yawning hole again, but all she could see was darkness.

'Mum?' she called, but there was nothing. She grabbed Isaac's arm, and they ran off the roof and down the stairs to the floor below.

'Will she be okay?' Isaac asked.

'I hope so,' Isobel responded, fear clutching at her throat. No matter what her mother had done in the past – the terrible things; the mistakes she'd made – she'd put her own life in danger to save Isobel and Isaac.

They rushed into the corridor, looking up and down at the row of locked classrooms. Where the hell could she be? 'Mum?' Isobel called, her voice bouncing eerily around the empty space.

'Gran?' Isaac's voice joined hers, twisting and turning around it.

'Here.' A weak response finally came from one of the class-rooms. Isobel turned towards it, relief flooding through her. Thank God her mother was conscious.

'Is it this one?' Isobel pointed to the locked door in front of them, and Isaac nodded.

'I think so. Gran? Are you in there?'

'Here.' The voice came again, weaker now, and Isobel shivered. It felt like her mother and the Square were bound together, their fates intricately woven. If one ceased to exist, so would the other. Isobel met her son's eyes. 'We have to get in there.'

Isaac took off his padded winter coat and wrapped it around his fist, then slammed it through the glass panel in the door. Then he carefully reached through and unlocked the door, swinging it open from the inside.

'Mum!' Isobel rushed to the dark sharp in the middle of the floor. 'Are you okay? The ambulance is on the way. It'll be here any minute.' She knelt beside her mother, who was lying at an awkward angle with her leg bent back behind her. Her face was pale and a trickle of blood ran from underneath her head, but her eyes were open. She blinked as she stared from Isobel to Isaac and back again.

'I'm okay,' she whispered. 'I'll be okay, don't worry.'

Isobel took her mother's hand and squeezed, emotions running through her as she noticed Isaac taking her mother's other hand.

'You'll be fine, Mum,' she said, wincing as her mother's face contorted in pain. Thankfully, though, her breathing seemed steady and her eyes were still open.

Distant sirens filtered through the silence, and Isobel turned to Isaac. 'Go meet them at the front and show them where we are, okay?' He nodded and hurried out of the room, the sound of his steps fading.

'I should have listened when you said it wasn't an accident. I should have believed you.' Her mother sounded breathless, and Isobel shook her head.

'Don't talk, Mum. Just try to relax.'

'Cecily.' The word eked out of her mother.

'Cecily will be all right, Mum. She'll be okay.'

'No.' Her mother struggled to sit up, and Isobel gently pressed her down again. 'The attack. Isaac. It was Cecily.'

Cecily? Isobel drew back, sure her mother had it wrong. She must not be thinking straight. 'Mum, I think it might have been Alex. He told me he wanted to hurt us. He wanted to hurt our family.'

'No.' The voice was raspy but had such conviction that Isobel had to believe her. 'He might have wanted to hurt me, but he never hurt Isaac. Cecily told me herself. She wanted you both to leave. She was desperate to have something of her own. She wanted to scare you; scare Isaac. And...' Her mother shifted, closing her eyes with the effort of it all.

'That's okay, Mum. You can tell me everything later.' Isobel squeezed her mother's hand tighter, trying to take in what she'd revealed. Cecily, her own sister, had almost killed Isaac to get what she wanted? No wonder she'd tried to stop Isobel investigating further. Isobel had been right when she'd wondered if Cecily had really cared about Isaac at all. All that talk of visiting him, of trying to keep things under wraps to help him... She'd been worried about herself, and Isobel had actually felt *sorry* for her. Nausea and anger roiled through her as questions pounded her brain. Had Isaac known it was her? Was that why he hadn't said anything? Because he was worried what it might do to the school, just as she had been?

Because he was worried it might destroy his family?

'I'm so sorry I didn't protect Isaac,' her mother said, her eyes opening again. 'I'm sorry I didn't protect you. I love you. Believe me. *Please.*' As Isobel knelt there, she realised that no matter what else her mum might have done, she *did* believe that underneath it all, her mother loved her... and Isaac too. Tonight had shown that when it came right down to it, she'd risk her own life to save theirs.

Tonight had shown that she did care more about her family than herself.

Red and blue lights flashed into the classroom, and Isobel ran to the window and looked out. 'The ambulance is here,' she said, kneeling down by her mother again.

'Will you come with me to the hospital?' Her mum's eyes were wide and fearful.

Isobel held her mother's gaze, her mind spinning. She didn't want to be angry or bitter. She didn't want the past to twist her life any longer. She looked up into the glowing night sky then back down at her mother, thinking that somehow, in the midst of all of this pain, they'd managed to find a way out of the darkness. They weren't trapped any more.

'I'll come,' she said.

FORTY-THREE

ISOBEL

Eight months later

Isobel wiped the sweat from her forehead, then stared up at the school, shielding her eyes from the glare of the August sun. She turned to look at her mother beside her, then Isaac. They'd all come together today to remove the gold plaque bearing the school's name that had been on the front of the building since it started. Alex had allowed the school to finish the year before he'd spend the next year converting the premises to the school he'd open in his sister's name. Burlington Square School would be gone, wiped off the map forever, just like Alex had wanted. She hoped that would bring him some peace.

Isobel gazed back at the building, emotions swirling inside at the thought of Alex. He'd tried to contact her several times, but she hadn't wanted to talk. She felt sorry for suspecting he'd hurt Isaac, but she'd been stunned by his revelations and the depth of anger and pain he felt. And while she could understand his emotions – it was probably why they'd connected so quickly – she was working too hard to let go her own pain to risk being dragged into someone else's.

Alex had connected with Henry, though, after talking to

Henry's mother first and telling him what had happened to Leana. And Henry finally had the sibling he wanted – he'd become closer to Isaac, raising his confidence and encouraging him to come out. Isaac no longer felt the need to hide who he really was, and he and his boyfriend Jez spent every spare minute together. His nightmares had stopped, he'd returned to photography again, and Isobel couldn't be prouder of her son. He'd carried so much on his own, but he was stronger than she'd given him credit for. And now she was strong enough, too, to give him the independence he deserved – and to trust him to talk when he needed her.

'Okay.' Her mother turned to look first at Isaac and then Isobel. 'Here we go.' Clutching an electric screwdriver in one hand and a cane in the other, she slowly climbed the steps, then lowered the screwdriver head into one corner of the sign. As the screw loosened, Isobel watched her mother closely. She'd expected today to be heavy and sombre, but instead her mum seemed lighter somehow – the same way she'd seemed when she'd decided to sell the family house and move into a smaller flat with no stairs. Despite recovering well from the accident, she tired easily and her back still caused her a lot of pain.

A screw popped out, and her mother brandished the screwdriver in the air. 'Here, Isobel. You do the next one.'

Isobel smiled and went up the steps, taking the screwdriver from her mother and removing the screw. Her mother touched her arm, and Isobel met her eyes. The woman in front of her now wasn't the one she'd idolised as a child, but it wasn't the woman she'd wanted to destroy either. She was working every day to find herself – to discover who she was away from the mantle of headmistress and to build a solid relationship with her family.

And Isobel had changed too. She wasn't running from the past any more, though sometimes, despite her strength, she felt almost buried under the weight of all that had happened. She'd lost everything when she'd run away and had never really let herself grieve. Even after she'd returned, she'd used anger and pain to propel herself forward. And now... now, the rage was gone, leaving only a deep well of sadness and loss. But with every day that passed, she could feel more and more of the light shining in.

She and her mother both had a long way to go, but they'd already come so far.

'Okay, done.'

'Isaac?' Her mother beckoned to her grandson. 'You can do the next one.'

Isaac nodded and loped up the stairs, then took out the third screw. The plaque swung back and forth, hanging off the remaining screw. Isobel tilted her head, thinking of the final member of the family who wasn't here: Cecily. They hadn't heard from her since that night at the school. Her flat had been emptied; her possessions packed away. While part of Isobel still wanted to rail at her sister for what she'd done, Isobel hoped that wherever she was, she was finally living the life she wanted.

'One left.' Her mother drew in a breath. 'I'll do it.' Isaac handed her back the screwdriver, and they all watched as she removed the last screw and lifted the gold plaque from the wall. They went back down the steps and stood in silence, staring at the bare facade. The building remained, and yet the school was no more. It was a reminder that no matter how strong any wall might be, it could never provide protection from the secrets and pain inside... from the secrets and pain inside *yourself*. But once you ventured outside – once you broke free from the prison of the past – there was a chance of becoming something better.

Isobel turned to look at her mother, then over at Isaac. She still didn't know what the future held, but for the first time in ages, it wasn't something to fear; something to endure.

It was something she was finally free to claim as her own.

A LETTER FROM LEAH

Dear reader,

I want to say a huge thank you for choosing to read *Why She Left*. If you did enjoy it and want to keep up to date with all my latest releases, just sign up at the following link. Your email address will never be shared and you can unsubscribe at any time.

www.bookouture.com/leah-mercer

I hope you loved *Why She Left*. If you did, I would be very grateful if you could write a review. I'd love to hear what you think, and it makes such a difference helping new readers to discover one of my books for the first time.

I love hearing from my readers – you can get in touch on my Facebook page, through Twitter, Goodreads or my website.

Thanks,

Leah

www.leahmercer.com

facebook.com/AuthorLeahMercer

twitter.com/leahmercerbooks

ACKNOWLEDGEMENTS

A huge thanks to Laura Deacon and the whole team at Bookouture for their support and encouragement. Thank you, too, to my agent Madeleine Milburn, and to all the bloggers and reviewers who have read my books through the years and continue to support me – it is greatly appreciated. And, lastly, thank you to my husband and son for always being happy to discuss plot, covers and characters with me!

Made in United States
North Haven, CT
27 December 2021

13567596R00162